"Oh, come now," Mabh murmured sweetly, "let us be friends." The water within the circle she traced grew dark, and Sonny could see shadows and shapes flickering in the depths. "Wouldn't you like to see what our darling girl is up to?"

In spite of himself, Sonny knelt back down on the grass and glanced into the Faerie queen's improvised scrying pool. He had no wish to spy on Kelley. Still, he found he could not look away when he saw glimpses of her soaring over the Central Park Lake on dark, glimmering wings, an expression of fierce elation lighting up her face. He saw the flaring darklight of her wings and then saw the howling tornadoes of Mabh's Storm Hags descend upon the scene. The wild, dangerous look on Kelley's face made her look so much like her mother that it gave Sonny a hollow feeling in the pit of his stomach. But not nearly as much as the last, lingering image that flared up in the water—the image of Kelley throwing her arms around another man.

LESLEY LIVINGSTON

Darklight

a novel

An Imprint of HarperCollins*Publishers*

For my mom

Darklight
Copyright © 2010 by Lesley Livingston
All rights reserved. Printed in the United States of America.
No part of this book may be used or reproduced in any manner whatsoever
without written permission except in the case of brief quotations embodied in
critical articles and reviews. For information address HarperCollins Children's
Books, a division of HarperCollins Publishers, 10 East 53rd Street, New York,
NY 10022.
www.harperteen.com

Library of Congress Cataloging-in-Publication Data
Livingston, Lesley.
    Darklight : a novel / Lesley Livingston. — 1st ed.
      p. cm.
    Sequel to: Wondrous strange.
    Summary: After a dangerous encounter in Central Park, actress Kelley
Winslow, who has only recently learned that she is a Faerie, journeys to the
Otherworld and begins to untangle the strands of a magical conspiracy with
far-reaching consequences.
    ISBN 978-0-06-157542-6
    [1. Fairies—Fiction. 2. Actors and actresses—Fiction. 3. Fantasy.] I. Title.
PZ7.L7613Dar 2010   2009014264
[Fic]—dc22   CIP
                                                                              AC

Typography by Sasha Illingworth
10 11 12 13 14 LP/RRDH 10 9 8 7 6 5 4 3 2 1
❖
First paperback edition, 2010

TITANIA [Awaking]: What angel wakes me from my flowery bed?

BOTTOM [Sings]: The finch, the sparrow and the lark,
The plain-song cuckoo gray,
Whose note full many a man doth mark,
And dares not answer nay;--
for, indeed, who would set his wit to so foolish
a bird? who would give a bird the lie, though he cry
'cuckoo' never so?

TITANIA: I pray thee, gentle mortal, sing again:
Mine ear is much enamour'd of thy note;
So is mine eye enthralled to thy shape;
And thy fair virtue's force perforce doth move me
On the first view to say, to swear, I love thee.

BOTTOM: Methinks, mistress, you should have little reason
for that: and yet, to say the truth, reason and
love keep little company together now-a-days; the
more the pity that some honest neighbours will not
make them friends. Nay, I can gleek upon occassion.

TITANIA: Thou art as wise as thou art beautiful.

BOTTOM: Not so, neither: but if I had wit enough to get out
of this wood, I have enough to serve mine own turn.

TITANIA: Out of this wood do not desire to go:
Thou shalt remain here, whether thou wilt or no.
I am a spirit of no common rate;
The summer still doth tend upon my state;
And I do love thee: therefore, go with me;
I'll give thee fairies to attend on thee,
And they shall fetch thee jewels from the deep,
And sing while thou on pressed flowers dost sleep;
And I will purge thy mortal grossness so
That thou shalt like an airy spirit go.
Peaseblossom! Cobweb! Moth! and Mustardseed!

Friday, November 13
1903

The old man lay crumpled on the flagstones in front of a Park Avenue brownstone, his lifeblood oozing from five small holes in his neatly buttoned tweed vest like sap from a maple tree tapped in spring. Standing over him, pistol still smoking in his fist, was a man with glassy eyes—vacant of rational thought.

A *thrall*, thought the dying man, and he wondered briefly who among his kind had stooped so low to send the poor, mindless mortal slave to do their unpleasant bidding. The old man's eyes rolled upward, gazing past the face of the thrall into a sky of blue so bright, it squeezed tears from the corners of his eyes. He remembered when he had first set foot in this world. And his *was* the first. Others from his realm had followed, but he had been the one to lead them there.

He had been the foremost of the Fair Folk, the most powerful, the one to discover a passageway between that other realm and this one. He had created the Four Gates, one for each Court in the Otherworld, for each turning point of the seasons; doorways through which his kind could pass freely to savor the delights of this fresh new world.

That was in the days before mankind had stretched out his hand, before the forests had given way to the ax, before meadows had been paved over and rivers dammed. The old man had learned to live with humanity. And so had the Faerie who'd followed him: finding ways to coexist, in the same way that green things push their way up through cracks in the pavement.

He had moved the Gates from place to place over time, for one reason or another—war, or progress, or plain old Faerie boredom. He could still remember when the mortal populace of this world had referred to the Beltane Gate as the Hanging Gardens of Babylon. That was before he had hidden it in the deep green forests of Ireland.

The Lúnasa Gate was still called Stonehenge—and most likely always would be. The Gate of Imbolc, now far in the north, had never had a human name, no matter where it had existed. Gwynn ap Nudd, the inscrutable king of the Court of Spring, had preferred it that way.

Now, with the relocation of the Samhain Gate, the old man

had done his finest work. His creation would be marveled over by the mortals of the New World for centuries to come. And even still, they would never know its true purpose—that it housed a Faerie secret, a portal to the Otherworld. But they would flock to the Gate, and they would call it by its human name: Central Park.

"Andrew."

The old man blinked up at a tall figure silhouetted against the sky.

"Andrew, old friend . . ."

"Ah," the old man gasped, struggling to rise up on one elbow. A trickle of crimson flowed from the corner of his mouth. "You are here."

"Be still, Andrew." The tall man knelt on the sidewalk and put a gentle hand on the old man's bleeding chest. "I will help you."

"Yes." Andrew Haswell Green, a philanthropist and a father of New York City, one of the driving forces behind the creation of Central Park, sighed contentedly. "It is well that you are here."

"What can I do?"

"Carry a burden for me."

"Anything."

"Thank you, old friend." Green put his hand on the other man's sun-browned brow. For a moment the little gray court-yard in front of the brownstone lit up with warm, forest-dappled sunlight. The chilly November air filled with the

3

heady scents of growth and harvest, fermentation and vegetal decay. The other man gasped and his eyes went wide, but he did not flinch or pull away.

The bestowing did not take long.

When it was over, the other man laid his oldest friend down gently on the stones and stood. Then he turned and walked north past the ornate edifice of Grand Central Terminal, in the direction of the park. To where the trees now whispered *his* name.

The shiny black carriage rolled to a stop on the other side of the street. Its occupant drew back the heavy velvet window curtain, hissing in frustration at the sight of Andrew Green's body, already emptied of life . . . and power. The passenger knocked on the roof of the carriage. The street was still empty, but that wouldn't last long. In the distance could be heard the faint sounds of voices raised in alarm.

The carriage driver stepped down from his perch into the street. The heels of his polished, silver-buckled boots rang on the pavement as he walked over to kneel beside the body on the sidewalk. After a moment, the carriage driver stood and returned, bearing four silver hairs plucked from the dead man's beard. They were stained with bright blood, twisted into four loops, and knotted together.

The shouting was closer now. Without another glance back, the lone occupant of the black carriage pulled the curtain closed and signaled the driver to move on.

I

"**O**, now be gone; more light and light it grows."

"More light and light; more dark and dark our woes!"

The lovers shared a brief, poignant embrace.

"And . . . *scene*!" the director called in a precise English accent. "I want to cut the rest of the lines up to Lady Capulet's entrance—Mindi, make a note in the cue script. Juliet, *upstage* hand, please. Romeo, watch your *diction*." He checked his watch. "It's ten o'clock, so we're done. We'll pick it up here next rehearsal, people. Check the call time on the notice board, and don't be late. I'll have notes for you all before we start, so *don't* think you've gotten off easy. Now go home and *look* at your *scripts*."

Kelley Winslow packed up her gear and hung up her rehearsal skirt on the back of her dressing-room door. "Good night, everybody!" she called out as she slung her purse across her body and headed toward the stage door of the Avalon Grande Theatre.

"Night, kiddo." Gentleman Jack Savage smiled at her from the doorway to the greenroom. The veteran actor raised his cup of coffee in salute. "Hell of a job tonight. Your balcony scene is gonna knock their socks off, Juliet."

"Shoes, *maybe,*" Quentin, the director, said dryly as he rounded the corner from the backstage area. "I'll reserve judgment on any sock-knocking until *such* occasion as you remember that quarter turn *up*stage when your nurse calls. And put a little *passion* into the snogging, hmm? He's *Romeo,* for heaven's sake. Not some distant relation your great-auntie forced you to kiss at a wedding."

"I'll work on that, Q." Kelley stifled a laugh as Alec Oakland—Romeo—made kissy-faces at her just out of the director's line of sight. He disappeared into his dressing room before Quentin could find him to berate his performance.

"Yes, well, you've only got three weeks." Quentin sniffed. "I *suppose* miracles could happen . . ."

From anyone else the criticism might have stung, but coming from Quentin St. John Smyth, that comment was pretty much the equivalent of a four-star review in the *Times*.

6

"You need me to get one of the boys to walk you home?" Jack asked, smiling at Kelley with fatherly affection. "I'm sure Alec wouldn't mind. . . ."

"Nope. I'm good." Kelley gave the older actor a hug and shouldered the heavy oak door open. "See you."

"Be careful out there, Kelley."

"Don't worry about me, Jack." She waved as she stepped outside. "I can take care of myself." She could—maybe more than the average almost-eighteen-year-old. Kelley had toughened up a lot in the last few months.

As the stage door closed behind her, Kelley stood for a moment on the stone steps, staring up at the darkened silhouette of the old church that had been converted into the Avalon Grande Theatre. *What to do with the rest of the evening?* she wondered.

She'd planned to avoid going near the park, just as usual.

But the April evening was intoxicating. A perfect night to take in the delights of early spring flowers—and besides, she still had some of her longer Juliet speeches to get down cold. She'd done her best line work in the park during the last show. It couldn't hurt to take a brief stroll.

And maybe . . . just maybe . . . Kelley sighed.

Sonny had been gone for almost half a year. *An eternity,* thought Kelley. And on such a beautiful night, when the air itself seemed almost brimming with its own subtle magic, it wasn't beyond the realm of possibility that he might find his way back to her that very night, was it?

Before she'd really decided one way or another, Kelley's sneakers seemed to make up her mind for her, and she turned and headed up Eighth Avenue, toward Columbus Circle—the nearest entrance to Central Park.

Soon after Sonny had returned to the Otherworld—the Faerie realm—Kelley had discovered that anytime she entered the park, the temptation to play around with her power was just too strong. Maybe it was because that was where she had first met Sonny . . . or maybe it was because the park wasn't just a park. It was also the Samhain Gate: a doorway to the Otherworld. Most people didn't know it existed, but Kelley Winslow wasn't "most people."

Neither was Sonny Flannery. Sonny was a member of an elite fighting force known as the Janus Guard. The Janus were all changelings—humans, taken as children from different times and different places to live among the Faerie in the Otherworld. These particular changelings had been appointed guardians of the Samhain Gate by Auberon, the Winter King of Faerie. Kelley's father.

When the Gate had opened last fall, the Janus had been significantly busier than they had been in other years, all because Kelley's presence in New York City had caused something of a ruckus. A deadly Faerie war band—the Wild Hunt—had been freed from enchanted slumber, Sonny had been transformed into their terrifying leader, and Kelley had been forced to bargain away one half of her Faerie birthright—the power she had inherited from her father—in order to save both Sonny and, pretty much, the entire mortal realm.

In the aftermath, Auberon had required Sonny to return to the Faerie realm in order to deal with the remnants of the Hunt, still rampaging through the Otherworld.

After Sonny's departure, Kelley had found herself occasionally spending time with the other members of the Janus Guard. They knew her secret, and that meant she could be herself with them. It also made her feel somehow closer to Sonny when she was around them. She knew that what he had gone to do—what he had been forced to go and do—was important. Kelley had experienced firsthand the devastation the Wild Hunt was capable of. Still, all she wanted was for Sonny to come back to her. Kelley knew in her heart that, once his task was accomplished, Sonny would make his way back to the mortal realm. He'd promised her that.

Strolling these familiar paths, Kelley fought the urge to reach up under her hair and unfasten the clasp on the silver chain that held a charm around her neck. The charm was made of green amber and shaped like a four-leaf clover; she'd worn it all her life. It was the only thing holding in check the power that still ran through Kelley's Faerie blood.

Her mother's power. Dangerous power.

The last time Kelley had been wandering alone in Central Park, she'd been careless—when a cop on horseback had come trotting into view and surprised her, she'd been hovering about six inches above the grassy surface of the Sheep Meadow. Fortunately it had been a moonless night, so the officer hadn't noticed her slightly elevated state. Although she could have sworn the horse looked at her sideways. . . .

It wasn't an experience she was anxious to repeat. So in recent months she'd begun to avoid the park altogether—and, in doing so, managed to mostly ignore the seductive call of her Faerie heritage. It helped that she'd been so busy with the new play lately. The company's last show, *A Midsummer Night's Dream,* had been a smash hit—thanks in large part to her performance as (ironically enough) Titania, the Fairy Queen. And this production of *Romeo and Juliet* aimed to top that. It would be a breakout role for Kelley if she could pull it off.

Kelley reached the Ladies Pavilion on the shores of Central Park Lake and mounted the steps. Her four-leaf clover firmly fastened around her neck, she leaned on the railing, gazing out over the still water.

"This bud of love, by summer's ripening breath . . ."

She murmured her lines and pictured Sonny climbing a trellis to her balcony.

". . . May prove a beauteous flower when next we meet.
Good night, good night! As sweet repose and rest
Come to thy heart as that within my breast!"

"O, wilt thou leave me so unsatisfied?" asked a voice in the darkness.

Kelley glanced up, startled. "Uh . . . ," she stammered, flustered at being taken off guard.

The moonlight pouring down onto the pavilion steps illuminated her like a spotlight.

"Sonny?" Kelley peered hopefully into the darkness of the surrounding woods, trying to make out where the voice had come from. No . . . not Sonny. Sonny wouldn't joke with her like that. It had to have been one of her fellow actors from the theater screwing around. "Alec?" There was still no answer. To cover her momentary unease, Kelley laughed a little. "Fine, I'll play your silly game," she said, and answered back with her next Juliet line: "What satisfaction canst thou have tonight?"

"Well," the voice answered, "I'll take that pretty necklace, for starters."

Kelley put a hand to her throat as a stranger stepped out of the shadows and into the light. It wasn't Alec Oakland.

"And I'll take any other jewelry you got. I'll take your wallet, too, just for the hell of it. And your watch, if it ain't a knockoff." The man radiated casual menace as he ambled toward her. He was lean and tattooed and wore a dirty denim jacket and motorcycle boots.

Great, Kelley thought, a knot of fear tightening her stomach. *A mugger with a taste for Shakespeare. This could only happen in Central Park.*

Running a hand through the long, shaggy hair that curtained his sharp face, the man said, "Didn't anyone ever tell

11

you this is a dangerous place after dark, little girl?"

"I'm not a little girl." Kelley snapped. A flare of anger nudged her apprehension aside.

"Ooh. Touchy." The man grinned unpleasantly.

Kelley felt the uneasy thrill of something dangerously close to excitement tingling along her spine. The sensation washed away the rest of her fear, even as it left her anger untouched. *Do it,* a voice whispered in her head, sounding like her mother's. *Let loose. It'll be worth it just to teach this jackass a painful lesson.*

"Look," Kelley said, holding up a hand. "I don't want any trouble. And—believe me—neither do you."

"Oh, I live for trouble, little girl."

Kelley almost laughed at that. "Not this kind," she said.

Of course he just sneered at her warning.

She felt a kind of heat blooming deep in her chest. "Trust me," she said. "You should go now."

"Let me guess." He continued walking toward her in a predatory fashion, one hand disappearing behind his back. "You know kung fu?"

"I don't need kung fu."

"Stop screwing around now and you won't get hurt," the mugger snarled, suddenly brandishing a knife. "Hand over the lucky charm! No tricks."

"Silly rabbit," Kelley said coldly, going with the breakfast-cereal theme, "tricks are for kids!" She reached up and yanked hard on the silver chain around her neck. The catch came loose, and brilliant purple light flooded the pavilion, spilling out onto shores of the Lake. From within the heart of the flaring nimbus, Kelley watched the man's expression shift suddenly in the dark blaze of her Faerie wings. He dropped the knife and took off running as if the hounds of hell were at his heels. Having once been chased by *actual* hellhounds, she understood the reaction. She almost felt sorry for him.

Shoving the charm into her pocket, Kelley stepped down onto the grass and bent to retrieve the weapon—a polished iron blade with a carved black ebony-wood handle. Grimacing with distaste and holding the thing between two fingers by the hilt, she stuffed it in the side pocket of her shoulder bag. It wouldn't be a good idea to just leave the thing lying around in the park.

When she straightened, her mugger was nowhere to be seen. Kelley smiled to herself and inhaled deeply. The spring air was sharp in her nostrils, and everything took on a diamond-bright clarity to her eyes. Opening her arms wide, Kelley felt her Faerie strength surge. She leaped off the ground and soared up into the sky. High above the Lake, she paused.

Her assailant had fled north and was hidden from her sight by the densely forested terrain of the Ramble. Kelley hovered on the night wind for a moment, enjoying the rush of excitement and power she had been denying herself, and then a flash of movement caught her eye. She folded her wings like a hunting hawk and plummeted toward the ground in a steep, arcing dive. She navigated a twisting path with reckless abandon, narrowly avoiding slamming into trees as she tried to chase the creep down, but he was nowhere to be found. Caught up in the thrill of the hunt, Kelley snarled in frustration at the loss of her quarry and beat the air with her wings. When she found herself in the narrow ravine of the Gill, she paused, hovering, listening.

Then something hit her from behind, square between her wings, and drove the breath from her lungs. The light from her wings flickered and dimmed, and she fell from the air, landing painfully on the rocky streambed of the cold, tumbling waters of the Gill.

Her concentration shattered by the fall, Kelley thrashed around wildly, trying to right herself and figure out what had hit her. Suddenly she realized that she was not alone in the water. She tried to scream but her throat filled with water as dozens of slimy, taloned hands grasped at her, dragging her down.

Nyxx! Kelley thought, panicking.

She knew that there were scattered Fae living in the mortal realm, and the Janus had warned her about which ones to avoid—and nyxx neared the top of that list.

Their scaly limbs wound around her arms and legs. Her brain screamed, telling her how stupid she was. Her mugger had been more right than he'd known when he'd said the park was dangerous after nightfall. Kelley had arrogantly thought to teach him a lesson and instead had flown straight into danger of another kind.

She kicked violently, dislodging the nyxxie that tore at her pant leg, and scrambled toward the stream bank. But then Kelley realized that the water-dwelling fae were not her only problem. Shadowy shapes moved in the trees and among the steep rocky outcroppings. There were eyes everywhere, staring at her with inhuman hunger. Kelley froze, paralyzed with fear.

Just then the moon cleared a bank of clouds and shone on a bluff in the near distance behind the menacing beings. The silver light perfectly silhouetted twelve figures, standing like statues on the ridge.

The Janus Guard.

Awesome! Kelley thought, almost shouting with joy. Adrenaline and Faerie magick coursed through her veins. She was spoiling for an all-out fight. She heard a command barked in a deep, sonorous voice—that would be Aaneel, the leader of the Guard—and Kelley saw the figures fan out, moving with precision and purpose.

Tiny, pretty Cait, ponytail swinging, slashed a slim-bladed rapier through the air. Selene targeted shadows with a compact bow from the vantage point of perching on a low tree-branch. Kelley saw Camina and Bellamy, twin sister and brother, working in lethal tandem. Maddox's tall, lanky shape moved with surprising speed and grace as he chased down a creature that darted through the undergrowth, growling like a bobcat. In the distance, someone was singing as they fought—Godwyn, Kelley thought, as the fiercely cheerful sound floated in the night air.

Kelley climbed halfway up the steep bank to join in the

fight. There was a sudden roar of warning. She turned sharply as another nyxxie leaped for her like a vicious, human-shaped barracuda—all razor-sharp teeth and sinewy body. The creature knocked her back into the water, grappling and twisting. The foaming waters of the Gill carried them both swiftly downstream, away from the sounds of fighting.

She punched the nyxxie hard in the stomach and floundered away to try to reach dry ground. Finally she gained solid footing on the rock, and space enough to gather her wits. Kelley stretched out her arm. Her fingertips crackled with eldritch energies as she wound up and threw a handful of raw, unformed magick like a fastball at the surface of the stream. The water erupted in a boiling geyser, and when the roiling subsided, the nyxxie floated motionless, stunned by the blast, its seaweed-black hair spread wide on the surface of water.

Kelley's breath came in gasps, her muscles ached from landing on the rocks, and lacerations on her leg from the nyxx claws stung fiercely. But she knew she was grinning from ear to ear. She hadn't felt this truly alive in months. She clambered along the rocks back upstream. The Janus had spread out, and in the darkness Kelley could just make out where running fights with the nightmare creatures of Faerie—spiny things and twisty things and shadowy-slippery, menacing things—carried on unabated.

A full-scale battle raged. She realized that the roar of warning had come to her from a Janus Guard called the Fennrys Wolf—he'd hurled himself into the Gill to take on the rest of the nyxx, who thrashed and flailed in the water where she'd first been attacked like piranha scenting blood. All of their attention was on Fennrys. It gave Kelley time. She concentrated again on reaching past the thunderous gallop of her pulse to the place where her mother's power lay coiled and waiting for her to call upon it.

She felt the dark, sparkling lattices of her wings furl outward from her shoulders as firecracker sparks showered everywhere. Suddenly thunderclouds boiled in the skies above her, and fat, pelting raindrops began to splatter on the shore and surface of the stream.

Kelley hadn't actually known how she would *use* her power to help Fennrys out of his dire situation—she wasn't well-versed enough to even know what she *could* do—but that mattered little. Her Faerie magick had taken on a shape and purpose of its own making—and called for backup!

Kelley glanced upward as a deafening whine and hiss assaulted her ears. The sky directly above her head tumbled with black and purple thunderheads and three Cailleach—her mother's fearsome Storm Hags—suddenly appeared in a burst of lightning and thunder. The Hags were Mabh's most dangerous and powerful minions; they did Mabh's bidding. *And apparently . . . mine!* Kelley thought, startled.

The Cailleach were like the living embodiment of unpleasant weather—in this case, three whip-twisty funnel clouds. Kelley yelled over the howling wind for Fennrys to duck and cover. The embattled Janus took one glance over his shoulder

17

and dove for shelter behind a rock in the middle of the stream.

The nyxx weren't so lucky.

The Cailleach swirled together into one massive, tornado-like formation, plucked the whole tangled pack of thrashing fae out of the Gill, and spun away with them over the treetops, spitting lightning randomly about the park as they went.

The silence left behind in their wake was deafening.

Kelley stood staring after the retreating storm as the Fennrys Wolf waded ashore.

"Evening," he said, wringing out his shirt, one side of his mouth quirking upward in a shadow of his trademark mocking sneer.

"Hi, Fennrys."

"That was interesting." Fennrys nodded at the retreating tempest, now far in the distance, heading toward Harlem Meer at the far north end of Central Park.

"I guess so," Kelley murmured, still a bit stunned by it all. "I didn't know they could do that. I didn't know *I* could do that." She turned to Fennrys, her excitement in the aftermath of the fight building with the release of tension. "Call them like that. I mean—ever since November, they've been kind of hanging around, you know? But at a distance. Which I was cool with because, frankly, they creep me out. But . . . calling them just now? Okay—*that* was neat. And useful!" She was babbling, she knew—animated to the point of almost giddy. "And we won!" Impulsively she threw her arms around Fennrys's soggy neck in a victory hug.

"Yes," he said.

Kelley felt his shoulders stiffen as Fennrys hesitated for a moment before awkwardly returning her embrace. The Wolf wasn't what anyone would mistake for easygoing or affectionate, and if it hadn't been for her exhilaration, Kelley would never have even presumed to hug him.

"Yes," he said again, as he lifted Kelley's arms away and settled her back on her feet. "We did. But, if I were you, I'd be more careful where I chose to take midnight strolls. This place is dangerous after dark."

"That's what *he* said." Kelley looked around at the mess they'd made. There were broken tree branches everywhere and long slashes of claw marks marring the stream banks.

"That's what who said?" Fennrys asked.

"Some poor guy who tried to mug me." Kelley frowned. "He ran this way. I bet the nyxx ate him."

"Well, that'll teach him the error of his ways, now, won't it?"

"Fennrys!"

He grinned coldly in the face of her admonishment and waved a hand at their surroundings. "Should have taken his own advice, if you ask me. Ever since all that craziness during the Nine-Night, we've been seeing a lot more activity from renegade Lost Fae. The Gate blowing wide open like it did on Samhain Eve has emboldened them somewhat."

"I guess that explains why all of you guys are in the park tonight."

Fennrys nodded. "Aaneel says that, on top of the Lost Ones getting uppity, there are hairline cracks showing up in places throughout the Samhain Gate. None big enough for even a sprite to get through yet, but still."

"I guess that's kind of my fault. . . ."

"I didn't say that. I just said you should be careful. You especially."

"Thanks, Fenn."

"Just a bit of advice. Take it or leave it."

"No . . ." Kelley smiled sheepishly. She knew she should have taken more care. "I meant about rescuing me just now."

"Don't mention it."

"Right!"

"No, seriously. Don't mention it." Fennrys shook out his dark-blond hair and ran a hand through it, pushing it back from his forehead. "If anyone knew I was rescuing damsels, it would ruin my reputation."

Kelley wasn't sure whether he was serious or not. "Well, thanks anyway."

"You're welcome, m'lady." He bent low in a courtly bow, and Kelley tried to get a sense of whether or not he was mocking her.

"C'mon," he said and offered her an elbow. "Let's go make sure the others weren't eaten or killed."

"See . . . this kinda thing?" Maddox said, breathing hard and leaning over, hands on his knees, as Kelley and Fennrys approached. "*This* is the kind of thing I was always nattering on about when I said things like 'Be careful, Kelley' and 'Maybe don't walk through Central Park alone at night, Kelley.'"

"I dunno, Maddox," Kelley said wanly, limping rather noticeably now that the adrenaline had worn off. "Fennrys seemed to enjoy the exercise."

Beside her the Wolf just grinned, sauntering away.

"Is it true what Fennrys told me about the cracks showing up in the Gate, Madd?" Kelley asked, digging her clover charm out of her pocket and fastening the chain around her neck once more.

"Yup."

"And Lost Ones are attacking people?"

"Well." Maddox shrugged. "Yeah. I mean—only *some* of them. Here and there. Like tonight."

Maddox always got a little evasive whenever the subject of the Lost Fae was broached. It was because of Chloe, Kelley knew. The Lost were Faerie in the mortal world. Either they had been trapped there when Auberon had first shut the Gate, or they considered perpetual confinement to the realms of Faerie to be imprisonment and had decided to "defect"— escaping through the Samhain Gate and quitting the Other-world forever.

Chloe was one of the Lost. She was also a Siren. An *ex*-Siren, if Maddox was to be believed. She had saved Kelley's life when Kelley had almost drowned in the fall. In the process of doing so, Chloe had learned that Kelley was the lost Faerie

21

princess stolen by a mortal woman from Auberon's Court almost a hundred years earlier.

Until that time, growing up in the Catskills under the watchful gaze of her "aunt" Emma, Kelley had never had the slightest inkling that she was anything other than human. But Chloe, being a Siren, had not been able to resist stealing the memory of a piece of music from Kelley's mind while she was unconscious, as payment for the rescue. A cheap price to pay to a Siren—they usually took every scrap of song that a mind could hold, and that would invariably cause irreparable damage. Death, most often. It was how they got their fearsome reputation in legends down through the ages. Chloe had long ago sworn off such behavior but had, it seemed, fallen off the wagon back in October when she'd rescued Kelley.

The theft had done Kelley no harm whatsoever, but that was because Kelley wasn't human—a secret that lay open to the Siren once she was inside Kelley's head. Chloe had gone on to barter the information she'd gleaned from Kelley's mind, trading the knowledge for another piece of music: she'd burrowed deep into Sonny's memories and stolen a lullaby, the only memory he'd possessed of his human mother.

As far as Kelley was concerned, Chloe was no better than a vampire. But Maddox had feelings for her, so Kelley usually avoided the subject.

"Let's get you the hell out of this park," Maddox said, ignoring Kelley's uncomfortable silence and putting a lanky arm around her shoulders. He was Sonny's best friend and had become almost like an older brother to her in Sonny's absence, especially in those first few months when Kelley had visited the park more frequently.

In the darkness they heard Fennrys snarling gleefully—he must have found something hanging around that was still worth hurting.

"C'mon." Maddox nudged her into a walk. "I'm sure the others can mop up the rest of this mess without my help."

Kelley nodded absently, just as sure as Maddox that the other Janus had handled the renegade Fae easily. They were all extremely good at what they did.

"I wonder how Sonny's doing," Kelley suddenly thought. Out loud. She could feel her cheeks redden a bit as Maddox looked at her, amused.

"I'm sure old Sonn is just fine," he said blithely. "While the rest of us are stuck here in the mortal realm, scrabbling around in the underbrush risking life and limb, Sonny's probably taking it dead easy, drinking Faerie wine and eating wild raspberries!"

II

Sonny Flannery swore an ancient, exceptionally foul oath and threw himself violently sideways—right into an enormous tangle of wild raspberry bushes studded with two-inch thorns as sharp as fish-hooks. The move may have lacked elegance, but it saved him from certain decapitation.

The hunter Fae that had almost swiped Sonny's head off bellowed in anger at the thwart. He'd obviously been pretty sure of a kill, and had it been any other adversary, he probably would have succeeded. But Sonny Flannery was a quarry of a different sort.

More hunter than hunted, even now.

The Wild Hunter had caught him unaware, yet Sonny had to admit that after months spent hacking through treacherous undergrowth, following trails of burned-out faerie woodland and the scattered bodies of dead lesser fae, relentless in his pursuit of the marauding remnants of the Wild Hunt, *this* contest looked to be more entertaining than most. Aside from the thorn bush—*that* was painful—Sonny was perversely enjoying the fact that this particular warrior Fae had sought to find Sonny before Sonny found him.

It is a deal more challenging to have the tables turned, he thought, struggling desperately to dislodge himself from the grasping branches before the hunter could wheel his mount and charge again. *At least this way, I won't feel quite so much like hating myself for what I have to do.*

The contest seemed like it might be almost even this time. This opponent, a worthy adversary. Still, Sonny had no intention of losing.

As the hunter's horse thundered to a stop, Sonny tore free his riding cloak from the bushes. Leaping to his feet, he ran for an open space between trees hung with Spanish moss. It was only then he realized that, in freeing himself from the thorns, he'd left behind the leather satchel that had hung from a strap across his body. It dangled uselessly from a thorny branch out of reach—full of the weapons of which Sonny was in dire need. The hunter wheeled his mount and charged again, straight for where Sonny stood unprotected.

Sonny threw himself to the side, throwing up his arm to protect his head as he hit the ground. The sudden hopelessness of his situation crashed like a wave in his mind—the hunter and his next pass would likely end the game once and for all.

But then a piercing whinny rang through the air, and Sonny lifted his head to see a kelpie—a faerie horse with a fiery red coat—come galloping furiously through a hawthorn brake, to shoulder aside the hunter's deadly charge.

"Lucky!" Sonny shouted in frantic relief, recognizing the creature he'd not seen since a certain Faerie princess had knocked him flying from that animal's back high above New York's Central Park what seemed like so many months earlier. Sonny leaped to his feet as Lucky whirled nimbly, but as the kelpie came to a halt directly in front of him, the creature reared suddenly, lashing out with his deadly hooves in the direction of Sonny's head.

Sonny hit the dirt just before the first kick would have smashed in his skull. "What in hell—," he cursed, but rolling onto his back, he saw that Lucky hadn't been striking out at him. Looming large above where he lay on the weedy ground, Sonny saw that the Fae hunter's mount—a thing of smoke and mist capable of landing surprisingly solid blows—rose up on its hind legs, right behind him.

The two creatures danced above where Sonny sprawled on the ground, dueling fiercely with their flashing front hooves. Keeping his seat with ease upon the back of his heaving steed, the Fae hunter laughed wildly and swung his sword at the prone form of the Janus. Sonny pulled his arms against his chest and dodged first one way and then the other.

Above him, the two faerie beasts pummeled the air and each other, raining down punishing blows. Sonny tucked into a shoulder roll as Lucky somehow managed to avoid mashing him into a fine red paste. He scrambled for the raspberry bushes—and the satchel that held, among other things, a compact crossbow and a quiver of iron bolts. Sonny had commissioned the gear from a mortal blacksmith in thrall to Auberon, the king of the Unseelie Fae. He was glad he had. Sonny's weapon of choice had always been the enchanted silver blade that the king had bestowed upon him along with his Janus status, but relying on the sword alone meant that he had to get close enough to his target to strike a blow. That hadn't usually been a problem for Sonny. But the Wild Hunt was not usual quarry. The bow had been commissioned as a backup plan.

It had come in handy more than once.

With Lucky flailing and rearing madly in his efforts to protect the Janus, Sonny plunged his hand into the bag and withdrew the crossbow and arrow case, dancing away before he was crushed by the dueling horses. With swift, fluid motions—the fruit of endless hours of practice—he cocked the bow, loaded the bolt, and in one sweeping movement, raised, aimed, and fired.

The short, thick arrow took the hunter in the shoulder,

and the impact knocked him from his shadowy horse. He hit the ground heavily, but was up on his feet with a quickness that made the motion almost a blur. Sonny noted that from the point of his shoulder where the arrow had lodged, the Fae's wraithlike appearance was changing. Solidifying. His mount— spooked by the fall of his rider—reared and, screaming, pounded away into the distance.

With grim determination, Sonny cocked and reloaded the bow.

The second bolt slammed into the Faerie hunter's thigh, and he roared with unbridled rage, falling heavily to one knee. Sonny pulled a bundle of three short tree branches bound with a red cord from the satchel and, with a whispered incantation, transformed them into the silver-bladed sword that was his signature weapon. He approached the hunter, easily parrying the pain-clumsy, one-handed blows the Fae directed at him and knocking the blade from the hunter's hand. His opponent was almost entirely corporeal now—the effects of the iron stuck in his flesh spreading rapidly. Still it was a surprise when, with a ragged, defiant battle cry, he launched himself in a tackle around Sonny's waist and slammed him to the ground, breaking his grip on his own sword, which flew out of reach.

This is new, Sonny thought, struggling to keep the strong, graceful hands of the hunter from closing off his windpipe. Most High Fae, unlike some of the more beastly inhabitants of the Otherworld, would have considered grappling with an opponent—even in the desperate moments at the end of a fight—as beneath them. But not this one. The only thing that was beneath *him,* in that moment, was Sonny. The Fae pinned him to the ground with the knee of his uninjured leg and, rearing back with a short dagger clawed from a sheath at his belt, made to slash the Janus's throat open.

In the last instant, Sonny raised his left arm in a block—hand open and fingers spread wide—and braced for the flash of pain as the knife sliced a long, deep gash in his palm. Blood splashed crimson on the Faerie hunter's surprised face, blinding him momentarily and causing him to drop the knife. Without even trying to dislodge the Wild Hunter, Sonny reached out his bleeding hand and grasped the black talisman shaped like a stag's head that hung, glittering, from a silken cord around the Faerie's throat.

Words of an incantation hissed from between Sonny's teeth. He plucked up the hunter's fallen blade and cut the talisman free from the hunter's throat. The Fae's expression turned from surprise to alarm. And then, as his gaze met and locked with Sonny's, to wonder. His beautiful golden eyes, suddenly bereft of battle madness, searched Sonny's face, and he began to laugh softly—a quiet chuckle that faltered as he fell away from the young Janus, to lie gasping on his side on the ground.

"I *see.* . . . ," he murmured. "Oh, now I see. . . ."

"See what?" Sonny panted, turning to face his adversary in these, his quarry's final moments. "What do you see?"

"I do not feel so bad now," the hunter wheezed, heaving to pull the breath into his laboring lungs. "Having . . . having lost to such a one as you. It was a good chase, was it not, noble lord?"

"Noble lord?" Sonny pulled back, startled, the bloodied charm slick in the tight knot of his fist. *The Fae must have fallen into a kind of delirium,* he thought. However, the hunter's expression remained clear-eyed and keen. "Why would you call me by such a name?" Sonny demanded. "I am not a lord. Certainly not noble."

The hunter opened his mouth to speak, but it was too late. He was already going—in another moment, there would be little left of Mabh's monstrous creation but smoke and mist and a haunting cry that drifted away on the wind.

Sonny averted his gaze so that he would not have to watch as yet another Wild Hunter faded to nothingness.

"Another one for the fire," Sonny said as he slammed his hand down on the oak table and sank wearily onto a bench. Gofannon the blacksmith—a mountain of muscle in a scorched leather apron—rumbled a greeting that sounded half composed of ash and smoke. He thrust a bar of raw iron into the heart of the forge and threw his heavy tongs down on the hearth as though they weighed no more than a pair of knitting needles.

When Sonny withdrew his hand, a glittering black stag-head jewel lay upon the worn wooden surface. Gofannon eyed the stone as if it were a poisonous viper. He drew a dirty oil-cloth rag from the pocket of his apron and picked the stone up in it. Moving swiftly for all his bulk, he stepped back over to the fire and tossed both rag and gem into the forge. Then he went and worked the bellows, pumping air until the flames burned almost white.

"You'll ruin the iron." Sonny nodded his head at where the metal bar had begun to misshape in the extreme heat.

"Plenty more where that came from," Gofannon grunted between his exertions. When he returned to sit with Sonny, he was carrying a small wooden box that he had fetched from a cabinet hanging on the rough stone wall, along with a clean rag, a dish, and a pitcher. "Give me your hand," he said, pouring water from the pitcher into the dish and dampening the rag.

Sonny's hand was wrapped in a strip of fabric torn from the hem of his riding cloak, the cloth stained through and stiff with blood. He laid his forearm on the table and waited silently while the blacksmith unwrapped the makeshift bandage.

Sonny tried to ignore the big smith's muttered expressions of consternation as—once he'd cleaned the dried blood away—Gofannon traced the thin white lines of close to two dozen other scars that ran across the breadth of Sonny's palm, in addition to the fresh, angry-red seam of his latest wound.

"How much longer is this going to go on, then?" Gofannon asked, his voice carefully neutral.

"There are twenty-seven hunters, all told," Sonny said, staring at his palm as if the scars could tell his future.

"Then you must be close to the end, judging by this."

"Three left. I think. They all start to blur together. In my mind *and* on my hand . . ."

The act of eliminating the Wild Hunt, Sonny soon discovered upon his return to the Otherworld with Auberon, was bound up in dangerous magick. His appointed task was not quite as simple as hunting their scattered numbers down, one by one. Not only were the hunters dangerous in and of themselves, but it was only blood magick that allowed Sonny to release a hunter from Queen Mabh's curse once he'd caught up with them. His own blood.

The smith's brows knit fiercely as he tended to the wound on Sonny's hand. "When you first told me of this task the king has charged you with . . . I should have counseled you against it."

"It wouldn't have made any difference, Gof. It wasn't something Auberon would have let me refuse. And besides, the waking of the Hunt was partly my fault. It's only right that I be the one to clean up this mess."

"Still. Blood magick is bad business, Sonny. Dangerous."

"Aye," Sonny agreed dryly. "And frequently painful, I can attest."

The gash on Sonny's hand cleaned, Gofannon twisted the stopper out of a squat, opaque green jar that he produced out of the box. He slathered a thick coating of pungent ointment onto the not-yet-healed wound and unrolled a length of linen bandage, wrapping it around the Janus's hand. "Faerie magick is a plague, Sonny. A sickness. Passion fuels it, and that is its very peril—because the more you use it, the more it uses you. I know whereof I speak, believe me. Even the simplest of spells can wound your soul, but blood magick is the absolute worst for it."

Sonny didn't need a lecture on the dangers of blood magick. Faerie magick, sourced in thought and emotion, was perilous enough—especially when the heart overruled the head. But blood magick had its roots in a deeper place. It came from the very core of a person's soul. It was easily corruptible and, as such, was almost never used to create—only destroy.

"It'll hook its claws into you, Sonny. Be cautious. Be wise."

Sage counsel, Sonny thought. Especially from Gofannon, who in centuries past had made a bargain with Auberon that had been neither cautious nor wise. Sonny had never learned the details, but he knew that the end result had been the smith's eternal servitude to the Faerie king. The fact that he kept an abundance of iron strewn about his forge was Gofannon's single rebellion—the hated metal was poisonous to Faeriekind—and yet Auberon had found a way to make even *that* serve his ends.

"I remember when I made that," Gofannon said, reaching out to tap the iron medallion that hung from a braided leather cord around Sonny's throat. "I've put more magick into those Janus charms than I ever thought I had in me."

"Blood magick?" Sonny asked, gently sardonic.

"Some," the smith acknowledged. "Not *mine*, though. Still, magick is magick, and it takes its price. Those iron trinkets took more than most."

Sonny fingered the intricate design on the face of the medallion, thinking how he could not remember the feel of *not* wearing it. Even though the changelings that made up the Janus Guard had been drawn from all Four Courts to serve the Winter King, Auberon had made sure to mark them as his own from the time he had enlisted them. No other Fae would dare even attempt to remove their medallions—and the fact that they were made of iron just served to emphasize that pointed fact.

"Speaking of iron . . ." Sonny stood, suddenly uncomfortable with the subject of what was, essentially, his slavery. He fetched an arrow quiver that he'd left by the door of the forge with his satchel. "I'll need another two dozen or so bolts for my crossbow." He tossed the near-empty holder onto the table.

"That's a lot of ammunition when there's only three of the hunter Fae left out there."

"These last few Hunters are getting more dangerous and more desperate." Sonny pushed a hand through the tangled wave of his long, dark hair. "And I didn't really appreciate having my arse kicked all over the Borderlands in this last fight. If I can incapacitate them from a distance first, so much the better."

The burly smith laughed, taking two mugs and a brown

earthen jug from a shelf by the door. Sitting back down at the table, Gofannon twisted the cork out of the jug and pushed one of the mugs toward Sonny's freshly bandaged hand. "Speaking of arses . . ." he said, "if I may offer a carefully cultivated observation, Janus? You look like the hind end of hell."

"You're being generous," Sonny said wryly. "Thank you."

"When was the last time you slept, Sonny?" Gofannon asked, peering at him. "I mean *really* slept—the whole night through."

"I don't remember. A few days ago. Maybe three?"

"And what is it keeps you awake night after night? It can't be just this hunting, surely."

"You said it yourself—this kind of magick gets its hooks into you."

"So does another kind of spell casting I know of. And it is even more dangerous." The smith shook his head. "I know the look. You, young sir, are in love."

Sonny did smile then. A pure and genuine smile. "I am," he said softly.

"Ah. Well then. Love is the Great Discombobulator. Especially among us mortals. I should have sooner guessed." Gofannon poured out two generous measures of golden liquid. "In that case, I will simply say this: joy and good hunting to you."

Sonny laughed wearily. "Insofar as it seems I won't be achieving the one without the other, I accept your toast." He took a long sip of the cool, smooth drink. It was like biting

35

into a fresh pear that had fallen into an ice-cold mountain stream.

Sonny gazed out the window toward a row of jagged hills that jutted above the nearby forest of snow-covered pines. The highest peak was topped with the spires and battlements of Auberon's palace, like glittering stalagmites. "How are things up there?"

"Why do you need to ask?" Gofannon sounded surprised. "Aren't you staying in the palace?"

Sonny shook his head. "There's a cottage near the woods of the Autumn Borderlands where I've been staying. You know—for those scant few days when I'm not off hunting maniacs. No, Gof, I may still work for the Winter King, but that is all. I won't shelter under his roof. He hasn't mentioned that?" Sonny asked, the tone of his voice both surly and a little wounded. Auberon had been the only father he'd ever known.

"I haven't seen his frosty lordship for a good long while," Gofannon answered. "Not since Samhain, when you returned from the mortal world. Any work he's had me do lately—and that has been very little—he's sent the Goodfellow down with his orders. And *that* tricky beast and I don't speak much in the way of civil discourse and the passing of time, these days."

"Is there anyone left that Puck hasn't managed to madden or make an enemy of, I wonder?"

The smith shrugged. "We used to be cordial. Friends even."

"What happened?" Sonny asked.

"He's a bloody thief is what happened."

"A lousy one, to hear tell of it!" Sonny laughed.

"Lousy or not, he'll steal the breeches off your backside if you're looking the other way. Bah!" Gofannon turned and spat into the fire. "Don't talk to me of the Goodfellow. He'll come to ill one day for his thieving ways, and I'll drink to it!"

Sonny was surprised to see the smith, usually so even-tempered, turn flushed with anger.

Gofannon moved away from Sonny, back to the glow of his forge. "I'll send word when the arrows are done," he said curtly, and picked up his hammer. Sparks flew as he began pounding at the white-hot ingot. The visit was at an end.

"Thank you, Gof," Sonny said, and slung his leather satchel across his body. When the smith didn't answer, he quietly opened the door of the forge and stepped out into the biting chill of a winter day.

III

"**N**o!" Kelley bolted upright in her bed, the blood-spattered images of her nightmare so vivid that they seemed to hang before her in the darkened air of her room. She took a deep breath, trying to slow the pounding of her heart, and pulled her knees up to her chest.

Oh, Sonny, she thought bleakly, *not another one . . .*

The late April breeze sifting through the cracked-open window bared sharp, chilly teeth, but in spite of that, Kelley's sheets were soaked with sweat, and she felt almost feverish. According to the blue glow of the clock at her bedside, she'd been asleep for less than an hour, but it seemed that she'd dropped straight into the ravening maw of her dreams. Again. But these dreams were different.

Kelley still preferred to think of it as dreaming. It *wasn't*, of course—not in the conventional sense. When they had first started happening, Kelley had written them off as garden-variety nightmares. Vivid ones, sure—but just nightmares. Now, however, she knew the visions that tormented her from time to time were glimpses of actual events. She knew, for instance, that Sonny had managed to hunt down yet another of the dwindling numbers of the Wild Hunt. Hunt him down and . . . kill him.

Kelley knew it was real—she had seen the bright blood splashed across the hunter's cheek as he gasped for breath, and she had forced herself to wake before the terrible moment when she knew she would have to witness the light fading from his beautiful eyes.

She had her mother to thank for the disturbing visions, but that was hardly surprising. Her mother had a lot to answer for.

Kelley reached for the glass of water on her bedside table and knocked a stack of playscripts to the floor. With a sigh she bent to pick them up. In among the scattered pages was a postcard from her aunt Emma that she'd been using for a bookmark; it was from Ireland. Kelley turned it over and gazed at the glossy image of green, rolling hills. Kelley still found it hard to believe that the "aunt" who'd raised her was actually Sonny's mother—and that she'd stolen Kelley as an infant, taken her from her cradle in the Unseelie court in the Otherworld before tumbling through time and space to wind up in New York City, more than a century and an ocean away from where she'd begun her perilous quest. Though Kelley still hadn't quite gotten used to these revelations, she had been happy that Em had decided to return to spend a few months in the country of her birth. From the sound of things, the trip had been good for her.

Kelley tucked the postcard back into its place and gathered up the rest of the fallen scripts. Sandwiched between copies of Shakespeare's *The Tempest* and a collection of Greek tragedies, she found a single folded sheet of paper. Her fingers trembling slightly, she unfolded it—page 26 from her old script for *A Midsummer Night's Dream*. She had told Sonny to keep the script as a good-luck charm, and he had sent that one page back to her on opening night with the words *I love thee* circled in gold ink.

Kelley swallowed the tiny sob that was building in her throat and, folding the page gently, pressed it to her heart for a moment, hugging herself in the darkness.

Shivering in the chill draft that seeped through cracks around the edges of the bathroom window, Kelley ran the tap and splashed water over her face and neck. She really didn't feel like going back to sleep.

When she looked up into the mirror, the green eyes that

stared back at her from her own face seemed to smile sadly.

"So you saw, then."

Of course she had. Mabh sent her the visions like clock-work—every time Sonny was successful in one of his deadly pursuits. It was like supernatural spam, straight into Kelley's mental inbox.

"Another one down. Now only three of the Hunt are left . . ." As Kelley's reflection spoke, the features began to alter subtly to become those of a woman with Kelley's same eyes, but older. How much older was impossible to tell. She was ageless, effortlessly beautiful, and more dangerous than anyone Kelley had ever known. Mabh. Her mother. The Faerie Queen of the Autumn Court sighed mournfully and continued as if Kelley weren't glaring daggers at her. "He'll be coming after *me* soon enough, I daresay. . . ." She somehow managed to infuse an artful tremor of fear into the music of her voice. "They'll cage me again like an animal."

"You assume I care," Kelley said flatly as she pushed the damp hair from her forehead and turned her back on the mirror.

"Kelley!" The silky voice turned petulant as a pouty child's. "I'm your mother."

Wearily Kelley plucked a bath towel from the rack by the tub and hung it over the mirror.

"I'll wager you didn't know your boyfriend was such a bloodthirsty little thing when you promised your heart and soul to him," Queen Mabh continued, her voice only slightly muffled by the thick terrycloth. "How's that working for you, darling? Has he broken your heart yet? Men will do that, you know."

"Stow it, *Mom*." Kelley felt her jaw tightening.

"Has he called? Written? Sent a bouquet of ro—"

Behind the towel the glass shattered under the hammer of Kelley's fist, mercifully silencing the sound of her mother's voice in a rain of tinkling shards falling into the sink.

"Right. That's it."

Kelley jumped, startled. She turned to see her roommate, Lady Tyffanwy of the Mere—better known in the mortal realm as Tyff Meyers, model and party-girl supreme—lounging against the doorframe.

"Winslow," she declared, "you need to have some fun."

"Tyff, I—"

"Unh!" Tyff put up a hand. "We're going out."

"But—"

"Kell . . . no offense"—Tyff sighed—"but honestly? Ever since Smiley hit the road back to the Otherworld, you've become a royal pain in the ass to live with."

"His name is Sonny. And I have not!" Kelley yelped in indignation.

"Have."

"I—"

"Look. Sure. You've been cheerful and chipper and patient and diligent and polite and on time for everything." Tyff turned on her heel and marched to her own room as she spoke, Kelley reluctantly following. "All of which tells me that you're wound tighter than a factory-fresh yo-yo string. Well—also the fact that you just broke our bathroom mirror with punching."

"Sorry abou—"

"Not the issue." Tyff threw open the doors to her vast wardrobe and began chucking bits of designer clubwear over her shoulders at Kelley. "In fact, *that* was the most interesting thing you've done in months. Now get dressed."

The River was an upscale boutique hotel in midtown, but most of the lower floors and lobby space were occupied by club-style lounges and an exotic-cuisine restaurant with, Tyff pointed out, a months-long waiting list. From the outside, it sure didn't look like much, Kelley thought. Inside the hotel, it was a whole different story.

The escalator was the only feature in an otherwise blank white lobby. Kelley stepped aboard the narrow moving stairs in the wake of her roommate, and together they were carried upward through a corridor lit by chartreuse fluorescent lights and into a hall that served as a reception area. It was vast and airy, dark with rich wood on all the walls. The ceiling seemed to disappear into leafy shadows overhead. A long concierge desk, carved with the shape of a twisted tree, was illuminated only by the flickering electric flames of an elaborate crystal chandelier that was festooned with hundreds of holographic images—like photographs, only they shifted and shimmered. As she passed, Kelley thought she saw a face in one of the portraits wink at her. But when she blinked and looked again, the grotesque face just seemed to be leering in general. She quickened her pace to catch up with Tyff, who was checking her jacket at a cloakroom off to one side of the hall. An impossibly thin, white-haired young girl staffed the desk—standing under a stuffed mountain-goat head that Kelley *also* could have sworn winked at her as she handed over her jacket.

Tyff grinned at the look on Kelley's face. "Come on!" she said, and tugged Kelley by the elbow down a long passageway lit, intermittently, at ankle level.

Kelley cast a nervous eye around at the River's patrons and extracted her elbow from Tyff's long-fingered grip. "I don't know about this. . . ."

"Stuff the nerves, Winslow. You said you'd come dancing tonight, and you are *not* backing out. I already told the big guy at the concierge desk not to let you leave without me. And he's really an ogre."

"You mean—"

"I mean a *real* ogre, yeah. He owes me a favor, and he's fairly enthusiastic about wanting to repay it. So he might accidentally break you if you try to go." She shrugged. "Ogres tend to have a little problem with fine motor skills."

"Nice."

"You said you wanted to have fun tonight."

"*You* said I wanted to have fun tonight! That is not the same thing!"

"I'm doing this for both our sakes."

"You're doing this because *you* like dancing. And torment-
ing me, apparently."

Tyff ignored Kelley's protests and shoved her gently up a
shallow staircase toward the main lounge. The level of illumination in that area was almost blinding by comparison to the
entrance—also a bit dizzying. The floor was composed of illuminated square panels. From the corners garish green, gold,
and purple spotlights swept the room, alternately obscuring
and revealing an intricate mural on the ceiling—a swirl of
leaves and flowers and snaking vines, surrounding a curled
abstract female form at the center.

Mismatched furniture gave an eclectic air to the place;
white leather settees and high-tech clear Lucite chairs molded
into antique shapes stood scattered among several enormous
felled tree trunks that lay diagonally across the floor and served
as bench seating. Here and there the gilded walls shimmered
with waterfall fountains.

Tyff grabbed them a couple of drinks from the long oak
bar and led Kelley through a maze of bodies swaying to
music. The club was packed, but in the corner Kelley saw a
high-backed gilt chair sitting empty, as though reserved and
waiting for some Hollywood starlet or New York celebutante.
She followed Tyff through a set of soaring double doors that
led out to a central courtyard overflowing with plants and
flowers. April was early for such a profusion of blooms, but
the River didn't seem bound by that particular law of nature.
The whole place was like one giant, fantastical garden, and

Kelley felt a bit like Alice down the rabbit hole—a rabbit hole full of Lost Fae.

Tyff led the way into the center of the courtyard, Kelley following in her wake, trying not to stare too much. The courtyard was lit only by dozens and dozens of candles scattered about in glass holders. The night air wrapped around them like a cashmere sweater—warm, soft, perfumed by flowers. Dancers swayed to the music that came from a band on a raised stage in the corner. A dark-haired Fae with an ethereally beautiful voice sang in a language that Kelley couldn't understand, her soaring tones somehow melding with an operatic score and an urban backbeat.

"I thought Herne's Tavern was where the Lost Fae went to party," Kelley said.

"The Tavern is where the Lost go if they want to get *away* from humanity. The River," Tyff waved a hand at the fantastical surroundings, "is where the Lost come if they want to get up close and personal with humanity!"

Kelley glanced about the place and realized that, in fact, the capacity crowd was equal measures of Fair Folk mixed in with unsuspecting New Yorkers looking to hang out in a hot clubbing spot with the beautiful people. Really beautiful people.

"C'mon!" Tyff shouted in her ear over the clamor. "Let's go see if we can find Titania—you gotta meet the queen!"

Kelley shook her head vigorously. "I really don't think I— I'm not—I'm not dressed to meet royalty, Tyff. . . ."

"You *are* royalty, Winslow."

"I'm still undecided on that point."

"It's not really optional, you know. You just are. And you look fine—obviously—you're wearing my stuff."

It was true. Even though Kelley felt bad from the last time she had borrowed from Tyff's huge wardrobe (they'd had to throw the Galliano dress in the trash, and Kelley still shuddered to think of it) she had to admit that the designer jeans and deep purple top that Tyff had thrust at her back in the apartment suited both her figure and her coloring, and the strappy sandals gave her some extra height that almost made her feel willowy.

"Anyway," Tyff continued, craning her neck to see over the crowd, "Titania's not like the other monarchs."

"What—scary and pathological?"

"You'll *like* her, Kell. She's really cool. Nice, even. And I've already told her all about you."

"She's not *here* here, is she? It's like the mirror thing my mother does, isn't it?" Kelley crossed her arms, determined to be obstinate. "Because I find that horribly creepy. It's like talking to a television set. And having it talk back."

"No, Kelley." Tyff sighed and blew a strand of shining, wheat-gold hair out of her ridiculously blue eyes. With her perfect skin, her hair and her eyes—not to mention the body—Tyff tended to stand out. Even in Manhattan. "She actually comes here. She owns this place."

"She owns the nightclub?"

"The whole hotel, actually. I think she won the land in a

47

card game and then she built a women's residence on it in the 1920s—mostly that was a facade; it was really a sanctuary, a place to stay for all the Seelie girls who'd gotten caught in the mortal realm when your bad-ass dad, King Auberon, shut the Gate."

Kelley frowned. "So Titania still comes and goes as she pleases—even though Faerie like you were stuck here?"

"Yup." Tyff shrugged a sculpted shoulder. "The kings and queens of Faerie aren't exactly bound by closed doors."

"But Mabh was bound—"

"Only *after* she'd already poured most of her power into transforming Herne and his buddies into the unstoppable monstrosity that was the Wild Hunt. Even then it still took the two strongest monarchs to bind one lesser queen and— well, as we all discovered last fall, much to the detriment of a particularly expensive item of my wardrobe—even *that* wasn't anything close to permanent." Tyff's eyes restlessly scanned the crowd. "There she is!" she exclaimed suddenly, and, clamping a hand on Kelley's wrist, dragged her back into the main lounge and over to the thronelike chair that was now occupied by the most stunning creature Kelley had ever laid eyes on.

Titania, the Queen of Summer, was nothing like Kelley had expected. Perhaps it was all the Victorian fairy paintings she'd seen over the years, or the fact that Tyff, a Summer Fae, looked like the ultimate sun-kissed California beach babe. But, whatever she may or may not have expected, Kelley found herself staring. The queen's beauty was utterly exotic. Her flawless complexion was the color of honey and ripe peaches; and her hair, piled high in a cascade on her head, was a rich, dark shade of chocolate, shot through with ruby and bronze highlights. Her regal head was set upon a long, graceful neck, and she wore peacock-hued silks that showed tantalizing flashes of burnished skin when she moved.

With a start Kelley realized that she looked almost exactly like the famous bust of the ancient Egyptian queen Nefertiti. Kelley had only a fleeting moment to make that comparison, though, before Titania turned and her dark gold eyes caught and held Kelley in a stare that felt like standing in a beam of late summer sunlight.

"So *you're* Kelley," she said, her voice fluid and fair as birdsong. "It is such a pleasure to finally meet you—come sit with me, my dear girl." She gestured to the chair next to her. "Tyffanwy, love—your Queen is parched. Be a dear?"

Tyff smiled and inclined her head gracefully. Then she shot Kelley a wink and flitted off to fetch her queen refreshment.

"All this unpleasantness last Samhain." Titania shook her head. "Such a pity. Such drama. I'm so sorry for you that you had to discover your heritage in such an untidy fashion. I hear that you had something to do with thwarting the risen Hunt?"

"I . . . I was just in the right place at . . . uh . . . the right time, I guess," Kelley stammered.

"I'm sure it was much more than that." Titania smiled.

Kelley thought fleetingly that maybe hanging out with the Fair Folk might not be so bad after all. Not if there were more Faerie like this. Tyff was right—she did like Titania.

The queen reached out and touched her cheek with real warmth. "You're too modest," she said.

"No. Really!" Kelley laughed. "It was kind of just dumb luck that I didn't wind up getting myself killed!"

"Terrible business." Titania's gaze roamed over the bobbing heads of the crowd. "Who was it, one wonders, who dared to wake the Wild Hunt?"

"You don't know?" Kelley didn't really feel like bad-mouthing Auberon just at that moment, but she wasn't sure what else to say. Her father had been the one to loose the Hunt. He had called the Roan Horse with Mabh's horn. Turned Sonny into a monster . . . But she knew that Titania and Auberon were frequent paramours—almost husband and wife at times—and for this reason Kelley figured that the queen wasn't really about to vilify Kelley's father in front of her. Kelley might have had some choice words about him herself, of course, except that she didn't know where the king and queen's relationship stood at this particular moment. And, anyway, Titania rescued her from actually having to say anything of the kind by waving the matter away.

"One hears rumors. Of course, I'm not sure anyone really knows *everything* that happened on that horrible night, my dear," she mused. "Best not to think about it too long. Madness, really."

"I'll say," Kelley agreed wholeheartedly. "That whole night is pretty much just like a bad dream to me, your highness."

"Of course. I'm so sorry to have brought it up." The queen leaned in to her then, like a confidante sharing a secret. "But *do* tell me about the boy," she whispered, her eyes dancing with fun. "The young hero—the Janus favored of the Unseelie king who hunts Mabh's creatures for him now."

"Sonny?"

"That's the one." The queen smiled, running her fingertip around the corner of her perfect mouth. "Out of all the changelings Auberon ever took into his Court, I was always a little surprised by that one. Now Aaneel—my sweet Indian boy—was exotic *and* the son of a princess. A very handsome child. I could understand why Auberon would desire him as a page."

Kelley blinked in surprise. She kept forgetting that Shakespeare had actually based at least some of *A Midsummer Night's Dream* on reality.

"But the young Irish boy always seemed so . . . normal to me." Titania's laugh was like water falling on silver chimes. "Common, even."

"He is not!" Kelley protested.

Titania raised a startled eyebrow at her, and Kelley had to restrain herself from leaping rabidly to Sonny's defense. *Common?* Was Titania even thinking about the same person as she was? she wanted to ask. But the Summer Queen was entitled to her opinion, and this *was* her place. Kelley didn't want to be rude. She also didn't want to get caught up in any sort of Faerie head games. Even though Tyff vouched for Titania, Kelley knew that messing with people's minds was a sort of national pastime among the Fair Folk. So she demurred, saying: "I mean—he's a Janus. They're not exactly common, are they? He's very strong, actually. And smart."

"I see." The queen tilted her head.

"And stubborn . . ." *And beautiful and funny and infuriating and a phenomenal kisser and*—Titania was staring closely at her, so Kelley shut up and tried to stop thinking about Sonny before she blushed crimson.

"Well, perhaps I've missed something in the boy." The queen waved a hand dismissively. "You seem to hold him in some sort of regard."

"Oh, well, I—"

"And naturally I respect the opinions of so bright a girl." Titania smiled her extraordinary smile. "And so talented, too. I attended your performance on closing night, you know. Lovely. I think you captured my essence brilliantly!"

And then Kelley *did* feel her cheeks reddening. The thought of the *actual* Titania sitting in the audience watching her pretend to be the Queen of Faerie! *Oh gawd . . .*

"But you must excuse me; I should attend to my other guests as well." Titania stood and looked down on Kelley, her golden gaze like a sunbeam. "Be merry and at peace in my house, child of Auberon, daughter of Mabh."

Kelley watched Titania disappear into the throng and was

surprised to see a figure she recognized standing at the edge of the crowd. "Maddox!" she exclaimed, leaping to her feet and waving him over, relieved to find a familiar *human* face. "I didn't expect to find you here."

"Hullo, Kelley," he greeted her. "Some party, huh?"

"I thought you Janus types didn't mix with the Lost Ones," she said, and then immediately regretted the jibe when Maddox's expression went stiff and awkward.

But Maddox recovered his composure almost immediately. "Well . . ." He waved a hand. "You know. We're not all horribly stuffed up like Godwyn."

"You mean 'stuck up'?" Kelley grinned.

"Yeah. That." He nodded, smiling, in his disarming fashion. "I've even got a few friends who are Lost Ones. Y'know?"

Right. Like Chloe.

"Hellooo there . . ." Tyff suddenly appeared out of nowhere, putting down a tray of champagne flutes and artfully elbowing Kelley out of the way as she extended her hand toward Maddox. "Kelley never told me she knew *real* men! How naughty of her."

In the glow of the whirling lights, Maddox blushed almost purple as Tyff's gaze raked over him. Kelley stifled a laugh.

"Care to dance, handsome?" Not like Tyff was presenting him with options. She already had him halfway to the dance floor.

"Uhh—shouldn't we keep Kelley company?" Maddox protested loudly enough to be heard.

"Sure!" Tyff yelled over the thundering backbeat. "C'mon, Kell! Come dance!"

"No, no! You go ahead, guys—I'll just stay here . . . until I can acclimatize myself to this place." Kelley cast a wary eye at the writhing mass of beautiful bodies. "Don't worry about me—go have fun. Seriously."

Tyff sighed and shook her head in frustration but, after a second, relented and gave Kelley a smile. She swung her hair over her shoulder and tightened her grip on Maddox. Together they disappeared into the gyrating crowd.

Kelley watched them go, a tiny sliver of envy working its way into her heart. She wished she could be that carefree. The song ended, and she heard Tyff's silvery laugh float over the heads of her fellow Fae and all the pretty, oblivious mortals. Another song started—this one more melodic. Not a slow dance, but not a frenetic one, either. Kelley found herself swaying slightly to the beat.

Someone tapped her on the shoulder. "Might I have this dance?"

Kelley turned, a polite refusal on her lips that died when she saw who it was.

"Fennrys?" she asked, surprised. "Okay—Maddox I can kind of understand, but what on earth are *you* doing here?"

"Slumming," the Fennrys Wolf said archly, casting a bleak eye around at the River's shimmering patrons.

Kelley crossed her arms and looked up at him. "You guys aren't here on some kind of stupid babysitting assignment or anything, are you? Because if that's what this is—"

"Nah," Fennrys said, glancing down. "Not really my style. Besides, I've seen you fight. You can take care of yourself." He smiled, an expression composed of a crooked twist of his mouth and a glint of mischief in his eyes. "So, how 'bout that dance?"

He didn't wait for her answer. Just plucked the glass from Kelley's hand and put it on the high table beside her. Then he took her by the wrist and pulled her out onto the floor. Even if she'd resisted, Kelley knew that she didn't stand much of a chance of successfully defying the Wolf's wiry strength. And then, she realized that she didn't want to resist. Tyff was right. Maybe she had been kind of a wet noodle lately. Maybe she'd been putting so much energy into waiting for Sonny to come back, she'd stopped having fun. And . . . Sonny would *want* her to have fun. Wouldn't he?

So she danced.

It was fun.

IV

Sonny slid off Lucky's back and gazed around sadly at the devastated grove of elm trees. Smoke-blackened stumps stood like rotting teeth, and the bodies of half a dozen dryads were strewn about, crushing the bluebells beneath them where they lay. The Hunt had been busy.

And he had come too late.

He knelt and lifted one of the dead wood nymphs in his arms and carried her to a sheltered spot beneath a lonely tree that had survived the Hunt's rampage. When he stood, anger had washed away his sorrow. As if in response to his fury, a wind—wild and tearing—whipped through the clearing and a huge, black warhorse plummeted from the sky like a meteorite, landing with ground-shaking impact and almost crushing Sonny where he stood.

Mabh, Queen of Air and Darkness, slid from the saddle onto the ground, her dark robes swirling about her like ink stirred into water.

Sonny clenched his fist against a sudden feeling of dread. He had not expected the Faerie queen to come after him herself. Perhaps she was feeling anxious now that only three of the Wild Hunters stood between her and a continuation of her imprisonment. But if she was, she gave no outward indication. The queen regarded the fallen bodies of lesser fae remotely.

"What a mess," she said, as if the place just needed a good sweeping up.

"The Wild Hunt's handiwork, lady," Sonny said.

"Naughty things. You'd think they'd nothing better to do." The disdain was heavy in Mabh's voice. She turned and regarded Sonny flatly. "Rather like you."

"I'm only doing my job," Sonny answered stiffly.

"Spoken like a true lackey, slave of Auberon."

The Queen's midnight charger, sensing the foulness of his mistress's mood, snorted and pawed the ground with a hoof the size of a serving platter, and Sonny heard an anxious whinny from Lucky.

"Think what you like, Mabh." Sonny bent and lifted another dryad, setting her body down beside that of her sister. "But someone has to clean up in the wake of the chaos you seem so fond of conjuring."

Mabh uttered a little laugh and, after a moment, seemed to let go of her anger. "You do know that it was not I who released the Wild Hunt from their slumber during the Nine Night."

"I know that, lady," Sonny answered, his voice carefully neutral. *And that is something that I will make Auberon pay for one day. . . .*

"Yet still you do your cold king's bidding," she mused.

"The Wild Hunt are too dangerous to be left free." Sonny sighed, too tired to play games with the Faerie monarch. "And, forgive me for saying so, but so are you."

"Well, it's nice to be appreciated, at least." Mabh laughed again, but it was a sound that was tinged with sadness.

That surprised Sonny.

"Oh, leave off." She waved him away as he moved toward the next dryad on the ground. The queen turned from him and grew very still for a moment. Lifting her palms to the sky, she closed her eyes.

Sonny closed his too, against the brightness that swept over them. When he could open them again, what he saw surprised him even more. The bodies of the dryads were gone. In the middle of the little clearing, a gentle swell of earth rose, crowned with six bright-leafed elm saplings. A new freshwater spring bubbled up at the foot of the burial mound, emptying into a tranquil pool that reflected the sky.

"A peace offering," said the queen. "Let there be truce

between us. For the moment, at least."

Sonny hesitated and then nodded agreement. *What choice do I really have?* he thought.

Mabh's presence filled the tiny grove with a heady perfume. Ripe, sweet, and spicy like apples ready for harvest. She was intoxicatingly beautiful, even among the Fair Folk. But her beauty could not quell or even compensate for the aura of chaos and danger that accompanied her. A conversation with Mabh was like playing tag with a grizzly bear.

"Come, sit with me and be civil." The Autumn Queen spun away, crooking one long finger over her shoulder, beckoning Sonny to follow her. At the edge of the glassy pool, she folded gracefully down to sit upon the bank. Reluctantly Sonny followed, sitting far enough away that he was almost directly opposite the little pond from her. He would not look directly into her eyes. He had made that mistake once before and was not eager to repeat it.

"I came here to find you," Mabh said. "To remind you that you did me a great favor once. I told you that I would not forget."

Sonny grimaced at the memory. "I wish you would. I made a mistake."

"I honor my debts, changeling." Her voice turned on its edge. "You'd be wise to let me."

"I meant no offense, lady," Sonny said, his tone sincere.

"Dear creature." The queen stared flatly at him for a long moment. Then the sparkle returned to her eyes and she laughed—a sound like wind chimes tinkling. "You'd be dead if you did. I say it plainly."

As plainly as the Fae ever say anything, Sonny thought.

She seemed to read his mind. "I do not double-deal as some do," Mabh said, her green, glittering gaze still flashing with merriment.

"Neither do you play entirely fair, lady," Sonny said, deciding to speak his mind with her. It was quite apparent that as hard as he tried to keep his thoughts quiet, they showed in his face. So he might as well be as up front as Mabh claimed she herself was being.

"You wound me," she said, pouting playfully.

"I'm supposed to be *hunting* you," he said, exasperation coloring his words.

"And here I am. Right within arm's reach. Wasn't that easy?"

"It would be, if there were anything I could do about it. Which, because the Wild Hunt still rides, there is *not*. As you well know."

So much of Mabh's dark, potent magick was tied up in the original spell that had created the Wild Hunt that it would prove useless to try to shackle the Autumn Queen again as long as any of the hunters remained on the loose. Sonny was well aware that, until he finished dealing with *them*, Mabh was essentially untouchable.

"A happy consequence, don't you think?" Mabh asked, trailing her long perfect nails over the surface of the water, gazing at her own reflection in the rippling surface. When he didn't answer, she continued, pleasantly conversational. "You were a deal more handsome the last time we met, Janus. Not quite so . . . scruffy. My daughter will be disappointed. You do remember my daughter, do you not?" She laughed at the expression on his face. "Not to worry. I'm sure she remembers you—at least, I think she does. I do try to keep in touch with the dear thing and, well, frankly, she hasn't really mentioned you in a few months. Young love. Such a fickle wind, don't you agree? Perhaps you should have thought twice before leaving her all alone in the mortal realm. Just like her father did before you, poor girl."

"Lady." Sonny ground his teeth together in an effort to stay civil to the Faerie queen. "You mock me—it is an ungentle thing for a queen to do."

"Touché, Sonny Flannery." Mabh smiled. The flickering nimbus of her wings shed dark, sparkling points of light that danced on the surface of the spring pool. "Such a fierce young thing you are. . . . Think about my offer. Under altered circumstances, I could find a use for such a one as you in my Court."

"You'll pardon me, lady, if I seem a bit weary of being used these days."

Mabh sighed. "Fierce, but humorless. All those years living under Auberon's chilly blue thumb have done you a disservice. I sometimes don't know what my daughter sees in you."

Kelley . . . Sonny ached at the thought of her.

Mabh gazed at him, a knowing glint in her eye. "If she still sees anything at all."

Sonny glared over the queen's shoulder, refusing to rise to her bait.

"And what about you, Sonny Flannery? Sent away from Court, so deep into this shadow-bound country, so very far away from the mortal realm and your ladylove. Why, you've become a virtual hermit, Sonny. A warrior monk. I wonder if anyone even remembers that you're out here, doing the good king's work. Or why."

"*I* remember."

"Do you think *she* still does?" Mabh asked softly. "Was this pointless quest worth leaving Kelley?"

"Don't speak her name!" Sonny was on his feet. He wasn't even aware of having stood, but suddenly he towered over the Faerie Queen.

"I will speak her name if I damn well please, fleshling," Mabh hissed up at him, her green eyes sparking like lightning. "You're not the only one who cares for her, and you're most *certainly* not the only one who's lost her!"

"I haven't lost her." He averted his face so that she wouldn't see the doubt in his eyes. Doubt that had not been there a moment ago. The thought of losing Kelley was unbearable to him. "She waits for me. She *has* to—"

"Perhaps." Mabh shrugged. "Perhaps not." She turned back to the little spring pool and drew a circle on the silvery surface.

Sonny remained standing, uncertain. *I should leave,* he thought.

"Oh, come now," Mabh murmured sweetly, "let us be friends." The water within the circle she traced grew dark, and Sonny could see shadows and shapes flickering in the depths. "Wouldn't you like to see what our darling girl is up to?"

In spite of himself, Sonny knelt back down on the grass and glanced into the Faerie queen's improvised scrying pool. He had no wish to spy on Kelley. Still, he found he could not look away when he saw glimpses of her soaring over the Central Park Lake on dark, glimmering wings, an expression of fierce elation lighting up her face. When the scene shifted, morphing into chaotic flashes of what looked like some kind of fight, Sonny leaned forward in alarm, straining to make sense of the jumbled images. Suddenly they cleared, and he saw Kelley, a mad wind whipping her hair in a fiery cloud about her head and frothing the surface of the waters that sloshed about her ankles. He saw the flaring darklight of her wings and then saw the howling tornadoes of Mabh's Storm Hags descend upon the scene. The wild, dangerous look on Kelley's face made her look so much like her mother that it gave Sonny a hollow feeling in the pit of his stomach. But not nearly as much as the last, lingering image that flared up in the water—the image of Kelley throwing her arms around another man. *Fennrys.*

Kneeling beside him, Mabh peered intently into the water, a wicked little grin curling her lips. "Ooh!" she exclaimed.

"See there! How delightful."

Sonny felt as though he'd been sucker-punched.

"She seems like such a romantic little thing. Very susceptible to knights in shining armor. Believe me—I *know* the
type."

The images in the pond faded, and the queen turned back
to Sonny. Tilting her head delicately on her long neck, she
regarded him with a languid head-to-toe glance as he struggled to compose himself.

Her laugh was low and throaty. "Of course . . . *you,* brave
boy, are looking rather more tarnished than shiny at the
moment."

Sonny shivered, avoiding meeting her eyes directly as
Mabh's gaze slid over his chest and up to his face.

Suddenly the queen rose and, gathering her cloak around
her, swept regally toward her waiting charger. Mabh mounted
her enormous horse with unaided grace and stared down at
Sonny.

Sonny stood, stiffly. His hands were clenched into fists that
he could not seem to loosen. He barely heard Mabh as she
spoke: "Think about what I have said. I *do* owe you a favor,
Sonny Flannery. And the favor of a Faerie queen is not something to be squandered."

"I'll take that under advisement, lady," Sonny mumbled,
turning away from Mabh's green-eyed stare, so like her
daughter's.

"While you're at it, run a comb over your head. Maybe

shave once in a while. Boys can be such grubby things, left to their own devices. I shudder to think what Kelley would say if she could see you now." Her horse pawed at the air, but Mabh hauled effortlessly on the reins, checking the great beast. She looked down at Sonny, the sculpted planes of her face lit by the midnight glow of her shadowy wings. "Love is not nearly as blind as you'd think, Sonny Flannery. Nor as patient."

His heart hurting, Sonny stood in the middle of the glade, watching as the Queen of Air and Darkness climbed into the sky on the back of her storm-cloud horse.

Then she was gone. Except for a breath of her voice on the wind.

"Joy to you," it whispered in mocking tones. "And good hunting."

V

yff caught Kelley's eye halfway through the third song. Or maybe the fourth—Kelley had the feeling that she might have lost track of time. The shake of Tyff's head combined with her self-satisfied grin told Kelley that her roommate approved of her dancing—even if she held reservations about her dance *partner*. Like most Lost Fae, Tyff had a thing against the Janus—particularly the Fennrys Wolf, with his reputation for the brutal approach he took to guarding the Gate.

Fair enough, Kelley thought. But he could also *really* dance.

The band downshifted from an up-tempo set and started playing a slow cover version of an old seventies glam rock song: Roxy Music's melancholy "Dance Away." As the other couples began to drape themselves over each other, bodies melding into bodies, Kelley stiffened. When Fennrys said "Let's get something to drink," her relief left her almost light-headed. And *not* disappointed. Not at all . . .

She followed him through the crowd as they went into another room, this one filled floor to ceiling with books and carpeted in vibrant shades of purple. Slender young women and hipster boys played pool on two tables covered in mauve felt instead of the traditional green. One of the girls made a difficult combination bank shot as Kelley passed, earning faint applause from her companions.

At the long mahogany bar, a group of impossibly hand-some young men stared with quiet watchfulness at Fennrys as he ordered two iced cappuccinos. The drinks arrived and the Janus smiled coldly at the watchers, raising one of the glass coffee mugs in a silent "cheers."

The rest of the Lost Fae gave them a wide berth. But distance certainly didn't preclude them from all staring at her.

Kelley sipped at her coffee, feeling like a particularly interesting fish in a glass bowl, until Fennrys finally sighed and said, "C'mon. This party's getting lamer by the second. I'll walk you home."

"Fennrys, I'll be fine."

"Yes, you will. Because *I*"—he jerked a thumb at himself—

"am in no way particularly eager to find out how young Irish would react to coming back from his little sojourn in the Otherworld only to discover that *you* had gone and gotten eaten by a nyxxie or had your head twisted off by a common mugger. He might be inclined to do the same to me."

"I thought you didn't like Sonny."

"I'm indifferent about *Sonny*."

Before she could figure out what that meant, the Fennrys Wolf had turned and was cutting a wide swath through the crowd, which backed away from him like a swiftly ebbing tide. Kelley put her coffee down and followed, not wanting to be left alone in the room full of stares and whispers.

Fennrys only grunted in halfhearted protest when Kelley insisted that they take a route that would again lead them through the park. He probably figured it wasn't worth the time and energy it would take trying to convince her otherwise.

Cutting through the park was Kelley's way of silently reinforcing the fact that she wasn't about to alter her behavior, in spite of the bodyguard treatment. Fennrys's presence was an impressive one, though, she had to admit. Even the ogre behind the desk at the River had only managed a fierce glower as Kelley got her coat from the check and scooted past him, unaccompanied by Tyff, who was still dancing.

The night wasn't particularly chilly, but the humidity hung bunched under the trees and made it feel that way. The rising mist on the path eerily reflected the lamplight like witch fire, making the park feel graveyard spooky. Kelley was silently glad for the company of her Janus escort—not that she was going to say so out loud. She couldn't help but think about that as they walked, though—about what it meant to be one of Auberon's Janus Guard.

Kelley slung her shoulder bag across her body, freeing up her hands so that she could shove them into her pockets. "Fenn . . . ," she said finally, her voice quiet in the night. "Does it ever bother you? What you do, I mean?"

"Killing Faerie?" he answered, not bothering to turn and look at her.

"You don't kill all of them."

He laughed—a rough, harsh sound, as though his voice was unaccustomed to it. "I don't even kill *most* of them," he said. "You get a bit of a rep as a battle-mad psycho killer, folk tend to do their best to stay out of your way."

"Oh . . ."

"But I *have* killed."

"Oh." Kelley swallowed. "Does it bother you—that Auberon turned you into . . . that?"

"Listen. I was taken by the Fae from a world that was governed by violence and death. If I'd been left there, I would have grown up a warrior, and I would have taken a lot of life. A lot of *human* life. Why should I bemoan the fact of what I am, when it is only a shadow of the beast that I could have become?"

"It might have turned out differently for you, is all."

"I was a Viking," he said quietly. "And I was a prince. I would have led men to war with other men, and I probably would have been very good at it. Or I might have died messily. It was that kind of world."

Kelley studied Fennrys's profile as they walked. He'd always seemed so sharp and hard to her before—all angles and planes. But the lamplight and the moonlight softened his features, made his rough, shaggy blond hair seem less like a mane. It made him look young. Almost boyish.

"Sonny's good at it, isn't he?" she asked. "Killing, I mean."

"He is and he isn't."

Kelley waited for clarification.

"Boy's got technique. Strength, speed, agility. He's a fine, precise instrument of war. But he doesn't *like* it. He likes the fight—and the hunt, the chase, the contest—but I've seen him hesitate in the instant before the sword falls in his hand. Dangerous way to go about things."

"I don't think he hesitates much anymore, Fenn." She hugged her elbows tight to her body as they walked, images from her recent nightmares flashing through her mind. "I think he may have . . . changed."

"Sonny hasn't gone and turned mean, if that's what you're thinking, Kelley," Fennrys said. "I'd bet real money on that. He doesn't have the capacity for cruelty."

"And are you *looking* for a capacity for cruelty?" asked a voice in the darkness.

Fennrys shoved Kelley behind him so fast, it almost

knocked the breath out of her.

"Because *I* might know a lad who'd fit that bill."

Kelley's heart thumped in her chest. She recognized that voice.

"Oh, goody, you brought company." The creep who'd accosted her the last time she set foot in the park stepped out of the darkness, turning his cold, dangerous stare on Fennrys. "I've got a bone to pick with your kind, dog."

The Janus's lip curled in a snarl. The mugger's long, thin hand suddenly snaked through the air in a convoluted gesture. Kelley leaped back as the ground beneath their feet suddenly turned to pudding and Fennrys sank almost knee-deep into the mire.

Faerie! Kelley thought, cursing herself for not having realized it before. Her "common mugger" was Faerie. And he'd been hunting her. Her insides turned to ice as Kelley realized the terrible danger of their situation—and she'd brought them to it through sheer mule-headed stubbornness.

Fingers of green mud clutched at Fennrys's legs, immobilizing him. He roared in rage, powerless to stop the Faerie creep as he sauntered forward, prancing lightly in his heavy boots, buckles jingling like cowboy spurs. The thick soles looked as if they could inflict an awful lot of damage, Kelley thought—and then wished she hadn't.

The Faerie attacked with the savagery of a soccer hooligan in a street brawl. His fingers still dancing a tattoo on the air, he leaped and spun, lashing out with one of those

71

booted feet in a whiplash kick. Fennrys's head snapped back, the skin above his left eye split open to the bone and gushing blood. Another swift kick snapped Fennrys's wrist. The Janus fell backward onto the oozy ground, stunned. Hooligan-boy grinned viciously, bouncing like a prizefighter on the balls of his feet.

"I'd have that set, if I were you," he murmured through a sneer, nodding at how Fenn's hand hung from his wrist at an odd angle. "Might heal all wrong. Might not heal at all if I kill you. Now . . . out of my way, dog." He flicked his hand sideways, and the softened ground bucked like a rogue wave in the ocean, hurling Fennrys twenty feet away into a thicket.

Kelley decided to end things before they got really out of hand. She reached up under her hair to the catch on her necklace, and tugged.

And nothing happened.

Kelley tugged on the clasp of her silver chain again, frantically, and willed it to come loose. It had been so easy the other night—as if the charm had been eager to come loose, to let her power run free.

So why can't I take the damned thing off now?

"Because I don't want you to, thief."

"What?" Her gaze flew to where Hooligan-boy's fingers were twisting faster and faster through the air, tracing patterns as intricate as Celtic knots that Kelley could almost see hanging in the darkness like silver fire.

"Oh, I'll take back what you stole, don't you fret," he said, his voice ruggedly musical. "But I can't very well have you blasting away at me with your mum's pretty purple power in the meantime, can I? Nah—you can just keep that little trinket fastened on tight."

Kelley tugged so hard on the delicate chain that it should have snapped. It didn't.

"See . . . this way"—the Faerie danced closer still, his tone disconcertingly conversational—"your power stays hidden and you stay helpless. Then, after I kill ya, I'll just cut your pretty little head off."

"You can *try,*" Kelley snapped.

Hooligan-boy laughed, flashing his long teeth. "D'you still have my knife handy, thief?" He drew his dancing fingertips in a line back and forth across his own neck. "The one I dropped the other night? It's not the sharpest blade—I'll probably have to hack a bit—but it'll do the trick."

Kelley swallowed thickly. The fear that she would not allow to show in her face was a tight knot in her stomach. The Faerie raised his hands higher into the air, fingers weaving intricate spells, and there was a sudden rustling behind Kelley—like the sound of millions of leaves shaken by wind, only she knew that the trees were just barely beginning to bud. She didn't dare take her eyes off the menacing creature in front of her to look.

"Thief," the Faerie spat at her again.

"You're delusional," Kelley said defiantly. "I've had this necklace since I was a baby. It's mine."

"*Dead* thief."

From just over her shoulder, Kelley heard a ferocious groaning sound—like a log cabin settling after an earthquake, only a thousand times louder. Some instinct told Kelley to get the hell out of the way, and she did—leaping to one side just in time to avoid the massive tree limb that slammed like a giant fist into the ground where she'd been standing.

"I underestimated you last time, missy," the Faerie said. "But I came better prepared this time." His eyes burned with a poison-green light, and the tattoos on his wrists and the sides of his neck writhed like strangling vines. He crouched and put the palms of his hands flat on the ground. The tattoos slithered off his arms and sank into the earth.

"Never just attack someone *in* a park," he said, "when you can attack them *with* a park."

Tree roots slammed upward out of the ground like impaling spikes all around her. Kelley dove out of the way to avoid getting skewered, gasping as the roots whipped around her ankles and thighs, stinging and bruising her.

She ran for all she was worth.

If she could just get to the edge of the park, flag down a cop, yell for help—something—

But the park wasn't going to let her out. Everywhere she turned, tree branches whipped through the air, catching at her hair and clothes. The ground rippled angrily, and grasses grew long, tangling her feet, tripping her as she ran. Kelley threw her arm in front of her face and charged on blindly until her lungs screamed and her brain didn't even know which way was east or west.

In a confetti shower of new blossoms, Kelley burst through a wall of flowering branches—a stand of ornamental trees on the fringes of Cherry Hill—and she paused for an instant, glancing back, certain that she'd outrun her pursuer. But suddenly, from behind her, rough-barked, many-fingered hands grasped at her torso and arms, wrapping around her face and silencing her angry cry.

Overhead the sky rumbled with thunder, and lightning stabbed down into the park. Her mother's Storm Hags! *Nearby, but not near enough,* Kelley thought in desperation. Another lightning bolt forked down, farther away now. Although they'd been shadowing her for months, it seemed as if the Hags couldn't get a lock on her position.

No backup this time.

The thought rang in Kelley's head like an alarm. If she didn't do something soon, she was going to die. She was helpless in the grip of the Faerie's charmed tree, and he was going to cut her throat. "D'you still have my knife handy, thief?" he'd asked her, and the question suddenly rolled like thunder through her head.

She did. She *did* still have it!

You bet I do.

Kelley twisted her arm beneath the imprisoning branches and managed to get her fingers inside the zippered side pocket of her bag that still hung from its strap across her body. Fishing madly, her knuckles brushed the ridged wood of the knife's carved hilt. She fumbled at it with slippery fingertips.

It was too late.

Kelley saw Hooligan-boy's grin appearing out of the darkness, gleaming at her like the Cheshire Cat from across the paved circle of the Cherry Hill turnaround. He sauntered forward a few steps, dancing his swaggering little jig as he came on. He was toying with her. The knife was in her hand, but the tree held her immobile. Then it began to squeeze.

There was nothing she could do. Her sight was going dim as the branches choked the breath from her body. Kelley opened her mouth wide, gulping at the air she couldn't draw into her lungs. She was suffocating.

Sonny, Kelley whispered in her mind. *Sonny, help me. . . .*

The edges of her vision were tinged with a crimson darkness, and all she could hear was the vicious cackling of her Faerie assailant. Her thoughts were becoming muddled with the lack of oxygen. An image of Sonny from one of Kelley's long-ago dreams, back when he had simply been a handsome, intriguing stranger to her, flared up in her mind: Sonny standing in a forest, his dark hair hanging loose, moonlight glowing in his beautiful silver eyes.

Sonny, Please! Kelley implored the dream image. *HELP ME!*

In the vision Sonny's head snapped up as if she'd shouted at the top of her lungs. The branches of the trees behind him framed his head like a many-tined crown. There was a sudden, blinding burst of forest-green light, and she felt the tree shudder and flinch.

Kelley was dimly aware that the Faerie had staggered back a step or two, confusion in his venomous gaze. The break in his concentration was only momentary, but his fingers paused in their twisting dance, and Kelley found that she could almost breathe again.

In that same instant Fennrys burst like a runaway freight train from out of the trees behind Hooligan-boy. His feet were bare and the legs of his jeans were caked with green mud. He hammered the Fae to the ground with a single blow and swept past, launching himself at the tree that imprisoned Kelley. The branches pinning her cracked asunder as, with a primal yell, Fennrys one-handedly tore the possessed tree literally limb from limb.

Her upper body freed, Kelley fell forward into Fennrys's arms, gasping for breath. It felt as though her rib cage had gone through a trash compactor, but glorious air surged into her lungs.

"Sonny," she gasped, disoriented.

"No, sorry." Fenn's smile was pained. "Just little old me."

"Fenn—behind you!"

Hooligan-boy had climbed to his feet and lashed out again in another roundhouse kick. The blow caught Fennrys on the shoulder, dislocating it with a horrifying sound. The Wolf hollered in agony and rolled out of the way, scrambling awkwardly across the grass. The enraged Faerie followed, fists balled and raised to strike, but his knuckles grazed only air. Fennrys was ready for him this time, and his good arm flew wide in a punch that caught the Faerie a cracking blow to the jaw and sent him sprawling. He hit the ground heavily and lay there stunned for a moment, a tangle of arms and legs, as Fennrys dropped to one knee, overcome by the pain of his injuries.

The tree holding Kelley tightened the grip of its remaining limbs, branches snaking back up over her torso, pinning her to the rough bark. Kelley wriggled one arm free and, clutching the knife from her purse, lifted the blade high and jammed it to the hilt into the tree branch wrapped around her chest. The tree recoiled violently, with a sound like screaming; thick, reddish sap gushed from a wound that splashed upward onto Kelley's skin—warm as blood.

The tree sap tingled where it touched her, and the four-leaf-clover charm flared hot against her breastbone. She looked down—the charm was coated in crimson sap. Beneath the sticky wetness, the four-leaf clover glowed brilliantly, cycling through vibrant shades of green.

The ground beneath Kelley's feet felt suddenly electrified, and the power that was locked inside of her surged outward from her core, down into the tips of her fingers like a river through a burst dam. Dark light blazed: a color like rage—not purple, not quite red—flooded the clearing, melding with the green light of the charm.

"No!" Hooligan-boy shrieked and threw a hand over his

face as if the light burned. "No, no, *no!*"

The malicious tree retreated completely and Kelley dragged herself free. She sliced at the air with her hand, and the darkness crackled and split, gaping wide in a rift that shimmered and spat sparks. Kelley wrapped her arms around Fennrys's muscled torso and launched them through her makeshift gateway, willing it closed behind them as the screams of the thwarted Faerie echoed in her ears.

VI

On the banks of a wide, tumbling river, Sonny upended his leather satchel, dumping a small pile of laundry and a few cakes of tallow soap out onto the ground. *Ah, the glamorous life of a Janus Guard, he thought.*

If he'd acquiesced to Auberon's wishes and stayed in the Winter Palace, such menial tasks wouldn't have been a concern. Even in the small cottage where he stayed, Sonny had a complement of helper sprites—tiny, winged fae that tended his hearth—but he was strangely loath to impose his housekeeping chores on them. Perhaps because he was feeling a little too much like a slave himself.

He knelt at the water's edge, just downstream from where a roaring waterfall cascaded down the face of a high cliff, filling the air with mist and fractured rainbows. From the corner of his eye he caught glimpses of the shining bodies of one or two of the river folk, leaping like salmon in the water. A swim before chores seemed like a good idea and so he took off his boots and stripped off his ratty linen shirt. Clad only in breeches, Sonny stepped down from the grassy shore, wading out toward the middle of the stream where the water was deeper. The cold water felt good to his sore muscles. He leaned back, closing his eyes, and drifted on the surface of the river.

Sonny, Please!

Kelley's voice rang out like a bell in his mind, and made his head snap up.

HELP ME!

He treaded water, glancing wildly around. He felt a sharp, terrible pain in his chest—as though his heart were on fire—and a sudden wash of brilliant green light left him momentarily blind.

She's here! something deep in his brain screamed at him. *Kelley's here!*

Sonny sensed the familiar firecracker-spark of her presence—flaring star bright in his mind's eye.

Suddenly the waterfall exploded outward with a noise like thunder, and a body—or was it *two* bodies, tightly intertwined—burst forth, hitting the surface of the water with a resounding impact.

Sonny caught a glimpse of fiery auburn hair and he dove, swimming frantically upstream against the river's flow. Opening his eyes underwater, he thought he could see her—bright hair and alabaster skin—where she floated near the river bottom, motionless and pale.

Kelley! Sonny swam as fast as he could. *Oh, Firecracker—no!*

He reached out a hand, and his fingertips brushed her wrist. The current was carrying her away from him. Sonny kicked desperately, closing the distance before she was swept out of reach. He got an arm around her waist and started to swim for the surface, dragging her behind him. Suddenly Kelley twisted in his grip, struggling violently against him and screaming—the muted sound billowing out of her in clouds of bubbles. Their heads broke the surface together and Kelley coughed and sputtered, fighting Sonny's hold on her as if her life depended on it.

"Kelley!" Sonny grappled with her flailing limbs, trying to turn her around so that she could see it was him. "Kelley—it's me! It's Sonny . . ."

Her head swiveled around and her eyes went wide at the sight of him. She threw her arms around him, almost dragging them back down.

"It's okay," he murmured into the tangled, wet mass of her hair. "I'm here. I've got you."

Kelley rasped out a word, the sound catching in her throat.

"What?" Sonny asked. "Kelley, what are you—"

"Fenn . . ." She coughed, pulling away from Sonny and trying to swim back out into the middle of the river.

Fenn, Sonny thought as he turned and saw that there *had* been someone. *Fennrys?*

A body was floating spread-eagled in the middle of the river, pulled downstream by the swift current. Floating face-down. *The impact must have stunned him,* Sonny thought. *He's going to drown.* He reached out a hand and grabbed Kelley hard by the shoulder.

"I'll go. You get to shore," he said, and pushed her in the direction of the strand.

"But—"

"*Go,* Kelley!" he ordered. "Wait for me onshore."

Sonny dove back into the water.

Swimming with powerful strokes, Sonny shut down every thought that wasn't directly focused on the task at hand. At least he tried to—tried very hard not to think about the fact that he was attempting to save a man whom he had very recently observed embracing Kelley in the mirror of Mabh's scrying pool. And he tried not to imagine what kind of circumstances had led to them tumbling through a rift into the Otherworld, arms and legs tangled around one another. . . .

Sonny surfaced briefly and got his bearings. Fennrys's seemingly lifeless form was only another ten yards in front of him. Sonny kicked off again and swam until he thought his lungs would burst. With almost the last strength left in his tired arms, he reached out a hand and snagged Fennrys's jacket collar. Managing to get an arm under the Fenn's torso, Sonny struggled to flip him over in the water. Finally he succeeded, noticing with a sinking heart that the Wolf's lips were blue. Sonny was running on fumes. And Fennrys was deadweight. They rounded a sharp bend in the watercourse, and even though the river narrowed and they were now less than twenty feet from shore, Sonny didn't have the strength left to fight the current's tow. He needed to get Fennrys to shore. And he couldn't.

That's when he saw Kelley, perched on a rock that jutted out into the water ahead of where Sonny and Fennrys floated. She must have cut across the spit of land that formed the inside curve of the river. It looked as though she was holding some kind of lumpy, uneven rope looped between her hands. She threw it to him just in time before he and Fennrys swept on past, and it was only when Sonny grabbed hold that he realized Kelley had knotted together the sleeves of all the shirts he'd left lying in a heap on the bank of the river. His laundry had become his lifeline!

"Hold on!" Kelley shouted, trying to brace against the sharp tug of Sonny and Fennrys's weight. She managed to tie her end to a stout tree and reeled the two men in to shore like fish. Together she and Sonny dragged the unconscious Janus up onto the ground, where Kelley elbowed Sonny aside and dropped to her knees. "Out of the way—I know how to do artificial respiration," she said.

Sonny wasn't entirely sure what exactly "artificial respiration" was, but it seemed to have something to do with kissing drowned men. Under other circumstances, he would have protested vehemently. As it was, he got out of the way and watched as Kelley desperately tried to breathe life back into Fennrys's inert body.

The minutes seemed to crawl by as she worked with fierce concentration, counting and blowing air into the Wolf's lungs. Sonny was about to tell her to stop. That it was hopeless. And then Fennrys's entire body arched off the ground, jerking spasmodically as he began to cough raggedly. Sonny helped Kelley roll him over onto his side, and river water poured out of his mouth and nose.

"That was fun," Fennrys gasped weakly when he could finally speak. "Let's not ever do it again."

VII

Together Sonny and Kelley helped Fennrys to his feet.

"I owe you one for the save, Irish," Fennrys said, his voice gravelly.

"Thank Kelley." Sonny shrugged. "She hauled us both out."

"Oh, don't thank me," Kelley said airily. "I was just gonna let you float downstream, Fenn. I thought you were dead."

"I wasn't dead," Fennrys snorted, one arm hanging at an unnatural angle from his shoulder, and his hand hanging even more unnaturally from that. "I was swimming."

Kelley looked at him. "You floated around the bend face-down. It really didn't look like you were swimming."

"It's just a little awkward doing a front crawl when your arm's half off, that's all." Fennrys winced. "But you know. Thanks anyway."

"No trouble at all." Kelley laughed, giddy with the sheer fact that Fennrys was still alive.

Sonny looked back and forth, seeming slightly bemused by the après-crisis banter. The joking drifted away as he and Kelley found themselves staring at each other. Fennrys cleared his throat in the silence and, when neither of the pair turned to look at him, wandered a few feet away as if to observe some particularly fascinating pattern in the bark of a tree.

"So . . ." After all the excitement, Kelley suddenly felt awkward and almost shy as she looked up into Sonny's face. "Um . . . Hi?"

"Hi, yourself," Sonny said, gently brushing a damp auburn curl off her forehead. Then he wrapped his arms around her in a fierce embrace. It was the best feeling she'd ever had. She was back in Sonny's arms.

After a long moment that wasn't nearly long enough for Kelley, he pulled back. "I thought I told you to wait for me."

"You mean here or back home?"

"Both."

"You might have noticed I'm not very good at taking instructions."

"I did notice that." He kissed her and smiled. "But in this case, I think I'm glad."

Kelley couldn't take her eyes off Sonny as they walked back to get the rest of his gear and her shoes—which she'd kicked off before her mad rescue dash. His dark hair was loose, longer than she remembered, and falling in his face. He was too thin. There were dark circles under his silver-gray eyes and a fresh, barely healed scar running from the plane of his cheekbone up into his hairline. He was pale. His torso was marked in places with bruises, fresh and faded, and more than a few scars, including the pale, parallel claw marks that he'd received rescuing her from a Black Shuck almost six months earlier. Sonny's hand was bandaged and his clothing worn and tattered. There were dark, rust-colored stains on his breeches (and—she'd noticed while furiously tying them together—on almost all of his shirts). In spite of all that, Kelley caught her breath at how beautiful he was.

She was still staring as they both bent down to retrieve their respective footwear. When Sonny looked up from tying the leather laces of his boots around his calves, he reddened a bit at her unblinking scrutiny. Trying in vain to smooth the wrinkles in the shirt he'd thrown on, he grimaced and said apologetically, "Today was supposed to be washday."

"I figured." Kelley grinned. "Sorry. I didn't mean to throw your whole schedule out of whack."

"No!" Sonny protested, moving like lightning to kneel

down and take her face in his hands. He kissed her smiling mouth and said, "It's no problem! I mean . . . I . . ."

She was laughing now.

"That was a joke, right?"

"Mm-hmm." She leaned forward and kissed him again.

He sat back on his haunches and chuckled. "I've been by myself a little too much lately, I think."

"Not anymore," Kelley said softly. She was in the Otherworld with Sonny.

"If you two lovebirds are done cooing, can we please go somewhere and set my bloody arm?"

And Fennrys.

Kelley's reply was preempted by a sharp whinny. She spun around to see a roan horse galloping out from the trees.

"Lucky!" she shouted. The creature pulled up and pranced excitedly before her, front hooves pawing at the ground. Laughing with happiness, Kelley flung her arms around the kelpie and buried her face in his mane. Lucky nuzzled her shoulder and head-butted at her in delight.

Beside Sonny, Fennrys gestured with his good arm. "Isn't that . . . ?"

"The Roan Horse, Harbinger of the Wild Hunt and Fearsome Bringer of Doom? Yeah." Sonny nodded. "Used to be."

"Thought so." Lucky kicked up his back hooves like a frolicking colt, and Fennrys snorted in disgust. "Evil really needs to step up its game."

Sonny smiled grimly. "You wouldn't say that if you'd been

the one riding him when the war horn blew."

Or the one watching it happen, thought Kelley, a shiver traveling up her spine at the memory. Both Lucky and Sonny had fallen under an age-old curse, originally woven by Queen Mabh as a means of exacting a terrible revenge on a mortal prince named Herne the Hunter. Mabh and Herne had once been passionately in love, but Herne had slighted the Faerie queen, and in fury she had cursed him and his companions to ravage the human realm in the guise of the Wild Hunt. Auberon and Titania had managed to throw down the Hunt that first time, and Herne had faded into legend.

Kelley herself had managed to stop the Hunt a second time. She was so glad to discover that Lucky had survived the encounter.

"So tell me," Sonny asked, "what on earth happened to you two, anyway?"

As Kelley began to explain, she led Lucky over to a small boulder, helping Fennrys to mount up. She told Sonny everything that happened before she and Fennrys had tumbled through the rift. Everything except dancing the night away with the other Janus.

Sonny listened carefully, asking questions at intervals: "What did the Faerie that attacked you look like?"

"Super creepy. Ripped jeans, weird tattoos, bad hair. And, come to think of it, really nice boots . . ."

"Where?"

"On his feet."

Sonny winced and rubbed his temples. "Where were you *attacked*, Kelley?"

"Okay, see . . . that was a joke."

"Where?" Sonny asked again.

Kelley sighed reluctantly. "In Central Park. I mean—hey—where else, right? It is, after all, my favorite place to be attacked." The sarcasm in her voice was a gentle admonition, designed to make Sonny feel suitably overreactive about his concerns. She could take care of herself.

And, if necessary, she could take care of him, too.

VIII

"It's nothing." Sonny lowered his voice so that Fennrys, following behind on Lucky, wouldn't hear him.

"Sonny . . . you're being weird." Kelley was staring at him, waiting for an answer to her question. "It's *not* nothing."

They had stopped in a nondescript clearing just off the path they'd been following. Sonny turned from Kelley, avoiding her searching stare, and concentrated for a moment. With a thought he lifted the veil from around his cottage, and the squat little house with its tiny, stone-fenced yard shimmered into view. Kelley blinked, her mouth in an O, and gazed at the place for a moment. But as Sonny reached for Lucky's bridle to lead him into the yard, she put a hand on his arm.

"What's *wrong*?" she asked again.

"You were hugging him!" he blurted. *You idiot,* he cursed himself silently.

"What? When?"

"When . . . when you came through the rift," Sonny stammered, not wanting Kelley to know that he'd been spying on her with Mabh. "You were . . . hugging."

Kelley slowly turned her face to look up at him. "Okay. See, that's something."

Sonny felt his heart sink. "It is?"

"No!" She almost shouted at him. "You were right the first time. That really *is* nothing! For one thing, it was dragging, not hugging. And for another, what if I was? I'm in the *theater,* Sonny. We hug everyone."

"I'm in the Janus Guard," he muttered stubbornly. "We don't."

"Aw, c'mon, Irish," Fennrys interjected, even though he had to do it through clenched teeth as he slid off the kelpie's back. "For my part, I thought it was more of a cuddle than a hug." He winked at Kelley.

She gave him a flat, annoyed stare. "Don't make me finish the job that Faerie creep started, Fennrys," she warned.

Fennrys laughed, a low growling sound in the back of his throat, and limped off toward the cottage.

A small, secret shame flared up behind Sonny's eyes, making him see red for a moment. It was irrational, but many-sourced: foremost was the fact that, when Mabh had shown him the vision of Kelley in the mortal world, she'd had her arms wrapped around Fennrys. Adding to the conflicting emotions was the fact that, while he and Fennrys had never been exactly close—certainly not as close as he and Maddox—the Wolf was a colleague. A friend, even, of sorts. And it appeared as though he had almost been killed defending Kelley.

While Sonny had been notably absent.

That's what made it infinitely worse—the fact that Sonny could only watch as Kelley's expression filled with sympathy when Fennrys ground his teeth in pain . . . and wish it had been *him*.

"Sonny?" she asked as his silence stretched long.

"What were you doing in the park?" he asked, taking her arm and trying to sound more casual as they walked toward the cottage.

"What?"

"When you were attacked. Why were you in the park?"

"I . . ." Kelley looked away, her cheeks coloring. "I just like to spend time there. Sometimes."

"With Fennrys?" The words were out of Sonny's mouth before he could stop himself, and he instantly regretted the asinine question.

"What?" Kelley's eyes flew wide, and she yanked her arm away. "No! No. He was just walking me home."

"Walking you home from where?" *Flannery, you idiot, stop!*

Kelley crossed her arms over her chest, stopping just inside the door of the little house, and her gaze went a bit flinty at the interrogation. "If you must know, I was at a place called the River—"

"What? Titania's place?" Sonny rounded on Fennrys, who was lowering himself gingerly onto the narrow cot in the corner of the cottage's single room. "Damn it! What were you thinking, taking her there?"

"Whoa, whoa, whoa!" Fennrys protested. "*I* didn't take her anywhere, Irish." His pale eyes gleamed with amusement. "I just kept her company once she got there. Somebody had to show the lady a good time—"

"Fenn," Kelley interrupted sharply as Sonny spluttered in outrage, "you can slip into unconsciousness from the pain *any* time now, okay?"

"I have an unfortunately high tolerance." He shrugged apologetically.

"You want to test that theory?" she said acidly, glaring at him, and went to sit in the little window bay.

Fenn chuckled.

Sonny fetched the large wooden box he kept well-stocked with first-aid supplies. "Get up and go stand against the wall," he told the Wolf brusquely.

"That's right, Irish," Fenn murmured—just softly enough so that Kelley couldn't hear—as he rose stiffly. He leaned back, bracing his good shoulder against the wall of the cottage. "I almost died saving your girl."

Sonny ignored the goad. Fennrys was a jackass. Always looking for a fight—even within the ranks of the Janus Guard—and Sonny refused to indulge him. "You might want to look elsewhere for a few moments," he suggested to Kelley, and firmly grasped Fennrys's arm, careful to avoid his broken wrist. Holding it out straight, he told the other Janus to lock his elbow. "You want something to bite down on?" he asked.

Like a gag?

"Nah. I'm a straight-up hero."

Or my fist . . .

"Hold still, hero," Sonny said in a flat voice and, gripping Fenn's arm, thrust the dislocated shoulder joint up and in, snapping it back into place with a sickeningly meaty *pop*. The muscles in Fennrys's neck bulged and his eyes rolled white with flaring agony. But the only actual sound he made was a barely audible gasp as he sank down the wall. Sonny watched as the Wolf's gaze slid over to where Kelley sat on the window-sill to see if she was watching. It was pretty obvious that he was expecting her to be massively impressed. She just shook her head.

"Are you done trying to be stoic, Fenn?" she asked.

"Wh—what?" Through the fog of pain (which he was clamping down on—stoically), Fennrys blinked up at Kelley, his expression bemused.

Sonny grinned smugly.

"And Sonny?" Kelley continued. "A little compassion is a sexy thing."

The grin crumpled and died on Sonny's face.

"Boys," she muttered in disgust, and turned away, staring out the window and thoroughly ignoring them both.

"She always that touchy?" Fennrys whispered through clenched teeth, as he moved toward the narrow bed and settled down carefully with an unstoic groan of pain.

Sonny just looked at him, undecided as to whether he should thank him for helping Kelley or hit him over the head.

IX

The air remained thick with animosity between the two Janus Guards, even after Sonny had managed to splint and bandage Fennrys's wrist. Kelley had gone from sneaking glances over her shoulder at the procedure to watching outright as Sonny worked with deft assurance: fashioning a sling for Fenn's wounded arm, tying the cloth—none too gently—around the other Janus's neck; running another strip of cloth around his torso, tying that off too; immobilizing Fenn's arm against his chest. It reminded Kelley in no uncertain terms that the Janus were seasoned warriors—and used to dealing with the consequences of their vocation.

The sun was near to setting as Sonny finished the job, and Kelley noticed that tiny little winged specks of light had begun to drift about the room, setting alight the candles and lamps that were scattered on the few flat surfaces as the day grew dim outside. Two or three of the minuscule sprites drifted close enough to inspect Kelley where she sat—one brave spark even diving into her auburn hair, squeaking with what sounded like delight as it reemerged, and running a strand of her hair through the tiniest hands Kelley had ever seen. The teensy creature was soon joined by several of its fellows, and Kelley had a hard time keeping a straight face as they burrowed and yanked and dove in and out of her curls as if they were waves on a beach.

From the corner of her eye, she noticed a stack of rumpled paper lying on the tiny table beside the bed, next to an oil lamp. As a fire sprite coaxed the lamp to life, the flame from the trimmed wick cast enough light to gleam off the two brass fasteners left holding the pages together, and illuminate a few of the words on the top page. *A Midsummer Night's Dream*—it was her old script. She'd told Sonny to keep it. For luck. For her . . .

He still has it.

And he kept it beside his bed.

Oh, Sonny . . .

A warm glow filled Kelley that had nothing to do with the tiny fire sprites now hovering in a curious cloud all around her head. She *hadn't* imagined things. Hadn't embellished over the months he'd been gone. What they had felt for each other had been real. It still was—she was sure of it!

She looked up and was startled to see Sonny's gray eyes fastened on her face as he put away the first-aid gear. He had seen her looking at the script, and she could tell from his expression that he had read her thoughts. She felt her heart flutter as the corner of his mouth turned up and a fierce heat flooded his gaze that made her own cheeks turn from blush to blaze. She smiled back and moved to go to him.

But as she stood, Kelley felt a breeze on her shoulders, and the curtains hanging at the sides of the open window blew inward. Motes of dust danced in the reddening shafts of light from the setting sun, glinting with a subtle green glow as they drifted through into the shadows of the room. And then a voice from beside the fireplace hearth said: "I see time works differently in the mortal realm, too, now."

"Bob!" Kelley jumped back, startled, scattering her impromptu crown of fire sprites.

"Bob?" Fennrys asked.

A notorious member of a powerful, ancient race of Faerie called boucca, Bob was better known by the name of Puck, and insofar as his true name could be used to compel him against his will, he did his best to keep "Bob" a secret. The fact that he only threw a sour glance at Kelley and snapped "You didn't hear that!" at Fennrys was symptomatic of some grave distraction that otherwise occupied his thoughts.

"What's wrong?" Kelley asked.

"I've been waiting for you for nigh on a mortal month now, lady," the boucca sprite remarked dryly. "Were the words *urgent* and *time is of the essence* somehow vague? Or perhaps less communicative than I'd hoped?"

"Umm . . ." Kelley blinked, confused. She looked from the Fae to the Janus Guards, both of whom wore less-than-helpful looks. "Okay, I'll go with *vague*. What are you talking about?"

"You haven't come here to meet me?" It was Bob's turn to look confused.

"No, Bob. Not that I'm not glad to see you, but—"

"Then what *are* you doing here?" he interrupted her brusquely.

"Why does everyone keep asking me that?" Kelley threw her hands in the air in frustration. "As if I don't *belong*. As if I'm some kind of interloper."

"Some would say you are." The sternness of Bob's expression did not soften. "Me? I was simply hoping there was forgiveness in you. I guess I was wrong."

"Okay." Kelley clenched her teeth and spoke slowly so that she could avoid losing her temper again—which seemed to be on a hair trigger lately anyway, even without cryptic Faerie chastisement. "I'm going to ask you one more time: What . . . the hell . . . are you talking about?"

The boucca's shrewd gaze raked over her. "You didn't get my messages?"

"No."

"Any of them?"

"No!" Kelley screeched. "What freaking messages?"

"I've been leaving them on the mirror of your dressing

room for weeks now," the boucca said, perplexed. "Secretly, but *you* should have been able to see them."

"I . . . oh."

"Oh?"

Kelley winced. "I . . . I switched dressing rooms. I traded with Alec because his didn't have a mirror in it."

"I see. And you did this because wardrobe gave you a particularly ugly Juliet costume?" Bob asked, his voice heavy with sarcasm.

"I did it because *Mabh* kept showing up in my reflection! She's all keen on these little mother-daughter chats." Kelley made a sour face. "It was driving me nuts! I told Alec it was some weird superstition I had."

"Excuse me." Sonny spoke up. "Bob, what is this all about?"

Bob's eyes flicked back and forth between Sonny and Kelley, coming to rest at last on her. "It's about your father, Kelley."

"You mean Auberon?" she said tartly.

"I mean your father. He's not well."

"Really," Kelley said, her eyes narrowing suspiciously.

"I think he may be dying," Bob said.

"What?" Fennrys struggled to sit up on the narrow cot. "He can't die! He's the bloody King of Winter."

"Don't be absurd," said Bob, rolling an eye at the wounded Janus. "Just because he's immortal doesn't mean he can't die!"

"What in hell does that mean?" Fennrys asked.

Bob sighed in impatience. "Faerie live forever only if something doesn't *kill* them, you great oaf." He turned back to Kelley and Sonny, who both stared at him, openmouthed. "What do you think *you* do for a living?"

"Well, yeah—but, I mean, he's the *king* and all," Fennrys muttered.

"How . . ." Sonny had gone an ashen color. "What's wrong with him?"

"I don't know!" Bob snapped. "I thought I just said that!"

"No, you missed that part," Fennrys noted.

"Well, I don't. No one does. He's been in a slow decline since that business at Samhain, but he's not about to ask anyone for help. If word of this were to get around—I mean a mere *breath* on the air that the Unseelie king had weakened—and you know as well as I that the vultures would start circling before you could say 'Bob's your uncle.' Which I'm not." Bob turned to Kelley where she stood frozen like a statue. "Kelley, you have to come home."

Kelley didn't answer. She just watched, feeling strangely detached, as Sonny nodded—seemingly without even a second thought—and moved toward the door.

"I'll go get Lucky," he said. "It'll be faster if we ride."

"Not you, Sonny." Bob lifted a hand. "You're to stay and finish your job here."

"But—"

"Boss's orders."

Sonny's mouth set in a grim line. "Fine. I'll get Lucky for Kelley, then."

"No."

Kelley saw Sonny glance back at Bob, as if he'd thought for an instant that it was the boucca fae who had spoken again. But the word had dropped from *her* lips.

"Sorry?" asked Sonny, perhaps thinking he had misheard.

"No," she repeated. There was a kind of pressure building behind Kelley's eyes—like the way the air felt back home in Manhattan just before the skies opened on a major thunderstorm. "I'm not going." She looked back and forth between Sonny and Bob. "Why would I want to?" Her gaze settled on Sonny. "Why would you want to?"

"He's my king."

"He's your keeper!" she scoffed.

"He's *your* father, Kelley," Sonny said in a quiet voice.

"He tried to kill me!" Her mouth was hanging open now in utter disbelief. Kelley couldn't believe her ears. "He woke the Wild Hunt, Sonny! In the middle of New York City—what—have you all *forgotten* that? Is living in this place so marvelous that you don't mind living as a slave?"

"What would you have me do?" Sonny's beautiful silver gaze was flat and lifeless. "He raised me. He cared for me. If he's dying—"

"Let him die!" she said, hearing the current of savagery in her own voice as if it came from someplace else. From someone else.

"Kelley—this isn't like you. You're not—"

"What? Ruthless? Like you?"

Sonny's head snapped back as though she'd slapped him.

"What?" he whispered, his expression stricken.

"I've seen you, Sonny . . ." *I should shut up. I should close my mouth up tight and just stop talking.* She knew that. "I've seen what you do when you . . . hunt."

"Kelley, I—"

"No!" Her hand sliced through the air. "I don't want to hear it."

"Hear what?" he asked her, the tone of his voice suddenly sharp as the sword she'd seen him wield mercilessly in the dreams her mother sent her. "What exactly is it that you think I've been doing here? What exactly do you think of *me?*"

"I don't know." *Shut up, Winslow.* "I don't really know you, do I?"

"I thought I knew *you* . . ." His eyes were full of misery.

"You didn't see!" Kelley choked on a sob, her mind flooding with memories of that horrible night in the park when she had stared into Sonny's eyes and seen nothing but a monster. A monster that had wanted her dead. Her father had done that. "You don't know what he did to you! Auberon deserves whatever he's got coming to him—"

"He's your *father*, Kelley."

"I don't care!"

"He's my king," Sonny said again.

"And what does that make me?"

Over her shoulder Bob said, very quietly, "It makes you a queen of Faerie. If he dies."

Silence like a deep winter snowfall blanketed the room. In the corner, Fennrys shifted uncomfortably on the cot. Bob and Sonny were still as statues.

Kelley shook her head, suddenly weary. "You know, I guess I can accept that sort of insinuation coming from you, Bob. You're Faerie, after all. All your kind care about is politics and power." She turned to Sonny. "But from you? It's like you've been living among these creatures so long, you've forgotten how to be human."

"No—you've forgotten, Kelley," Sonny answered her in a voice so low that she had to strain to hear him. "I never learned."

"Sonny . . ."

"Maybe a year in your world isn't enough to teach me what it is to be a mortal man." He stood straighter, spine stiff. "But growing up here I think I at least might have learned some of what it is to be a son—mortal or not. I'll come with you, Bob."

"I don't think—"

"I owe him that much." Sonny cut the boucca short.

"He tried to kill me," Kelley murmured again, the shock of disbelief at Sonny's actions settling over her. Smothering.

"And now he's dying," Fennrys remarked dryly, his keen-eyed gaze narrowed in her direction. "A less sentimental person than me might call that poetic justice."

Kelley went cold with anger. She turned on her heel and stalked out of the cottage, a luminous cloud of fire sprites following in her wake, like surrogates for the sparkling wings she could not now make appear.

Storming away from the cottage, Kelley kicked at a small rock bordering the path that led through the yard and sent it skittering into the bushes. Something small and spiny scolded her from under a shrub and lobbed the stone right back at her. Kelley hopped out of the way, startled by the reminder that she was no longer in her own world. And that things hadn't turned out as she'd imagined.

Her reunion with Sonny was supposed to have been a magical, floaty, sparkly thing. With kissing and tears—strictly of joy, mind you, wherein she cried prettily and without blotchiness— and more kissing. And maybe distant fireworks going off as some kind of backdrop to the moment.

"Yeah," she said out loud. "Not exactly."

She hadn't thought anything could come between them— certainly not her father! But now she worried that Auberon had taken Sonny away from her—not just *physically* when he'd commanded him to return to the Faerie realm, but also in other, more intangible ways. She wondered whether Sonny had changed in their time apart, or whether he remained the same and she was only now seeing aspects of him that she had not noticed before.

She couldn't stop thinking about her visions, in which she barely recognized the boy she'd fallen in love with such a short-long time ago.

Why is this all so hard?

Why couldn't she just wrap her arms around him and melt into his embrace as though only hours apart had passed between them?

"Why?" she asked.

Standing in the little yard, Lucky whickered in what sounded like commiseration. Kelley went over to him, stroking the kelpie's neck. She could feel where battle scars on his hide had healed, leaving behind raised ridges in the deep russet coat. His mane and tail were a mass of knots—not like before, when he'd had the enchanted beads tied into his hair with elf knots—but rather, just from a lack of care. He and Sonny both seemed to be suffering in that regard.

Kelley thought of the way Sonny had looked on the river-bank. Of the way the slanting sunlight had cast deep shadows under his silver-gray eyes. Of the stains—they were bloodstains, she knew, there was no sense pretending that they weren't—on his clothes. She'd noticed the bandage wrapped around Sonny's hand, and she shuddered to think of all the times she had seen him bleed—and shed blood—in her dreams.

So what? Kelley thought, suddenly angry with herself. *What's the difference? You knew what he was when you fell in love with him. It's not like he's changed, is it? He kills Faerie.*

Then again, she'd fallen in love before she'd even known that "Faerie" was what she was. But why should that matter? It wasn't as if Sonny were a danger to her . . . although her *mother* was certainly in his sights. Of course, her mother—and it still weirded Kelley out to think of Mabh in those terms—had her own agenda. And was, in her own right, just as dangerous as Sonny. More so, Kelley was inclined to believe—even though Kelley carried that same dangerous, seductive power within her. Would Kelley's Faerie heritage one day make *her* a target of "Auberon's bloodthirsty little lapdog," as Mabh routinely referred to Sonny?

"No! Of course not!" she told herself.

Lucky nudged at her gently, and Kelley dug into the damp shoulder bag that was still slung across her body. In the very bottom, her fingertips brushed the bristles of her hairbrush. She pulled it out and began to gently worry all of the knots out of the patient kelpie's mane and tail, brushing them to silk. Lucky's comforting presence, and the gently monotonous action of grooming him, helped Kelley calm down and get a handle on her spiraling emotions. When she was done, she ran the brush over his whole coat, until finally he stood there gleaming from head to toe, ears pricked up, tail swishing contentedly, an expression of bliss on his long, handsome face.

Kelley smiled and murmured, "This is that very Mab that plats the manes of horses in the night . . . ," quoting Mercutio's famous Queen Mab speech from *Romeo and Juliet*. "Which once untangled much misfortune bodes. . . ." She let the line drift away. Right. Misfortune. She'd forgotten how that line ended.

Kelley hugged herself, suddenly cold.

I am not my mother, she thought, her cheeks heating. *I'm not dangerous or reckless or cruel. . . .*

And she sure as hell wasn't her father—that ice statue masquerading as a person! No, she was nothing like Auberon, and she felt nothing toward him but disdain. Feeling suddenly lost, Kelley slid her arms around Lucky and leaned her forehead on his strong, warm neck, closing her eyes.

When a noise behind her made her turn, Kelley barely even bothered to conceal her disappointment that it wasn't whom she had been hoping for. It wasn't even Fennrys.

"Oh. Hi, Bob."

"Are you all right?"

"I guess so." Kelley sat down on the stone wall that encircled the yard.

The ancient Fae sat beside her. "Is there anything I can do?"

She shrugged. "Right now, I just want to go home."

"You're a sovereign of Faerie, Kelley. At least, you have the blood of one—two, I should say."

"But not the *power* of two. Not anymore." Try as she might, Kelley could not keep the bitterness from creeping into her voice as she thought about the moment when Auberon had taken away the power that she had inherited from his throne . . . and the horrid emptiness it had left behind.

"You still possess the gift of your mother's blood. That is *hardly* inconsequential. Go the same way you came: just make a door. Walk through." Bob paused, gazing at her with his keen, unnerving stare. "Then slam it behind you and never use it again, if that's what you want."

"You think I'm being cruel. About Auberon."

"In some ways, I think you're being very . . ." Bob fished for the right words for a moment. "Very true to the nature of your kind. If not the actual kindness of your nature."

Bob sure liked his wordplay, Kelley thought. But his tone was sincere and made her think about what he had actually said. He had been a friend to her in a very difficult time and he knew her. Her—Kelley. Not just Kelley the actress, or Kelley the Faerie princess. Bob, she had to admit, had a certain amount of insight into Kelley the person.

She thought about that as her gaze roamed restlessly over the wild and unfamiliar terrain. Here she was, sitting in a world that was—ostensibly—her home, and yet it was utterly, fantastically foreign to even her most basic sensibilities. The very air on her skin felt different. Alien. She saw weird, phosphorescent lights flitting in among the tall, spectacular trees, and felt unseen eyes on her—not hostile, just curious. Everything seemed to stand out in sharp relief. The scent of ripe apples and fallen leaves was a heady perfume in her nostrils, and all along the moss-and-pebble path that led to Sonny's pretty little cottage, pools of rainwater shone like mirrors, rimmed with frost as delicate as the lace edging on one of the fairy costumes from the theater. Kelley knew somehow, without even needing to ask, that the dell the cottage nestled in was near the place where the land crossed over from her father's kingdom and became her mother's. She shouldn't know that. There was no reason for her to possess that knowledge. The fact that she did frightened her a little.

She wished she were home in Manhattan. Or even back in the Catskills, where she'd grown up. Thinking she was human. Her hand went to the charm at her throat, fingers brushing the cool green-amber stones.

"D'you remember when I asked you if you could make it so that this never comes off?" She tapped the pendant. "So that I could never draw on Mabh's power?"

Bob nodded slowly. "I do. And I believe I counseled against such rash action."

"You did. Except, well, now it's happened. Whether I wanted it to or not."

"You mean the charm—"

"I can't take it off."

"But you are here!" Bob protested, not understanding. "You must have opened the Gate. I know it wasn't that Janus brute Fennrys, because only someone who wields the power of royal Fae blood can do that at will."

"Yeah, I know." Kelley lifted one shoulder in a shrug. "I think it might have something to do with that tree I killed—"

"You killed a tree?"

"It tried to kill me first."

"Perhaps you should tell me *exactly* what happened to you, Princess."

Kelley sighed gustily and gave Bob the "CliffsNotes" version of her adventure in the park, while all around her Sonny's fire sprites danced in her hair. The evening stars began to peep through the creeping dark.

"This man who attacked you," Bob said finally, once she was finished her tale. "Describe him for me."

"He was some whacked-out Faerie guy." Kelley shuddered a bit, remembering how frightened she'd been. "I thought he was just a mugger that first night."

"And both times he appeared you were just walking through the park?" Bob asked.

"Yes."

"On the path?"

"Yes!"

"You didn't kick over a toadstool in a Faerie Ring or step on a patch of bluebells or anything?"

"No, Bob. I left the park flora entirely unmolested." Kelley laughed without humor. "Which is not to say that it returned the favor."

"Hmm," Bob grunted. "What did this 'whacked-out Faerie guy' look like?"

"Biker couture. Skinny, shaggy hair, jeans, and tattoos . . . plus, y'know, the aggressively green thumb."

"Vivification, yes," Bob said. "Impressive. Especially on that kind of scale."

"Vivi—?" Kelley blew a strand of hair out of her eyes. "Okay. Whatever."

The boucca's pale green forehead furrowed faintly. "I don't suppose your assailant was wearing exceptional quality footwear?"

"Yeah," Kelley answered, startled. "Boots. Like motorcycle boots. Shiny black leather, silver buckles."

"*Seven* silver buckles."

"I didn't exactly stop to count."

Bob didn't even crack a smile. "If you run into him again, I suggest you don't." The ancient Fae's expression had grown very dark indeed.

"What . . . *was* he?"

"Leprechaun," he said. "Bad one."

"Are you sure?" Kelley asked. The image of a leprechaun from children's storybooks and cereal boxes simply didn't tally with the scary, skinny man who had attacked her in Central Park.

But Bob nodded, sounding as sure as if he'd fought the creep himself, as he said, "I had a lot of time to contemplate his identifying features throughout the course of almost an entire century of honeyed fermentation—remind me to tell you that story sometime." His eyes went cloudy with memory. "He used to be a fairly natty dresser—three-pointed buckskin hat and a long coat. But, whatever his fashion sense nowadays, it sounds as though his personality has not exactly mellowed with the passage of time. Still the same mean, miserable son of a bitch. Tell me"—Bob's brow furrowed in thought—"if he cast a spell so that you couldn't remove the charm, how on earth *did* you manage to cross over?"

"Well, when the—er, when the leprechaun brought the tree to life, it tried to suffocate me. The tree, I mean. I stabbed it with his knife, and it—well, it sort of . . . bled all over me." She tapped the clover charm. "All over this."

Amber is the blood of very old trees, her aunt had once told her.

"Aha! Borrowed magick!" Bob exclaimed. "*That* explains how you were able to rip open a passageway. Sometimes, even the odd mortal gets lucky—or unlucky—that way. If he poured a bunch of magick into vivifying the tree that held you fast, then it probably reacted against the magick stored in your charm. Even with most of your own power hidden by the clover, what you had sticking out around the edges was obviously enough to spark off the power that was bleeding out of the tree. Sort of like a fuse on a—"

"Firecracker," Kelley said, the word whispering through her mind in Sonny's voice. "Right . . ."

"*I* was going to say stick of dynamite." Bob looked at her sideways. "But you take my meaning."

"Sure." Kelley understood now the mechanism by which she had managed to draw upon her power. What she didn't understand—and what, in that moment, she decided not to mention to Bob—was that she'd also experienced the incredibly potent vision of Sonny. And that, in the moment before she was able to draw blood from the tree, that vision had seemed to intervene, somehow. "It seemed like this guy was slinging an awful lot of magick all over the park."

"Aye, well. The Wee Green Men are some of the oldest, strongest powers in all of the worlds."

"Wee Green Men?" Kelley snorted. "You're kidding, right? There was nothing particularly wee or green about this guy. Heck—you're greener than he was, Bob."

"They're called that because they are the sons of the Greenman."

"The old forest god?" Kelley asked, remembering the giant, leafy creature who had raised his mug of whiskey to her and winked with a kindly, twinkling eye. "I think I met him at Herne's Tavern back in October. He was really sweet."

"His progeny are *not*," Bob snapped. "Neither the Wee Green Men nor their sisters, the glaistigs—those we call the Green Maidens—are the sort you want to run into in dark alleys. Horrible creatures, all of them. They are like the untamed saplings of a tree that spring up wild in a garden— choking out the other, more desirable growth. The Greenman was all about balance. His children, be they leprechaun or glaistig, are far more interested in chaos."

"Great. And now one of them is after me." Kelley reached up again to touch the charm at her throat, her fingertips playing over the cool surface of the stones. "You know, Emma told me you gave her this, to hide me when I was a baby. But you never actually told her where you got it from, did you?"

"It might have slipped my mind. . . ."

"Bob. Am I in possession of stolen goods?"

The boucca shifted uncomfortably. "Ownership is such a *human* concept—"

"Bob!" Kelley sputtered.

"I never expected he'd find you!" Bob threw his hands in the air. "But ever since Samhain, well . . . word of you has gotten out."

"Thanks for the warning."

"Sorry." Bob smiled weakly.

"You know—I'd cheerfully give it back to him if I thought he'd actually listen to me long enough to undo the whole binding-curse thing."

"Which brings me to my next point." Bob's expression went a bit grim. "Even if the leprechaun troubles you no further, unless you can find a way to remove the spell on the charm, you may never be able to access your Faerie power on your own. You'll be as good as mortal for the rest of your life."

Kelley wasn't exactly sure how she felt about that. On the one hand, she felt something like a vast sense of relief wash through her. But, on the other, she could almost hear a furious shriek of outrage deep inside herself.

"I wish I could lie to you and tell you that your father might help you remove the binding," Bob said. "Then maybe you would come with me. But I can't."

"Oh." Kelley swallowed hard, determined to suppress her flaring emotions in the same way that the clover charm now suppressed her flaring wings. Kelley's wings had once been silvery, shimmering things, in those first few days when she had newly discovered her Faerie magick. Her father had taken those—leaving her with only her mother's magick—and the only wings that she could manifest now were dark as midnight. Auberon had ripped those first wings away, along with the Unseelie power he'd sucked out of her. She hoped he choked on it. "I understand. He won't help me."

"You don't understand at all." Bob stared at her blandly. "Auberon can't help you. He's too weak. Of course, you *could* still pay him a visit—you know; 'in the neighborhood, thought I'd drop by,' that sort of thing—"

Kelley shook her head. "If he can't do anything for me, then there's no reason for me to go see him."

"That's a little harsh, Kelley. Don't you think?"

"I really don't," she said. "*I* remember what happened on Halloween. I'm surprised you've forgotten."

"I haven't *forgotten*," he answered. "I'm just no longer certain I *understand* what I remember. Someone once said. 'There is nothing either good or bad but thinking makes it so.'"

"*Hamlet.*" Kelley smiled. "Seriously—just how well *did* you know Shakespeare, Bob?"

"We frequented the same pubs. That's all. Sometimes he'd bounce ideas off me for one of his plays. And, of course, he'd frequently stiff me with the bar tab." He patted Kelley's knee. "Well, I have to be getting back to Court." He tried one last time. "He'll be disappointed you didn't come. . . ."

"Fine. Whatever. He's no use to me." Kelley was a little surprised to hear herself saying those words. She shook her head. "I'll find my own way back somehow. I know of at least one person who'd probably help me."

"For a price!" Bob scoffed. "I know what you're thinking, and it's really not a good idea."

"You said the only one who can help me is a Faerie Sovereign," Kelley snapped. "And since my father is out of commission, I guess that leaves Mommy Dearest. Loathsome an idea as that may be."

"There are four kingdoms of Faerie, you know, Princess," Bob reminded her. "And while Sonny may have his hands full with the Hunt at the moment, I'm sure the Fennrys Wolf is marginally well enough to guide you to Spring or Summer. If that is what you want."

Kelley glanced reluctantly over her shoulder at the cottage. She wasn't sure she could go back in there. Not after the things she had said to Sonny. After the way he'd looked at her. *Coward* . . . No. She'd been right. She wasn't the one who needed to apologize. Was she?

Bob regarded her sideways. "Do you want me to go and send Fennrys out?"

"Yes, please." She nodded, grateful and just a little bit ashamed of herself all at the same time. "I should get going."

The ancient Fae laid a hand upon her shoulder and said, "Good fortune go with you then, Princess. I hope."

X

"You know you're an idiot, right?" Fennrys asked, his eyes closed and his good arm propped behind his head.

"Shut up, Fenn."

Sonny crouched on his haunches in front of the fireplace. It was cold. Dead. All of his helpful little sparks had followed in the wake of the angry Faerie princess as she had stormed from his house.

"I need a drink," Bob announced loudly as he came back inside after his talk with Kelley. A talk which Sonny had guiltily observed from behind the curtain in his window, knowing full well that it should be *him* out there—and yet he'd been unable to make himself go. Bob went into the tiny alcove that served as a kitchen and rifled through Sonny's cupboards. "Aha!" he exclaimed, triumphant, producing forth a dust-coated bottle and three glasses. He set them down on a little table, pouring the contents out in equal measures. He handed a glass first to Sonny and then to Fennrys, who propped himself up against the wall, his long legs reaching almost to the end of the cot. Bob took a sip of wine and said, "I'd forgotten how much she was . . . like that."

"Like what?"

"Like her father."

Fennrys grunted in amusement. "I'd think twice before telling her that to her face."

"I'll drink to that." Bob toasted the Wolf.

Sonny went to the window again and twitched aside the curtains just long enough to catch a glimpse of Kelley's bright hair, lit by a twinkling constellation of fire sprites in the twilight. He shook his head. "I don't know, Bob. I don't see Auberon just now so much as I see Mabh. And I'm not entirely sure that doesn't worry me." It was true. The wildness in her eyes. The quickness to anger. The hint of cruelty when she spoke of the king. Of letting him die . . .

"That's talk, boyo." Bob astutely interpreted his silence. "What she said about her Old Man Winter. Just talk."

Sonny had no reply to that. But he wondered—was it really?

"Speaking of talk," the boucca said, gazing out the window

toward where they could see Kelley sitting on the low stone wall, shoulders hunched around her ears, "isn't that what you should be doing with her?"

"I don't think she wants me around her just now," Sonny muttered.

Bob and Fennrys exchanged glances. "Idiot," they said in unison.

Fennrys finished his wine in one swallow, a satisfied sigh escaping his lips.

Sonny threw back the sparkling libation, too, only barely tasting the exquisite stuff. A large part of him was still smarting—angry from Kelley's intimation that he'd become some kind of heartless instrument of the Unseelie king.

Bob swallowed another generous mouthful. Then he held out the glass at arm's length and poured out the sparkling dregs onto the dirt floor of the house, leaving behind a damp little circle on the earth. "An offering to the household fae," he said. "Maybe this will convince them to come back inside and tend your hearth. Maybe they'll do a load of laundry for you, too." Bob stared pointedly at Sonny's disastrous apparel.

Sonny ignored him and went back to crouch in front of the unlit fireplace. It was getting dark in the cottage. And cold. Gloomy. He stared hard at the charred remnants of a birch log in the hearth, as if he could ignite a blaze with his eyes.

With a frustrated sigh, Fennrys dug around in the pocket of his jeans and threw a cigarette lighter at Sonny. "You can sit there and light a fire on your own, or you can go outside and get your girl—and your fire sprites—back. Whatever gets your cheery little blaze going. I'm happy with either, frankly, if it keeps me from catching a chill."

Sonny picked up the lighter where it lay on the floor. It took a few moments to coax a flame out of the charred logs, but the minute Sonny added fresh fuel to the grate, the little fire flared into bright, brilliant life.

And there were images in the flames.

Sonny leaned forward—watching the scenes that shifted and danced in the hearth as though projected there. One of the first things he'd done upon taking up residence in the little cottage was to cast a warding enchantment all around a perimeter distant enough to his house to give him ample warning if anything unfriendly approached. And it *would* have given ample warning, too—if only Sonny's fire had been going sooner.

"Seven hells," he muttered through clenched teeth.

Fennrys limped over to the hearth to see what had caught Sonny's undivided attention. "At *least* seven," he agreed.

They could see several flashes of crimson, moving through the undergrowth beneath a stand of maples that Sonny recognized as being not far off.

Bob came and peered over Sonny's shoulder, stiffening in alarm at what he saw. "Now that is bad news on legs."

"Redcaps," Sonny said grimly.

"Friends of yours?" Fennrys asked.

"Not mine. Hardly anyone knows I'm here. And this place

is too strongly veiled." Sonny stared hard at the fire. The squat, troll-like creatures were easily identifiable by their blood-dyed caps and hideous features. Standing only a few feet high, with thick, stumpy limbs, they moved with a surprising amount of speed and stealth. They looked as though they were stalking something. The redcaps had stopped, pausing at a fork where the path split. Sonny watched as the redcap in the lead went down on one knee and minutely examined the ground. He pawed at the earth with one gnarled finger, tasting the dirt and spitting it out. Then he turned and exchanged words with someone hidden in the shadows beneath the trees. Nodding to his fellows, he led them silently up the overgrown arm of the path.

"Shit," Sonny swore softly.

"What?"

"They're definitely tracking something. And they're tracking it straight here."

"How far away are they?" Fennrys asked.

Sonny didn't take his eyes off the flames as he said, "Not far enough."

"Lads," Bob said, backing away from the hearth, "I must be on my way. I'd say it's been fun, but you both know that Faerie aren't capable of lying."

"You're leaving?" Sonny asked.

"Oh yes." The boucca nodded at the ward fire. "I'll not wait around for *that* company to come calling."

"Aw, come on!" Fennrys protested at the dire look on Bob's

face. "Between the three of us, surely we can handle a couple of redcaps."

"I'm sure between the *two* of you, you can at that." Bob patted Fennrys on his uninjured shoulder. "Good luck, now."

"Bob—"

The ancient Fae held up a hand, interrupting Sonny. "Oh no. I'll not be sticking around to help you on this one. Sorry."

"But Bob—"

"I am *sorry*, lads. Truly. But this is where my sense of self-preservation grabs me by the scruff and sends me packing." He pointed at the wavering picture in the flames. "See that shadow yonder up the path? Behind your little troll buddies? *That*'ll be the captain of this little excursion. The mind behind their muscle, if you will, and I am well and truly in *his* bad books. I'll not be crossing paths with that one again. Not if I can help it."

"Oh, crap," Fennrys groaned, looking closer. "Not that sodding leprechaun again."

"No." Bob said. "It's worse. It's his brother."

The Wolf straightened up and looked down at Bob. "I fought the one. How could the other possibly be worse?"

"Oh, he's meaner, drunker, more homicidal. Or, in my case, probably faeriecidal." In his agitation, the boucca's size and shape were shifting more than usual. It made him look almost as though he were bobbing up and down. "Imagine your leprechaun playfellow on a serious whiskey bender and there you have his brother. As a matter of fact, drink is his *only* weakness—he's a slave to it," Bob continued with nervous haste. "On the upside, it caused the Old Man to lay a curse on him and his brothers—I'll tell you about it someday, amusing story—but on the downside, it tends to render him wildly off-kilter and mentally swinging in the wind."

"Bob—wait!" Sonny's voice stopped the boucca in his tracks. Bob stood there, fidgeting and skittish.

"Can he be killed?" Sonny asked.

"No!" Bob's eyes went wide with alarm. "I mean—perhaps if you were to get extremely lucky—but you don't *want* that kind of luck!"

Fennrys and Sonny exchanged confused glances. "Why not?" Fennrys asked.

"Green magick is some of the most powerful magick there is. It doesn't just go *poof* when a leprechaun dies. It destroys everything in its path until it finds a new home. In fact, if you even see one of them on the verge of expiring, I'd suggest running as far and as fast as you can!" Bob's gaze shifted toward the images in the hearth and he gave a little yelp of fear. "Speaking of which—I'd really rather not be here when that rotten sod comes knocking."

"What about their sisters—the Green Maidens? They sound like fun. Can we kill those?" Fennrys asked, ever the pragmatist.

"Oh. Yes, of course. They are far more numerous than their brothers and share their power among them, so it is much weaker. Still—I'd avoid them altogether. They're liable to kill you first. Now look. As I'm pretty sure the entire Wee Green Clan still holds a grudge against me, I'd like to take this opportunity to bid you adieu." Bob spread wide his arms, and the tips of his fingers started to glow with a pulsing, verdant light. "Oh! I almost forgot"—he nodded at Fennrys—"the princess asks that you guide her to the Court of Spring or Summer so she can go home. I suggest you leave with all due haste. Tell her 'happy trails' for me. Can I go now *please*?" he begged Sonny.

"Yes, yes," Sonny said. "Go on."

Without waiting for further encouragement, the boucca slapped his hands together. There was a burst of brightness, and Bob faded rapidly from view until only a handful of green dust motes were left hanging in the air. Then they, too, swirled dizzyingly and funneled up Sonny's chimney, out of sight.

"Gimme a pair of boots," Fennrys said.

"What?" Sonny glanced down at the Wolf's feet, still bare under his muddy pants. "Oh, right."

"And a weapon of some sort might come in handy."

Sonny took a sword in a plain leather scabbard down from a rack on the wall and handed it over. Then he quickly fished an old pair of lace-up boots out of a trunk at the foot of his bed and tossed them to Fenn, who awkwardly put them on, one-handed, stuffing the laces down the fronts.

"Dainty little girly-feet you got there, Irish," he said,

grimacing, as he jammed his left foot into the too-snug boot.

"You're just jealous because *my* feet don't look like I stole them off a dead ogre," Sonny muttered, his attention on the ward fire.

Fennrys drew the sword from its sheath and tested the heft of the blade with his good arm. "How many redcaps do you want? I call dibs on beating the leprechaun at least to within an inch of his life."

"No way," Sonny protested.

"All right, don't pout. You can have the Wee Green Man, then, and I'll take the trolls. But if that's the case, then I get all of 'em!" The Janus grinned fiercely. "Last time I ripped apart a redcap, I remember it made a satisfyingly crunchy sound. So let's go."

Sonny put a hand on Fennrys's chest—or, rather, on the sling that wrapped across his chest—with actual regret. "No, Fenn," he said. "I'll handle this alone. Even though I'd love to have you stick with me, just so you could do something stupid and reckless and wind up dead because of it." Sonny flashed a smile at the thought.

"You're all heart, Irish."

Sonny stared at him. Fennrys stared back, seeming to sense what Sonny was going to say next: "Besides . . . if things go south, I want you to be there for Kelley."

"Right." Fennrys paused. Then he held out his good hand and they clasped each other's forearms.

"Now, go. They'll be here any second."

Fennrys hesitated at the door. "Aren't you even going to say good-bye to her?"

"I . . . no." Sonny frowned, thinking back to all the times he'd tried to protect Kelley—mostly in spite of herself. "I know her. If she thinks I'm trying to get her out of here—if she senses there's trouble on the way—it won't matter how mad she is at me. She's going to want to stay and fight."

"Is that such a bad thing? I've seen her in a scrap. Girl's got guts and I—"

"No!" Sonny snapped. The thought of Kelley in danger made him almost panicky—like he couldn't breathe or see properly. "Just . . . just get her out of here. Get her home. Please."

"Your call." Fennrys shrugged lopsidedly.

Sonny nodded his thanks and went for his satchel. He drew forth the bundle of branches, spoke the whispered word that transformed them into the shining silver sword, and turned back to Fennrys.

"Take care of her, Fenn," he said.

The Wolf didn't stop as he crossed the threshold. "What d'you think I've been doing the whole time you've been gone?"

Tall and lanky, the leprechaun stepped into the darkened cottage with the exaggerated, childish care of a career drunkard. He wove unsteadily on his feet, and his bleary, feral stare drifted over to where Sonny stood invisible. The Janus felt that glance with a shock that was like a blade in his chest, and he gasped soundlessly—he'd veiled himself as strongly as he could.

Damn.

The lurching Fae slurred an order over his shoulder and then stepped all the way over the threshold. Sonny had hoped that he might be able to lure the leprechaun's entire mob into the cottage, where he could keep them occupied for at least enough time for Fenn and Kelley to get a decent head start. Well, that wasn't going to happen now.

Without even needing to tear through Sonny's veil, the leprechaun launched himself into the air in a sideways barrel roll and caught the Janus two blows on the side of the head with both feet—one right after the other in lightning suc-cession. Sonny's sword dropped from his hand and skittered across the floor. The Faerie picked it up, giggled, and threw it out the window.

Then he went after Sonny again.

The way the leprechaun careened around the room made it impossible to predict where the next flailing, windmill attack would come from. In short order, Sonny's head felt as though it were coming loose from its moorings as the blows landed with uncanny accuracy. Both his arms ached from blocking kicks and punches, and some of the ribs on the left side of Sonny's torso were either cracked or bruised enough to feel that way.

The leprechaun backed off for a moment, grinning madly at Sonny through a curtain of tangled hair. "Now, boyo," he said in a slurring lilt, "s'very thoughtful of ye to hang back and keep me company while yon girlie thief and her mongrel doggie scamper away through th'woods. Has she stolen anything of yours yet? Your heart maybe? Such a tasty wee thing she is." He laughed lasciviously. "Let's commiserate on'r losses—here, give us a hug!"

The creature launched himself across the space between them, picking Sonny up in a crushing bear hug. Sonny brought his knee up into the Fae's rib cage and head-butted him sharply, ignoring the pain that bloomed in his own skull. The leprechaun staggered back a bit, and Sonny's feet touched the ground again. Leverage regained, the Janus lunged sharply forward, running his adversary into the wall. There was a flash of poison-green light from the Fae's wild eyes, and he fell forward onto his hands and knees on the dirt floor. Sonny readied himself for another attack. It never came.

Instead the leprechaun's nose began twitching like a rabbit's. The Faerie was staring in horror at the damp patch on the dirt floor where Bob had poured out the dregs of his wine. Sonny remembered what Bob had said about a curse.

"No," the creature moaned. *No, no. No!* His voice grew ragged, frantic with emotion that sounded dangerously close to madness. "Waste . . . such *waste* . . ." The leprechaun suddenly began to weep bitterly.

Bob hadn't exaggerated when he'd called the leprechaun

the slave of drink. Wide-eyed in revulsion, Sonny watched as the mad creature began scraping up handfuls of the wine-dampened earth, shoving his fingers into his mouth and sucking through his teeth to leach out the minuscule amount of liquid from the muddy grit.

Recalling what Bob had also said about the consequences of killing a Wee Green Man, Sonny backed away soundlessly, trying not to attract the Faerie's further attention. It seemed he didn't have to worry. The leprechaun was so consumed that he didn't even notice as Sonny grabbed his leather satchel, dumped out his laundry, and replaced it with his arsenal. At the last moment, he remembered his good-luck charm—Kelley's script. Plucking it silently from the little table beside the cot, he shoved it into his satchel along with the weaponry, glancing briefly at the ward fire as he did.

It looked like the band of redcaps had abandoned the cottage yard and were on the move. They were not traveling the same path that Fennrys and Kelley had taken—rather, they were hurrying along the one that led not directly to the river but to the top of an overhang above the little margin of shore near the waterfall. It was a perfect place for an ambush.

Sonny moved swiftly to the door, closing it gently behind him, and took off at a run to the small meadow around the back of the cottage where Lucky grazed.

"I'm not going any farther until you tell me what the hell is going on!" Kelley shouted.

"I thought you wanted to go home." Fennrys's voice was thick with frustration. They were arguing. It was like music to Sonny's ears for at least two reasons. One, Kelley was still very much alive. And, two, Kelley was mad at Fennrys.

"Yeah, but I don't want to kill myself to get there. Or you! I mean look at you—you can barely stand. Why are we running?"

Thank the gods, Sonny thought, relief surging through him as Kelley's voice echoed off the crevasse walls up to where he'd ridden Lucky. They'd gotten there in time—barely. The funk of redcap stink was so thick in the air that the trolls had to be very close by—somewhere in the woods at the edge of the precipice, waiting to ambush Kelley and Fennrys from high above where they now stood arguing.

"Ow!" Sonny heard her exclaim. "Let go of my arm, Fennrys. I'm warning you—"

"Kelley, would you please, for the love of the gods, just shut up and run?"

"Fenn, if you're not telling me something—oh god! Is Sonny in some kind of danger?"

Yes, Sonny thought as he found himself flying through the air, knocked from the kelpie's back by three or four redcaps that had launched themselves at him from the trees overhead.

He hit the ground and rolled, grasping for purchase in the sparse grass at the cliff's edge, his legs dangling. The redcaps squealed, suddenly realizing what a precarious situation they were in, and tried to climb up Sonny's torso and over one another as the lip of the cliff crumbled and they began to fall. Sonny twisted in midair and managed to land on at least two of them.

When he got to his feet, all he could see for a moment was Kelley staring at him, mouth agape.

"Sonny!" she cried, sprinting toward him. He held his arms open for what he meant to be a good-bye embrace. But Kelley dodged past him, scooped up a fallen tree branch that lay on the strand, and clobbered one of the redcaps. The branch shattered in two over the creature's ugly, lumpy head just before the vicious little troll would have plunged a long-bladed knife into Sonny's unprotected back. The creature slumped back into a heap onto the ground.

"Thank you," Sonny said in astonishment.

"I'm sorry I left without saying a proper good-bye," Kelley said, the broken makeshift club gripped in her white-knuckled fist.

"I'm sorry I let you," Sonny said, and opened his arms again. But as Kelley moved toward him, a flash of movement from above made Sonny grab her by the shoulders and thrust her toward Fennrys instead.

It seemed there wasn't going to be time for a proper good-bye after all.

"Fenn—get her out of here!" Sonny barked, looking up. "Now!"

The rest of the redcap pack barreled over the precipice high above, cannonballing down onto the beach, punching craters in the earth as they landed—deadly, spiked boots first.

Out of the corner of his eye, Sonny saw Fennrys grab Kelley around the waist and half drag, half carry her upriver as fast as he could. Then there was no time left for anything other than the fight.

XI

"*S*onny!" Kelley shouted and struggled like a maniac in Fennrys's iron grip as she saw Sonny brace himself for the onslaught of the horrible-looking creatures that seemed to pour down out of the sky.

Holding Kelley around the waist with his one good arm, Fennrys dragged her down a steep slope toward the river and the waterfall that tumbled in a foam-and-rainbow curtain down a sheer rock face.

Kelley screamed ferociously for him to let her go, but her voice was a tiny bird call compared to the thunder of the falls. Fennrys hauled her toward what appeared to be the solid, impenetrable wall of boiling-white water, dove straight into it . . . and then burst *through* it.

The noise from the wall of water abruptly silenced as they entered what appeared to be an underground cave or tunnel, and the entrance behind them vanished, shimmering like a mirage and turning into a wall of solid, sparkling rock. The Wolf set Kelley back down on her feet, and she turned around and punched him hard in the chest.

"Damn you!" She stalked back to the wall that had been their way in. It was no longer a way out. Sonny was there, somewhere. On the other side. Fighting those things. Still clutching the broken branch end, she hammered it at the rough stone, but the wood just splintered uselessly. "Open it, Fennrys." Kelley rounded on the Janus. "Open it or so help me, I'll—"

"I can't."

His tone of voice silenced the argument in her.

"That doorway swings in only one direction," he said. "We don't have any choice but to keep going forward. And you can punch me all you like, but it will not change that simple fact."

She saw in his face, and heard in his voice, that he was telling the truth. He really couldn't reopen the door. "But Sonny—"

"Can take care of himself." Fennrys stared at her, unblinking. "If I didn't think that, I wouldn't have left him. I'm a Janus. We don't abandon our fellows, no matter how idiotic

137

we might think they are." He turned on his heel and started walking. "Now come on. Unless you'd prefer to waste all that effort he's putting into saving you."

It felt as though they'd been traveling forever. As they trekked through an underground landscape that was like nothing Kelley had ever seen before, she'd been forced to let go of her anger toward Fennrys. She knew that it would be pointless to ask him to slow down. Or to stop. Or to go back. So she clenched her jaw against the jarring pain every time she stumbled in her strappy sandals on the uneven, rocky ground, and followed silently. Through twisting, labyrinthine caves and tunnels, Fennrys led her at a punishing pace, and she knew it was because Sonny had as good as ordered the Wolf to protect her. That thought made her feel both secretly warmed and rebellious at the same time.

"Y'know," she muttered, half to herself, as they walked, "I don't *need* saving. I'm perfectly capable of taking care of myself."

Ahead of her the Wolf snorted. "Yes, yes. You're very brave," he said sharply. "Never mind *you*—did you ever stop to think that your being there 'helping' Sonny fight could get *him* killed? We're trained for this sort of thing, Kelley. You're not."

"I didn't see *you* clobbering any trolls back there."

"Right. Nice shot. Beginner's luck. Whatever. If it was *me* back there, I'd say take your stick and have at it. I wouldn't give a damn. But Sonny *does* give a damn. A huge one. For him, you're not a help in a scrap. You're nothing but a distraction. And *that* makes you a liability—the kind that leads to unfortunate, often fatal, mistakes."

"I . . . I didn't think of it like that."

"I know you didn't," Fennrys said in a milder tone. "Now come on. We've got a long way to go."

The tunnel walls and vaulting caverns were covered with sparkling luminescent crystals that gave off a softly shifting light. Streams ran alongside them through some of the tunnels, the waters dark and mysterious, swirling and eddying to reveal flashes of swift-swimming fae. Kelley noticed, whenever they traveled beside one of those streams, that Fennrys made sure to keep her well away from the edges of the water.

At intervals the cavern branched off into what seemed to Kelley a hundred different passageways, but Fennrys always seemed to know which way to go. Occasionally he'd stop at a fork in a tunnel to lift his head and sniff at the air for a brief moment or two. Then it was back to leading her through the fantastical passageways at a near run.

When they finally emerged from the crystalline, twisting caves, it was deep night, so deep that it was almost morning again. Kelley remembered that time worked differently—or not at all—in the Faerie realms. She wondered what time it was at home, and her hand went automatically to the pocket of her shoulder bag where her cell phone lived, to check the time. The zipper was open and the pocket was empty—she must have lost the damned thing in the river.

Not like I can really phone home from here, anyway . . .

She breathed deeply of the chilly blue air. A sickle moon shone above the slender treetops, casting more light on the landscape than even a full moon did back home. The branches of the trees were bare—more bare than they were back in the mortal realm, where April was starting to tease the leaves out from slumber. Here, the land looked as if it were held suspended at the ends of winter's chilly fingertips, moments before free-falling into spring.

Which was apparently where they were—and not, it seemed, where Fennrys had meant to lead them.

"Spring. Damn," he swore softly. Then less so: "Damn it! Damn, damn, damn!"

"Fenn?"

Fennrys turned on his heel and started back toward the river. Kelley followed in his footsteps, but she bumped into him when he stopped abruptly. The cave entrance was gone. The river continued on in an unbroken line into the distant hills, the edges of the water trimmed with lacy ice, sparkling coldly.

"Fennrys?" Kelley wanted to know what was happening, but the Wolf's normally unflappable demeanor was . . . well, flapping.

He muttered something in a vocabulary that made Kelley's ears burn and said, "Right. Come on then."

"Is something wrong?"

"No. Yes. Not for you," he answered unhelpfully. "Maybe."

"Where are we?" she asked.

The Fennrys Wolf, warrior, Viking prince, and fearless Janus Guard swallowed convulsively and said, in a very quiet voice, "Home."

"We're *where*, exactly?" Kelley asked again. They were following a wide road of smooth stones and thick, fragrant moss.

"We're in the Vernal Lands. In the Kingdom of Spring. The shadow lands opposite your mother's."

Kelley had already deduced that the Vernal Lands, domain of the Court of Spring, was the *last* place in the Otherworld that Fennrys wanted to be, but she strove for what she saw as the bright spot in the situation. "So we're far away from my mother, at least," she said. "This is good. Right?"

"Wrong. This is . . . not good."

"That's not exactly encouraging."

"I haven't been back here since Auberon chose to make me a member of the Janus Guard. My former lord and master"— his voice was tinged with a sharp edge of sarcasm—"was less than agreeable with *that* arrangement."

"And who is your 'former lord and master'?"

"His name is Gwynn ap Nudd. He is the king of the Court of Spring." They crested a rise in the land, and Fennrys pointed with his good hand at the architectural impossibility rising up in front of them. "There is where I grew up."

A pale yellow sun rose over the hills at their backs, illuminating weeping willows that swayed gently in the breeze. On some of the branches, icicles still hung like ornaments, dripping onto the frosty grass. Banks of spring-blooming flowers lined the wide path, leading the way to the fairy-tale palace. It was like Oz, or Sleeping Beauty's castle. Or Rivendell. More like, all of those others were pale imitations of *this*—as if the human imagination had once seen this place in all its glory and forever after strived to return to it. Or re-create it.

"You grew up *there*?"

"Yes." Fennrys glared at the castle reproachfully. "It wasn't my idea, but yes."

"But it's so pretty." Kelley looked back and forth from the palace to her companion as they walked, having a hard time reconciling the place with the person.

"Yeah. Very nice. And not even close to where I wanted to wind up just now. Damn it all."

"Where did you mean to go?"

"I *meant* to lead you through the crystal caves to the Summer Court—I was sure I'd followed the right way."

Kelley frowned. "Sonny doesn't seem to trust Titania."

"Sonny was raised by Auberon, who spends most of *his* time and energy mistrusting Titania." Fennrys shrugged. "When he isn't busy trying to get her to climb into that big chilly bed of his, of course."

"Riiight." Kelley *really* didn't need the visuals. "Um . . . look! Flowers."

"Hyacinth," Fennrys said, and cast a baleful glare at the

fragrant blooms. "And those ones there are paperwhites," he said, pointing. He caught a glimpse of her staring at him in astonishment and growled, "I hate hyacinths."

Kelley bit her tongue to keep from laughing at his expression.

They traveled the rest of the way in silence to the palace's terraced marble steps. Squaring his shoulders, Fennrys led her up to a pair of tall, slender doors made of polished silvery wood. He raised a bunched fist to hammer on the doors, but they opened of their own accord before he could land the first blow. Fenn sighed and gestured with a courtly sweep of his good arm for Kelley to precede him.

Kelley stepped inside the palace doors, and a reed-thin slip of a Faerie girl emerged from an alcove, walking with a ballerina's grace. She wore a diaphanous, spring-green gown that, from the waist up—Kelley was shocked to see—would have gotten her arrested in New York, were it not for the pale blond hair that fell in an artfully obscuring fashion over her shoulders. The top half of her ensemble contrasted dramatically with the almost demure nature of her long, layered skirts that swept all the way to the floor, making it seem as though she hovered along the ground, rather than walked. The outfit managed to make Kelley, in Tyff's torn and muddied designer jeans, feel both under- and over-dressed.

"M'lord Fennrys," lisped the sylph in a shy, childlike voice, her lips barely opening to let the sound out. "Welcome home. We've sorely missed your presence here."

Fennrys gave her a barely cursory nod and turned away, asking, "Where is your master? Tell him the lady Kelley, daughter of Winter and Autumn, wishes an audience."

"This way," she murmured, gesturing with one long arm. Kelley thought she saw—for the briefest instant—a pure, red gleam in the Faerie girl's eyes. "He awaits you both."

The Fae waved them deeper into the palace, glancing sideways at Kelley as she passed, and then falling in behind them, following at a discreet distance. Kelley tried to shake off the creepy feeling the girl gave her. It was only natural, she supposed, that the Fair Folk would have heard about her after the events of last autumn and been curious. Still, she could feel the girl's eyes on her like drill bits boring into the muscles of her back as they walked, and she wished ill-humoredly that she could manifest her wings and flash-blind the staring girl for a moment.

Fennrys stalked ahead of them. He obviously knew the way without needing to be shown, and Kelley was bursting with curiosity to know what it had been like growing up in this place.

When they turned a corner and entered suddenly into a vast room, all thoughts of idle chat flew from Kelley's brain.

The Great Hall of the palace of the Court of Spring was like a soaring forest of birch and willow trees, leafless and petrified into pillars of slender white marble arching high into a watercolor sky. Far overhead, where the delicate branches of the stone trees came together, they formed a latticework that

144

supported a shimmering ceiling made of millions of shards of rainbow-colored glass.

Casting her gaze around as they walked the length of the sumptuous hall, Kelley wondered how Gwynn's palace compared with her father's. *With Auberon's,* she mentally corrected herself. Before she had time to wonder how Gwynn himself would compare, he stepped through an archway that led onto a dais where stood a silver throne.

The king was tall and thin and looked as though a stiff wind could snap him in half or a heavy rain wash him away. His hair was like fine black silk, tied in a tail down his back, and his eyes were the color of sapphires, startling against the whiteness of his skin. He wore a long, sweeping robe the color of midnight overtop of a bluish white tunic, belted with silver. He did not smile when he looked upon her.

"She has Mabh's eyes," he said.

"Actually, my mother has her own eyes. These are mine," Kelley snapped, the words leaving her mouth before she had time to think.

"And her temperament."

Beside her, Kelley noticed that Fennrys wasn't saying anything. His signature cocky swagger had been missing from the minute he'd realized they'd taken a wrong turn coming out of the caves. Well, *she* was not about to be cowed.

"Do you always speak about people standing right in front of you as if they weren't there?" Kelley asked, her tone politely conversational. "Is this the hospitality of the Court of Spring?

Seems a bit chilly to me, as though you might still be waiting for the thaw."

Silence filled the hall, and Fennrys shifted uncomfortably. Kelley wondered for a moment whether she had been too bold and then decided it didn't matter: she was the daughter of a queen. And a king. She would not be talked down to.

The Faerie king descended from his dais.

"Please," he said, and held out his arm for her to take. "Forgive me. You are quite right. That was uncivil of me, and you have traveled far." Gwynn led her gently toward a little table and a couple of chaise lounges—the kind that belonged in rooms where people didn't ever actually sit down to lounge. "Jenii," the king said over his shoulder to the lovely girl, "refreshments for our guests."

Kelley eyed the furniture skeptically. The pieces looked more like an art installation than furniture—also made of silver, with a delicate and lacy design like newly unfurled leaves and shoots, upholstered with damask and accented with richly embroidered cushions that looked far too precious to put any weight on.

"Be at peace here. Sit down," Gwynn said.

Kelley let herself be lowered onto the chaise. It was surprisingly comfortable.

"Welcome to the Faerie realm, lady." The King of Spring's voice was low, musical, and soothing. "We had hoped that, upon your arrival, you would grace us with a visit."

Kelley wondered briefly how, exactly, Gwynn had known

of her "arrival"—he made it sound as though she'd just stepped off a private jet, rather than tumbling violently through a rift and almost drowning in a waterfall—but she didn't ask. Kelley figured that Gwynn must have some sort of system like her mother's scrying mirrors in place—all the Faerie monarchs probably did—and she didn't feel like letting him know how uneasy that thought made her.

Gwynn lowered himself elegantly down onto the chaise across the low table from hers and gestured for the Wolf to do the same. Fennrys shrugged and threw himself carelessly onto the other remaining couch, hoisting a booted foot up onto the seat with what seemed like active disdain of the delicately embroidered cushions.

The Faerie girl returned, her long skirts whispering across the floor, bearing a tray of gently steaming cups and a long-necked bottle of clear green liquid.

"Nice place you have here," Kelley said stiffly, as the sylph poured a splash of the green liquor into each of the cups, causing the steam to billow and fill the air with a spicy, intoxicating aroma.

"It is much diminished from what it once was, but I thank you." Gwynn elegantly waved off her compliment.

"I don't understand. What do you mean, diminished?"

"Has no one ever bothered to explain any of the history of your people to you, Princess?" Gwynn asked, handing her one of the cups.

Kelley felt her cheeks coloring. Loath as she was to admit

it, her ignorance of Faerie was pretty comprehensive. Aside from the stories—folktales, really—that her aunt had inundated her with as a child, most of which languished in the dustier corners of her memories, she knew very little about the culture of her "people."

Gwynn smiled wanly at her silence. "But, of course, mine is not a tale that you would likely be told. This realm—all of it—once fell under my dominion entirely. These, my halls, were once filled with life and laughter."

Kelley took a sip from the cup. It tasted like . . . the only way she could describe it was that it tasted like spring. She listened to Gwynn, intrigued and actually a little grateful. Here was one of the Fair Folk who was treating her like an equal. He didn't, Kelley decided, talk down to her and he was actually telling her stuff that he thought she should know. It was refreshing.

"Time was"—Gwynn rolled his own cup around between the palms of his hands, staring at the liquid within as if the story he told appeared to him in its depths—"that I, Gwynn ap Nudd, was the one and only king of Faerie. That was a long time ago. Before the Greenman had even discovered that the Fae could cross over into the mortal realm. Before he built the Gates. Before your father, Auberon, became powerful and the Faerie realm was split into the four Courts. Back then it was simply the realm."

"What happened?"

Gwynn did not answer her immediately, seemingly lost in

his memories of that time, so Fennrys spoke up.

"War," said the Wolf in a voice that Kelley could only interpret as wistful. As though he wished he'd been there, a part of it. "The younger powers rose up and threw the older one down. There were many factions and a long war, and when the dust finally cleared, Auberon and Titania were the ones left standing the tallest. They became the new rulers of the Faerie realms."

The king put his cup down on the table hard enough to make the liquid splash over the rim. "My changeling speaks truth. Bitter though it may be."

Kelley sipped at her drink. She almost felt embarrassed for a moment—as though she should apologize for the actions of her parents.

Gwynn shook his head and smiled gently at her, as though sensing her unease.

"I am sorry, Princess. It was a long time ago, but the memory is still sharp. I remained a king of Faerie, as you see, but in a role much reduced: left only with the shadow kingdom you see here—the Vernal Lands. Auberon and Titania split the lion's share of the realm between their two Courts, Unseelie and Seelie, and became rulers of Winter and Summer, respectively." Gwynn laughed then—a hollowed-out sound. "And all that while, as the others fought, your mother, Mabh, slipped in and built herself a kingdom in the Autumnal regions, gathering what power she could lay her fingertips on—which was, in hindsight, probably far too much."

"Sounds like Mom, all right," Kelley agreed. She found herself relaxing in Gwynn's presence. He certainly had her parents pegged, and it was nice to hear her own opinions validated by no less than a Faerie monarch.

"Indeed. I've always rather suspected *she* was behind the whole mess in the first place. Your mother does so love chaos and strife. At any rate, when all was finally said and done, accords were drawn up, treaties made, and the Four Thrones were created. The magicks of the land were divided, bound up into the Thrones and bonded in the blood of the Faerie kings and queens." Gwynn shrugged elegantly and smiled. "The Greenman created the Four Gates to the mortal realm in honor of the Four Courts, and with the excitement and novelty of having access to a whole new world and a whole new race of mortal playthings to keep them occupied, the Fair Folk were once again content. Peace reigned."

"I was one of those playthings," Fennrys said sardonically.

"Yes." The smile vanished from Gwynn's face, and he glared balefully at the Janus. "And even that was taken from me by the Winter King."

An uncomfortable silence hung in the air.

"Um . . ." Kelley fidgeted for a moment. Now might be the time to get down to the business of why she was there, she thought. "Your highness . . . I appreciate the hospitality. I'd like to ask a fav—"

"Allow *me*," Fennrys interrupted her brusquely, shooting her a stern, warning look.

Kelley closed her mouth with a snap. She'd almost forgotten how careful she had to be around the Fair Folk, even those who seemed genuinely helpful. It was never a good idea to be in a position to owe them anything.

Fennrys cleared his throat and said, "My lord, the lady Kelley seems weary, and I've been charged with her well-being. Perhaps she could take her rest here while you and I discuss the reason of our visit."

"But I'm not—" Kelley began. But the Wolf gave her another sharp glance. *Okaaay, maybe I am tired.*

"Jenii, please show the princess to a guest chamber," Gwynn said graciously, and Kelley allowed herself to be led away. Fenn knew what he was doing. He'd promised to help her get home. The least she could do was get out of his way and let him.

Jenii led her through a maze of airy rooms on the way to her chamber. In one sparkling glass-domed hall, huge silver planters stood arranged on pedestals of varying heights, most of them filled with dark, freshly turned earth. Some bore fragile spring flowers, some were barren of any visible growth at all, and a few of the planters looked as though they were rimmed with old, dirty ice crystals. The air was heavy with the fresh scent of flowers but also the bittersweet tang of decay. In some of the silver planters, Kelley saw brown, rotting vegetation—like the kind that was always uncovered at home when winter finally retreated, leaving behind dead thatch and furry patches of pink and gray snow mold.

One dish was set slightly apart from the rest, and as she

passed by, Kelley saw it was full of tall stalks of vervain in full bloom, bursting with tiny purple flowers. They were the only flowers she could see that were summer-blooming rather than spring-blooming. A promise—or perhaps a reminder—of the season to come, Kelley supposed. The heady, sweet odor of them was familiar somehow. It turned her stomach, but Jenii cast an inquiring glance on her, and she tried not to let that show on her face.

Kelley smiled brightly at her guide, hoping that Fennrys would hurry the heck up. Gwynn seemed nice enough, but his choice of staff gave Kelley the creeps.

XII

For the first time that day, Sonny was glad he wasn't wearing a good shirt. Redcap blood both stank *and* left behind a nasty stain. He wanted nothing more, in the aftermath of a hard-won fight, than to strip off his torn and much-abused breeches and shirt and dive back into the river to get clean. Of course, that would have been exceedingly reckless on his part. Dangerous creatures, lured by the scent of redcap blood, had begun to lurk beneath the waves, and a pair of long, greenish-white arms, hands tipped in fishhook-sharp talons, emerged to drag one of the wounded trolls from the shallows into the deep middle of the river.

Sonny whistled for Lucky, who'd been stuck up on top of the cliff when the trolls had attacked. The kelpie peered gingerly over the edge, and Sonny waved for him to head back down the trail.

"I'll meet you at the fork," he called, knowing that the Faerie horse would understand. He noticed as he walked that the cloud of fire sprites that had accompanied Kelley when she'd left the cottage with Fennrys were now bobbing gently around him.

Fickle little beasts.

He shooed them all homeward, with a warning that there was a possibility the leprechaun might still be in the cottage. The tiny sparks squeaked and rustled with outrage at the thought that a libation that had been poured for *them* had been consumed—floor dirt and all—by someone else. Off they zoomed in a grumpy little sparkling swarm, and Sonny couldn't help but smile; they all now shone with the same deep auburn blush as Kelley's fiery hair. *Apparently she made quite an impression,* he thought as he trudged wearily homeward in their wake.

Home . . .

What was that, really? The only home Sonny had ever known growing up had been the Court of the Unseelie Fae. Auberon's Court. He felt a strange emptiness. By the time he reached the place where the path split and the kelpie awaited him, Sonny had made a decision.

He ran his hand over Lucky's freshly burnished coat,

conscious of his own still-sorry condition. For weeks nothing had really seemed to matter but the mission, the Hunt. But all that had changed when he'd seen *her* again. Just the sight of Kelley had reminded Sonny of what was truly important to him. And, impossible as it might have proved to convince Kelley herself of it, he'd realized that one of those important things was her father. Maybe not to her—maybe *never* to her—but, strange as it seemed, to *him*.

Suddenly Sonny didn't give a damn what Bob had said.

If Auberon was dying, then Sonny was going home.

He passed several gwyllion as he rode: solitary Fae who sat at the sides of roads, watching passersby with too-large, glassy eyes. Solitary Fae were far more common among the Unseelie Fae than in, say, Titania's Court, where everything was just one big party all the time and the Faerie there trooped about in large, raucously festive gatherings. Stone-still except for the tapping of their long fingers, the gwyllion just stared unmoving as Sonny passed. He gave them a wide berth and knew that, if he had approached them, they would have done the same. But then again, they all did. All the Faerie.

The Fair Folk were not his folk.

The thought came, unbidden: Kelley was not his folk.

But neither was she one of them. Not exactly. Perhaps she never would be, now that she was, for all intents and purposes, bound into the guise of a mortal girl. At least, that was his incomplete understanding of the events that had taken place before she had come through the rift in the middle of his river. With Fennrys. He clung to the notion that sending her away again—with Fennrys—had been the right thing to do.

When he reached the palace, the house guard of the Unseelie Court all backed off a respectful pace as he passed— each one nodding, acknowledging his presence and his station as he stalked through the halls of the cold, glittering castle.

"Oh, I knew it." Bob's familiar, mocking tone waylaid him as he turned the corner at the top of a great stair into a hallway that led directly to the king's chamber. The boucca shimmered into view. "I knew you'd come. I should have told you he wanted nothing more than for you to join him quick as you could. You would have shunned the place like it was plagued with fleas. Humans. Contrary unto death." He shook his pale green head. "Good goddess. You look worse than when I left you. Who would have thought *that* possible?"

"Please don't get in my way, Bob" was all Sonny said.

"I haven't suddenly turned imbecile, my young Janus." Bob didn't appear to move a muscle, but suddenly he was no longer standing in Sonny's path. "I know that look. Stubborn as your mum, you are. And we all know how well my willpower stood up against *her*."

Not at all, Sonny knew. In fact, it was Emma Flannery's strength of character—and her desperation at the Faerie theft of infant Sonny—that had driven Bob to help her cross over into the Otherworld, where she had stolen another child back. Kelley. Hiding her in the mortal realm with the aid of a leprechaun's charm.

Bob shook his head as if to dispel the memory of those reckless actions. "Right then. Do as you must." He swept a low, only half-mocking, courtly bow in Sonny's direction and fell into step beside him as the Janus stalked past.

Black Annis, chief herald of the Unseelie Court and a formidable power in her own right, sat on a low stool to one side of the arching doorway that opened into Auberon's chamber. The Faerie's hair fell straight in a long dark curtain on either side of her face, reaching the floor and covering her gray robes like a cloak. She looked straight at Sonny with her blue-white, pupil-less eyes, and he actually thought he saw something like relief or gratitude flicker for a moment in her unnerving stare. And even though the sharp, strikingly beautiful planes of her face did not change, Sonny felt her unspoken welcome.

Auberon must be worse off than I feared, he thought.

Black Annis was not known for her sentimental side.

"He does not want to see you," she said, rising to her feet, her voice a wintry hiss.

Sonny locked eyes with her blank, glacial stare. "And so?"

"And so." She bowed, lips twisting upward, and stepped aside. "You may go in."

The tall doors swung open on the dark room. Heavy drapes were pulled across the windows, blocking out the cold white light of the Winter Court sky. The floor of the chamber was piled deep in furs, and Sonny's boots made no sound as he crossed to the alcove beside the bed, where he could make out the dim figure of his lord, sitting in a deep chair, with only a single candle to give him light.

Sonny knelt at Auberon's feet, his eyes on the ground. "My lord," he said quietly, the conflicting emotions roiling around inside of him muting the greeting.

"Strange." Auberon's voice seemed to come from a long way away. "I was almost certain that I had expressed—in most unequivocal terms—that you were to continue in the fulfillment of your quest to rid the realm of the Wild Hunt."

Sonny remained silent, his gaze locked on the hems of the Unseelie king's robe.

"Am I to conclude then from your presence here," the king continued, "that you have accomplished this thing? Is it time now for you to accompany me to the Court of Summer so that, together, Titania and I may bind the Autumn Queen?"

"There are three hunters left, and they aren't going anywhere," Sonny answered. "They hide more than they hunt these days, and it's not as if they can make more of themselves. Mabh can wait."

"Can she, now? The Queen of Air and Darkness has always been the wild card that threatens the balance of the realm, Sonny. Do not be so quick to dismiss her."

In the wake of that admonishment, the king sank farther back into his chair, and the silence stretched out in the room. Sonny stared at the floor as if his gaze could bore holes in it.

"My daughter," the king said, finally. "Puck tells me that

she has been bound into her mortal guise by a leprechaun's spell."

Sonny nodded. "That is as I understand it. If I could be with her—protect her—then perhaps—"

"You will do nothing of the kind!" For the first time in that audience, Sonny heard some semblance of the Unseelie king that he was accustomed to in Auberon's voice.

"But why? She is your daughter!" Sonny raised his eyes, finally, and was inwardly shocked at what he saw. His vision had adjusted to the dimness of the room, and he could plainly see the ravaging effects of illness etched on Auberon's regal face. The Faerie king's visage seemed to have lost its timeless quality. He looked . . . old.

Sonny swallowed the sudden knot of emotion that had lodged in his throat.

"Finish your task, Sonny," the king murmured, his eyes clouding, as though he saw things that Sonny could not see. Things in the future, or maybe in the past. "My daughter does not need you. She can take care of herself."

"Without her power? How can you be so sure? What if she is attacked again? What if—"

"*Please*, lad . . ."Auberon shook his head heavily, focusing his eyes on Sonny's face with what seemed great effort. "Do what I have asked of you."

Sonny nodded, subsiding, and struggled to keep his concern for the king from showing in his face. He did not wish to shame the proud man.

Auberon's gaze drifted back toward the window. "I didn't really expect that she would come," he said, and Sonny knew that he was still speaking of Kelley. "I suppose I shouldn't fault her for that. She has cause to be angry with me. Hate me. Beyond even the reasons she thinks are the right ones." Auberon laughed a little. "And, quite frankly, I am more than a little surprised to see you here, Sonny. For many of the same reasons."

"I had to come," Sonny said, quietly. "When Puck told me you were sick—"

"Bob. Yes, well. The Goodfellow tends toward exaggeration." Auberon waved a languid hand and shifted in his chair. "And at any rate, I thought you had forsworn these halls. I 'betrayed your trust,' didn't I?"

"Didn't you?" When the king didn't answer, Sonny threw his hands in the air in frustration. "Why didn't you call upon me when you fell ill?" he asked, trying another tack.

"You were busy."

"My lord—"

"And you are angry."

"Do I not have cause?" Sonny snapped. Every time he thought about Auberon's perfidy during Samhain, the wounds to his heart felt just as fresh as when he'd first found out. Now, finally, he would say it. "Tell me, my king. Do I not have a grievance?"

"Do you?"

"You called the Wild Hunt—"

160

"Did I?"

"No games, Auberon!" Sonny's voice cracked in anguish, echoing off the cold marble. "I am fed to the teeth with Faerie games. *Please*."

A deafening silence descended upon the room. Finally Auberon spoke. "Herein lies the heart of my problem, Sonny. My tragic flaw, if you will."

"My lord?"

"I am not in the business of justifying my actions. Not even to one such as you. That being said, I will also tell you that *I do not play games*." Auberon sighed and mustered a chuckle. "It is only that sometimes my expectations are . . . unrealistic. I unwisely assume of others that they employ the same kind of clear-eyed detachment and analysis that I myself bring to bear on a given situation."

"I don't understand."

"I know you don't." The king continued to stare into the middle distance, his dark eyes unfocused, his voice still soft. "I do not blame you. You are, when all is said and done, only human. But it would, perhaps, behoove you to trust your human senses—and *only* your senses—in this case. Cold, hard facts can often be a comfort, Sonny. Conjecture and assumption, while seductive, will ultimately leave you wanting." The king shifted restlessly. "You ran afoul of Mabh once because you *assumed* she meant one thing when she meant another. You rode astride the Roan Horse when you *thought* the danger of the Wild Hunt had passed. What other

161

assumptions did you make?"

Sonny thought back to that horrible night. He remembered the horn blasts calling to him—claiming him . . . Auberon stooping to retrieve Mabh's horn from where it lay in the grass . . . What had he really seen that night? He had not seen Auberon *blow* the horn. . . .

"Are you trying to tell me that you were *not* the one responsible for waking the Wild Hunt?" Sonny gaped at the king in astonishment. "But if not you, Auberon, then who?"

"I cannot say."

"Why not?"

"Because I truly do not know," the king snapped. "And it is far too dangerous a thing to speculate upon."

"Out loud, you mean."

"Even so."

"But you have your suspicions."

"Even so." The king rose and gathered his heavy fur robes around him with some semblance of his usual majesty. He cast a wan eye over Sonny's shabby appearance but declined to comment. Instead he just lifted his chin and stared down upon the Janus as if from a great height. "Finish your task."

"But, my lord, if there is some way I can be of more use here—"

"Then I would have you here."

"Yes, lord."

"Now go. I grow weary." The dismissal was not up for debate.

There was nothing else for him to do. Sonny rose, nodded a curt bow, turned on his heel, and left the chamber, Black Annis following soundlessly behind him like a chill wind at his back.

"What ails him, Annis?" he asked as the herald pulled the chamber doors shut.

"Something ails my lord?" The ghost of a smile did not touch her eyes. "Whatever gives you that idea?"

Sonny glared at her, his skull pounding with a headache brought about by the tension of the last day, aggravated now with worry about the man who, despite their current differences, had still raised him from a baby. Sonny's pulse thrummed behind his eyes.

"I do not know," Annis continued, before Sonny ran out of patience completely. "When he returned to Court after the Nine Night, there was something . . . different about him. A newness. A light. A strength . . ."

Kelley's light, thought Sonny. *Kelley's strength. After Auberon had taken her magick for his own so that she would never become a threat to him.*

"But it didn't last. He began to suffer weakness, and sadness. Now he is as you see him."

"Why hasn't he sought help, Annis?"

"He is proud. And he has many enemies who would be quick to try to take advantage of the situation, should the Winter King's condition become known."

"What can I do?"

"Do what he asks of you," she said severely, her gaze sweeping over him like a beam of frosty light. "And be careful. There are ill winds blowing through this realm, Sonny. May they die down soon and not breed a tempest."

XIII

Home. She was home.

Fennrys had done it. Gwynn had sent her home.

Back to New York City. *Sort of . . .*

Kelley stood in the middle of a wide road—Park Avenue, maybe, although it was hard to tell—and gazed around the city streets at buildings with outlines softened and blurred, details obscured by greenery. Thick, lush vegetation covered the sky-scrapers, climbing trellises of glass and steel. They reminded Kelley of pictures she'd seen of those jungle-covered cliffs in places like Hawaii, towers of rock thrusting hundreds of feet into the air like grasping, leafy fingers. To her left a crystalline waterfall tumbled down what had once been an office tower.

Overhead the skies rang with symphonies of birdsong, but down at street level, everything seemed deserted. Almost. Kelley had walked for about a half a block before she encountered the first of many "statues"—a couple holding hands, frozen in time. They looked like sculptures in a garden; ivy and moss had begun to creep over them, obscuring their features, trapping their feet forever, rooted to the crumbling pavement.

There were others—petrified, motionless as if they were chiseled from marble. A man in a suit on a bus bench. A newspaper seller. A young mother pushing a baby carriage that— Kelley noted with numb, detached horror—was lacking an occupant.

In its place grew a profusion of wildflowers.

A flash of movement out of the corner of her eye made Kelley turn in time to see a red fox darting into an overgrown bush, heavy with some kind of berry. Kelley heard a high-pitched giggle and saw, hiding behind the screen of bushes, the Faerie girl from Gwynn's Court, Jenii, smiling widely at her. Kelley saw that there was blood staining the jagged points of her sharp teeth. Sharp, bright green teeth.

The four-leaf-clover charm at Kelley's throat grew warm, and as she looked down, she saw that it had begun to sprout leaves. And more. Leaves and shoots, flowers and vines of all kinds flowed up her neck and across her shoulder. Winding down her arms, covering her torso and legs like a shimmering emerald gown. Until she stood there, a living topiary. The curling fronds of new ferns—crooked like beckoning fingers—unfurled from her shoulder blades, fanning out, filling the space behind her in place of Faerie wings. Her hair became corkscrewed, twisting in tendrils like the growth of new ivy, and the flesh of her hands and wrists shone pale and glistening like the translucent, curling skin of a white birch sapling. . . .

Suddenly, a shadow-black, old-fashioned carriage drawn by a monstrous dark horse came racing toward her. The air grew cold on Kelley's leaf-clad limbs, and her feet were rooted to the ground. She could not move out of the way. She would be crushed.

She heard the Faerie girl Jenii laughing wildly.

Then she heard the bellowing of a king stag. From somewhere behind her, a white-green brilliant light washed through the street, and a white King Stag—the same magnificent creature that had once saved Kelley's life—thundered past her, toward the careening carriage, antlered head lowered in its charge.

Kelley felt a sharp sting in the palm of her hand and, looking down, saw a single peach-colored rose burst into bloom, cupped in the cage of her fingers. As she gazed at it, it wilted and withered and fell away, leaving behind a pool of shining crimson blood. The blood evaporated, revealing scores of scars crisscrossing her palm.

The scars blazed with eldritch fire.

* * *

Kelley's eyes snapped open.

So . . . not home, then.

Definitely not. Sheer curtains floated out like billowing sails through a set of open doors that led to a balcony. She lay in a sumptuous bed, underneath a silken coverlet and almost drowning in feather pillows.

Right. She remembered now—she had left Fenn to discuss passage with Gwynn and had retired to this chamber to wait, crawling into bed and dozing off.

She swung her feet stiffly to the floor and stood. The room tilted perilously for a moment but then settled down. Her head felt a little fuzzy—as though she were still partly trapped in her dream.

Looking around, Kelley saw that her clothes—torn and stained with grass and mud from her Central Park encounter, damp from her dunk in the Otherworld river—had been taken from her. The jeans and purple top were nowhere in sight. Kelley sighed. She wasn't sure how much more of her roommate's wardrobe she could get away with decimating before Tyff plotted revenge, swift and terrible. In place of her tattered apparel, someone had left a shimmering gown draped over a chair.

When a thorough investigation of the room revealed no hidden closets and left her no alternative but to wear the gown or go naked, Kelley reluctantly slipped into the dress. *Let's see how long it takes before I can destroy* this *one,* she thought wryly. *At least it's not Tyff's. . . .*

Turning this way and that in front of a long mirror, she had to admit it was lovely, and almost—thankfully not *quite*—as revealing as the one Jenii had worn. Kelley started briefly, remembering vaguely that the Faerie girl had put in an appearance in her dream, then shook her head. Already the images were fading, fleeing back into her deep subconscious.

She discovered that her shoulder bag was still there, resting on a low stool, and the strappy sandals she'd borrowed from Tyff had been cleaned of mud and were neatly placed on the floor by the bed.

"Kelley?"

She jumped at the sound of Fennrys's voice, coming from the other side of the bedroom door. She moved to open it and waved him into the room.

"Hey—are you all right?"

"I guess," Kelley muttered. She'd be better if her head would stop swimming.

"How do you feel?"

She looked down at the elaborate gown and tried to blink away the wooziness. "Like somebody spiked the punch at the formal."

Fennrys laughed a little. "Serves you right for drinking Faerie drink on an empty stomach. Strong stuff, that."

"I had the weirdest dream. . . ."

"Not surprised. Did I not tell you that Gwynn is known as the Lord of Dreams?"

"No, Fenn." She smiled tightly. "You neglected to mention

that little detail. You also might have given me a warning about the eighty-proof refreshments."

"I thought your auntie would have told you all this stuff when you were a kid. My mistake."

"No. Not your fault. I'm still not used to reading fairy tales as nonfiction."

Fennrys subsided into silence, his gaze fixed upon her, and Kelley felt her cheeks redden. She felt practically naked in the flimsy dress.

"You look nice."

"Um. Thanks." She stopped herself from trying to cover bits of exposed skin with her hands. That would just be drawing attention to the obvious. She lowered herself carefully to sit on the stool and stuffed her feet into the sandals, fumbling with the buckles.

"So," Fennrys said, clapping his hands together. "Good news!"

Kelley looked up to see him smiling brightly. She thought about it and realized he looked weird when he smiled. Uncomfortable. She chalked it up to the fact that he had so carefully cultivated his gruff, sneering facade that the muscles of his face simply weren't used to the gesture. It just wound up coming off like a pained grimace.

She stood, slinging her bag across her body. She was anxious to get going. "What good news?" she asked.

"C'mon," he said, turning on his heel and leading the way through the twisting corridors. "Gwynn has agreed to open a rift to send you home."

"Us," she corrected.

"Sorry?"

"Don't you mean send us home?" Kelley asked.

"Oh . . . yeah." Fennrys shrugged casually as he loped along. "Listen—I'm going to stick around here for a bit."

"What?" Kelley gaped at him.

"I've got a few things to take care of." There was that disconcerting smile again. "But don't you worry—Gwynn has seen to it. He's whipped up a rift that'll set you right back down in New York. You'll be all right. You don't need me."

"I was under the distinct impression that Sonny told you to *take care of me,* Mr. Wolf," Kelley said, her tone mocking. She had to almost run to keep up with the Wolf's overlong strides as he stalked down the deserted halls.

"He did," he said. "I am." Fennrys stopped, turned, and stared at her for a moment. The ghastly smile faded from his lips and he said, "Trust me."

XIV

After his visit to Auberon, Sonny went to his old chambers in the palace. He had barely stripped off his tattered clothes and climbed into his old bed before his body gave way to sheer exhaustion. He dropped instantly into a deep, utterly dreamless sleep.

In the morning he bathed and called for one of Auberon's healers to be sent for. Sonny's body was one entire mass of aches, and he realized he would be of no use to anyone if he didn't start taking care of himself. After a thorough ministration of tonics, salves, bandaging, and a few extra stitches, the young Janus felt worlds better. At least he felt as though he could stand upright without tottering.

It was early afternoon when he finally made his way down to the stables. He was surprised—and not at all pleased—to see the Fennrys Wolf waiting for him, perched on a stool outside Lucky's stall, and wrapped head to foot in a thick woolen cloak to ward off Winter's chill.

"Where's Kelley?" Sonny stalked toward him, his hands already knotting into fists. "Damn you, Wolf—"

"Home." Fennrys raised a hand, forestalling Sonny's angry questions. "She's home, Irish. Safe and sound. Gwynn sent her there."

"At what price?"

"She paid none!" Fennrys snapped. "Damnation. Auberon does tend to breed his household up suspicious, doesn't he?" He sighed gustily with exasperation. "Do you know I was very nearly searched and manhandled on my way here from the main gate?"

"Very nearly?"

The Wolf grinned coldly. "Hard to manhandle a man who's more than happy to break your hand."

Sonny noticed that Fennrys was able to gesture with both his arms. The splint and sling were gone, and his injuries seemed to be fully, completely healed. It was a little surprising. With the extent of Fennrys's injuries, it would have taken a generous amount of magick to have accomplished such a thing. Perhaps, Sonny thought, the Lord Gwynn ap Nudd was no longer quite so put out with his Viking changeling for

173

leaving the shadow lands to join Auberon's Janus Guard as he had once been.

"I can't see why you'd be challenged in the Unseelie Court," Sonny said. "You're Janus."

"Yeah, well." Fennrys shrugged. "Some new staff since I was here last. Eager to make an impression, no doubt."

"Why didn't you go back with Kelley, Fennrys?" Sonny asked. "Now you're stuck here unless you want to go begging for a doorway again."

"I didn't beg the first time. Gwynn's not like *your* lord and master, Irish. He was more than happy to send Kelley on her way." Fennrys turned from him, a broody darkness flashing in his eyes.

Sonny wondered just what had transpired between Kelley and Fennrys since he'd sent them away together, but there was also a large part of him that quite simply didn't want to know. "So why *did* you stay?" he asked.

"Dunno." Fennrys blew on his knuckles, trying to warm them. "Thought, y'know, maybe you could use my help. With the Hunt. What's left of them."

"You're joking. *You* want to help *me*?"

"We're brothers-in-arms, Sonny." Fennrys stood and paced restlessly. "And, truth is, I'm bored out of my mind in Manhattan. Nothing to do there but jump at shadows and put up with Aaneel's pompous yapping: 'There're cracks in the Gate! Remain vigilant! Protect the puny humans! Eek, a mouse!' It's tiresome."

Sonny regarded him skeptically, but he knew one thing was true—Fennrys was nothing if not a man of action, and it was easy to see how a lack of ravening monsters to fight on a regular basis would grate on someone like him.

"What if the leprechaun goes after Kelley again?"

"Then there're eleven other Janus there to take care of her, and I *told* her to stay away from the bloody park. She's stubborn, not stupid. You should give her a little more credit."

That stung. "Suit yourself," he snapped. "My little sojourn here hasn't exactly been a bundle of laughs, either, you know. Especially lately. The Wild Hunt? Now that only three of them are left, there's not nearly as much havoc they can wreak. Mostly it's all track and trap now. And that in itself is boring, dirty work."

Fennrys didn't say anything, just continued his restless pacing back and forth in front of the stalls. He reminded Sonny of a caged animal.

"On the other hand," he said, relenting, "I suppose I *could* use a hand setting those traps."

"Right." Fennrys stopped in his tracks and blinked at Sonny. "The sooner you get done, the sooner you can get back to your Faerie princess, right?"

"Right. That's the idea."

"So it's settled." Fenn put out a hand, and Sonny clasped it and shook. "Now can we please get the hell out of here? Cold as a witch's teat, it is."

Sonny shook his head and signaled to the stable keeper. "A

175

Northman with no tolerance for winter weather."

"My people knew how to dress for the cold. It's all about layers. And this cloak may be stylish, but the wind cuts right through it," Fennrys said, tugging the wooly folds close around his throat.

"You've got that thing wrapped so far up under your chin, it looks like your head is resting on the back of a sheep," Sonny said. "Mighty Viking prince, my arse!"

They finished saddling the horses, checked their gear, and mounted up. There was one place where Sonny needed to go before they headed back into the grim, dangerous regions of Mabh's kingdom.

"Two dozen. Solid iron—purest Fae bane. And I can make more if you need them. Although, if you need them, you're probably not in a position to come back and get them." Gofannon barked out a harsh laugh and tossed the compact leather quivers full of crossbow bolts lightly onto the work-table as if they were full of feathers, not iron. Sonny noted that they made a satisfying clanking sound.

"Fennrys," Gofannon greeted the Wolf as he stepped through the low door into the forge, trailing behind Sonny at some distance.

"Gofannon," Fennrys answered, nodding, leaning on the door post and seeming impatient to get going.

"Didn't know Sonny had Janus help on this little venture," the smith rumbled. "I'm glad. Rough business."

"Well, Irish can always use someone to keep a watch out for him. Make sure he doesn't incur any more catastrophic curses than is absolutely necessary."

"If I remember correctly," Sonny muttered, inspecting the bolts before shouldering the quivers, "it was *your* suggestion that I use the Roan Horse to travel faster on Samhain Eve. And that's when things went horribly awry, shall we say. So it's really *your* fault."

"I might have been joking."

Sonny glanced up, mildly amused. He noticed that Fennrys was still standing beside the door and he hadn't taken off his traveling cloak. The heavy wool was still swathed around his neck and shoulders, even though the heat of the forge had painted a sheen of sweat on the Janus's brow.

"What?" Fennrys shifted uncomfortably as the other two men turned to stare at him. "Can we get going? No offense, Gof, old man, but I can think of a few other things I'd rather be doing right now. Like killing something. C'mon, Irish. Grab your little toy arrows and let's get out of here."

They left the forge and rode briskly, in silence, for what seemed like hours. Fennrys seemed content to simply follow Sonny's lead for the time being. While Sonny didn't exactly resent the company—in fact, he knew that he would probably need the help to finish his job—he'd spent so much time alone that he was, he had to admit, rusty at the simple art of conversation.

They crested a rise and saw the purple hills in the distance that marked the entrance to the shadowy Borderlands. Between there and where they were, the forest was, in places, on fire. The Hunt had been busy in his brief absence.

A deep anger flared in Sonny's chest. He turned and looked over his shoulder at the other Janus. The expression of almost rabid anticipation on Fennrys's face—the absolute spoiling for a fight—was a bit much for him.

"Now, you listen to me," he said brusquely. "Don't do anything stupid and get yourself killed."

"Aw. You care."

"Not about you I don't. But this is my campaign, and all you're there to do is watch my back. And *that's* what you'll bloody do. I expect you to watch my back, you hear?"

Fennrys snorted. "Don't be such a baby. What—are you afraid to die or something?"

Sonny pulled Lucky up short and swung around to face Fennrys. "I'm not afraid to die. I just don't want to die surprised. And I swear to all the gods, if the last thought that goes through my mind is *What the hell was that?* I will hunt you down in the afterlife and punch you in the face throughout eternity."

Under the light of the moon, bloodlust shone in the Faerie huntress's eyes. Her beautiful face, half hidden under her silver helmet, twisted with rage, and she struggled madly against the slender chain that held her fast, suspended between the gnarled trunks of two trees like a dragonfly caught in a spider's web. The chain was strung with wicked iron barbs that bit deeply into her torso and arms where the plates of her armor had been torn away by the mad battle that had raged over half of the shadowed lands, but she barely seemed to notice. She was not used to being prey—only predator.

Sonny and Fennrys had already chased her and another hunter in a running fight all over hell's half acre. Of course, Fenn's discipline had lasted only so long, and eventually he had charged off headlong after the other hunter to engage in combat by himself—even after Sonny had strictly admonished him that they should stay together. The hunters were too dangerous, but of course Fennrys hadn't listened. Sonny, for his part, had stuck to the plan. He had driven the huntress toward the trap the two Janus had set earlier.

And now, their trap sprung, Sonny dismounted from Lucky's back and strode toward the huntress, the silver-bladed sword in his hand.

From somewhere in the distance, Sonny heard a snarl of rage and the sounds of fighting. Fennrys must have caught up with the other hunter. He ignored the sounds and moved in to finish the task at hand—the Wolf could take care of himself, damn him.

Only the cold iron of Sonny's snare kept the Faerie huntress tangible. Moments before she had been nothing but a creature of smoke and fire on a rampaging wraith of a steed. The metal made her flesh and blood. But it could not make her warm. Her gaze was empty of everything save hunger and cold rage. Sonny averted his own eyes so that he would not have to look directly into the black depths of hers.

"Make an end of it then, changeling," she snarled. "Finish it."

The sweat ran down Sonny's arm, making the grip of his blade slick. He tightened his fist. The Faerie stared down at him and, for the briefest of moments, her expression changed. The hollowness and the fury disappeared, replaced by a flood of grief and remorse.

"I beg you," she whispered.

Sonny swallowed the horrible pain that always clawed up his throat from his heart in this moment. He gripped the glittering black jewel that hung from the cord around her neck and raised his blade to grant her request.

He heard another howl of pain. Closer this time.

Then the world exploded in a burst of red stars—and just before everything went absolutely, utterly black, Sonny's last thought was *What the hell was that?*

XV

Kelley spat out a mouthful of turf and pushed herself slowly to her hands and knees. She was in Central Park—the one place she knew she should be actively avoiding. Every bone in her body ached and her vision was blurred. Which still didn't explain why she could see the park only in narrow strips, through what looked almost like a Stonehenge-ish ring of tree trunks. She blinked and realized that they weren't trees. They were legs. Kelley looked up slowly and saw that she was surrounded by a group of people, silhouettes in the moonlight, standing in a containing circle all around her.

"Bryan," said one of the figures in a steely tone that was not made gentler by the music of its accent. "Do a perimeter check. Beni, go with him. Make sure nothing came else came through *this* time."

Kelley heard the two Janus Guards moving swiftly off into the distance as she struggled wearily to her feet. A pale face loomed out of the darkness at her.

"Hello, Ghost," she said.

Ghost was the only changeling in the Janus Guard who had been taken from the mortal realm by Queen Mabh. The experience hadn't been particularly normalizing for the young man. Ghost gave Kelley the willies. His dark fathomless stare slid over her face.

"You look like your mother," he said bluntly. "More and more every time I see you."

"I really wish people would stop saying that," Kelley muttered. She felt a bit ridiculous, standing there in that beautiful gown for no reason, but she tried not to show it, ignoring the chill in the air that raised gooseflesh on her bare arms.

Another face appeared beside Ghost's, his copper-hued skin camouflaged by shadow and the orange glow of the park lamps. "Miss Winslow," Aaneel greeted her, his normally warm tones stiff with formality.

"Gosh. I missed you, too." The Janus must have deduced what had happened after she and Fennrys had left Maddox at the River, Kelley thought. Cait, she knew, could use her magicks like a forensics agent for the FBI. It seemed, however, news of their little adventure hadn't gone over particularly well. "You guys make a lousy welcome-home committee, you know?"

Aaneel ignored the sarcasm. "Where is the Fennrys Wolf?"

"He stayed behind. In the Spring Court."

Godwyn turned his head and spat into the bushes.

"I see," said Aaneel.

"It was *his* idea," Kelley said. "He said he'd come back soon. Aaneel—what is this all about? Why do I get the distinct feeling I'm in the Janus doghouse for something?"

"The portal you opened last night stayed open long after you were gone. Things came through that I don't even have names for."

"That's impossible—I shut it. I know I did—"

"You're wrong."

"I'm sorry—"

"You're dangerous!" The Janus's eyes blazed.

"I was in *trouble,* Aaneel! So was Fennrys," Kelley snapped. "If I hadn't gotten us through that rift, we'd probably both be dead right now!"

"And whose fault would that be, Kelley? Didn't you learn anything from that first attack? If you hadn't come back for a second night of playing around in the park, then maybe—"

"I *said* I was sorry."

"You don't know what you're dealing with."

"Well, no kidding!" Anger flared in Kelley's chest, hot and hurting. "It's not like this whole Faerie princess gig comes with some kind of instructional video, you know. And it's not like *you* guys have offered any kind of real guidance or anything. The Janus Guard is really only occupied—like, what?—one night out of the year?"

"More than that these days, it would seem."

"Right. And you're so very busy-busy that nobody in your little club could possibly find the time to maybe show me some of the ropes? Help me avoid some of the pitfalls that create situations like this? Instead of pretending all this time that I was human, maybe you guys should have been trying to help me learn what it is to be Faerie."

"You are not our responsibility. We are none of us Fair Folk."

"Yeah—and for most of my life, I didn't think *I* was, either! You at least know what it *means* to be one. You know more than most—more than me."

"It's not in the mandate of the Janus to teach you how to be what you are."

"Sonny's Janus. He would have helped me."

"Sonny's not here. Thanks to you. Now neither is Fennrys, and that is also thanks to you. I'm sorry, Kelley—I'm starting to think that I was wrong about you. Maybe you just don't belong in this world after all."

Kelley felt as though she'd just been slapped. Hard. She looked around from face to face. Godwyn pretty obviously agreed with Aaneel, but he was coldhearted to begin with. However, Kelley was surprised to see that neither Selene nor

Camina could meet her gaze. Camina's twin brother Bellamy shrugged in helpless sympathy. And Perry offered her a half-smile, but no more than that. Cait's brow creased in a troubled frown that Kelley could not decipher.

Ghost just stared up at the moon, utterly indifferent.

Maddox didn't look at her either. But that was because his eyes were locked on Aaneel. And his stare was flinty and cold.

"Maddox"—Aaneel met his stare and matched it, steel for steel—"go with the twins and do a patrol round of the upper half of the park. Normally I'd send the Wolf, but it appears that he's not available."

Maddox glared at him for another long moment and then with a nod—not to Aaneel but to Kelley—he turned and headed north, picking up Camina and Bellamy in his wake.

"Miss Winslow." The Janus leader turned from her, heading toward the Central Park Pinetum. "I trust you can find your way home on your own. I need all my people here. Good night." He gestured to the other Janus, who melted into the shadows at his command—and Kelley was left standing there, an unsaid, acid retort burning on her tongue.

"Miss Winslow, I trust you can find your way home on your own . . ." Kelley muttered in a mocking simper. "Jerk!"

"Yeah." Tyff stuck the tip of her tongue out the corner of her mouth as she carefully applied a second coat of color to her toenails. "I think I might have mentioned to you that those Janus guys are a bunch of self-righteous ass-hats, you know."

"Like it's all *my* fault or something that the Gate's become all crackly! How am I even remotely responsible for that?"

"Hey, did you hang that dress up in my closet? I'm taking it as payment against all current and future wardrobe wreckage."

"Yes, I hung it up in *your* closet."

Tyff shot her an amused look at the tone of her voice.

Kelley jabbed mercilessly at the remote, silencing the TV. "I *totally* saved *everybody* on Samhain Eve! Hello? Has everyone suddenly forgotten about that?"

"Kelley, I wouldn't get my panties in a bunch over what some Janus crybabies think if I were you," Tyff said as she closed up the tiny bottle of pearlescent enamel and waved her hands over her dainty feet. "It's not worth it."

"Not all of them are crybabies," Kelley said, feeling the need to defend the vocation if only on Sonny's account.

"Look, Sonny's okay—even I'll admit that. But it strikes me that his okay-ness is sort of in spite of what he does, not because of it." Tyff shrugged. "I mean—*most* of those guys? All they've really got going for them is that they're Auberon's goon squad, so they're untouchable." She thought about it for a moment. "Except for Maddox. And maybe that big, yummy blond one that you were dancing with at the River. Now—those boys are touchable."

"Tyff!" Kelley spluttered. "Stop that!"

"What"—Tyff twitched an eyebrow at her—"you mean to tell me that you don't find that Fennrys guy the least bit attractive?"

"No."

"Not even a teensy bit?"

"No!"

Tyff blinked at Kelley, her expression suddenly unreadable. She shook her head a little as if she weren't hearing things properly. "Oh my gods," she said, all trace of playful teasing gone from her voice. "Kelley, did you just lie to me?"

"What? No!"

"There! You did it again!"

"Tyff—what are you talking about?"

Tyff was almost bouncing up and down on the couch with excitement. "Lie. Right now. Say something obviously, patently untrue! Tell me I'm ugly."

Ookay . . . Kelley decided the only thing to do was play along. "You're hideously deformed."

"Holy crap! It's true!" Tyff leaped to her freshly pedicured feet and did a little dance.

"Not it's *not*, Tyff!" Kelley gaped at her roommate. "I only said that because you told me to!"

"No!" Tyff argued gleefully. "I mean it's *true*—you can *lie*!"

Kelley could only stare at her in bafflement.

"Kelley," Tyff explained to her as if she were a slightly dim six-year-old, "Faerie can't lie. It's just a thing. But you can!"

"Oh." Kelley deflated utterly. *So that's what this is about.* "Don't you lie all the time, though?"

"What? I do not!"

"Isn't sarcasm lying?"

"No, Kelley. Sarcasm is sarcasm. That's why it's called sarcasm. But *real* honest-to-goodness lying? That is like the best party trick *ever* for a Fae!"

"Big whoop."

"Is it the charm, do you think?" Tyff was way too excited about Kelley's newly discovered talent.

"I dunno." She glanced down at the little four-leaf clover, suddenly self-conscious in the face of her roomie's scrutiny.

"Wow." Tyff bent down to take a closer look at Kelley's necklace. She put out a hand but stopped before her finger had quite touched the stones. "That is one seriously hardcore piece of magickal technology." She glanced up at Kelley. "If you ever manage to take it off again—can I borrow it sometimes?"

"What? Why?"

Tyff regarded indulgently. "Hon, not being able to lie can sometimes be a serious impediment to relationships, you know."

Kelley snorted. "That's the most jaded thing I've ever heard. Even coming from you, Tyff."

"Yeah? Wait till you're seventeen *hundred* years old and some guy asks you your real age. See how far *your* second date goes."

"Great." Kelley sighed and sank back into the cushions on the couch, thoroughly depressed. "I guess this means I'm a weirdo. More of a weirdo. Even among Faerie. Super."

"I guess this *also* means you really *do* find the Wolfman kinda hot. Now there's something to think about, Little Miss Liar-Liar-Pants-on-Fire."

Kelley shook her head and tried to change the subject before she actually started blushing. "You know, if I ever *do* manage to get the whammy off this stupid charm, you're gonna have to show me how to actually use my power. I mean *really* use it. Then maybe I can avoid situations that inevitably end in tears and dry cleaning."

Tyff didn't answer back right away. Kelley looked at her and saw that the lovely Faerie's expression had gone dead serious.

"What?"

"There's something I don't think anyone's ever told you about Faerie magick, Kell," Tyff said in a quiet voice. "Something I think you should know."

"And that is?"

"That it's all tied up with what's inside of you. Head and heart, mind and soul. Who you are and what you want—that's what fuels it. That's what shapes it." Her eyes darkened, clouding with memories. "That's what makes it dangerous."

"Is that why I hardly ever see you using magick?" Kelley asked, intrigued.

"You hardly ever see me using magick because magick sucks, Kelley. Seriously. And if you let it . . . it can destroy you." Tyff's laugh was brief and brittle. "Me? I just let it destroy everyone I loved. Once upon a time."

XVI

"Don't lie to me, little Janus."

Sonny rubbed his shoulder along the side of his face where the invisible fist had hit him. Hard. "Why would I do that?" he asked with a profound lack of concern. Regardless of the fact that Mabh had been pummeling him enthusiastically with her magicks since he'd regained consciousness in her grim stone hall, he was silently far more worried about the fact that he could no longer feel his Janus medallion hanging about his neck. He must have lost it in the fight—and he felt its absence like a physical ache. All of the Unseelie magick that Auberon had gifted him was bound up in that talisman. Without it he would be forced to rely exclusively on his human abilities in a fight. But he wasn't about to let Mabh know of his concerns. "Why would I lie?"

"Because you hate, fear, and generally distrust me," answered the Faerie queen with a charming smile, kneading dainty knuckles, as if she'd actually been physically hitting him.

"So does half the populace of the Faerie realm, lady. That in no way makes me unique. Or particularly prone to lie to you." Sonny struggled to heave himself back up onto his knees. It was a bit awkward, what with his hands being bound behind his back. "If I knew where Kelley was, and I did not wish to share that information, I wager I'd simply be inclined to tell you to sod off."

Mabh flicked her wrist, and the resulting blow almost sent Sonny reeling back into unconsciousness again. It would have been the third time in very recent memory. He lay on the stone floor for a moment, squeezing his eyes shut against the pain, struggling to stay cogent. He could hear Mabh's footsteps as she paced in a circle around him.

"I cannot find my daughter, fleshling," she said. "My Storm Hags tell me that she is quite hidden from them. Almost as if she never existed. That has me worried. And I tend toward violence under worrying circumstances."

"Perhaps you should get therapy, then, lady. You seem to worry an awful lot," Sonny said through clenched teeth, tensing for the next blow. It never came. Instead, when he dared to open his eyes again, it was to see the queen crouched in front of him, peering at him with a frank and lively curiosity that seemed to override her anxieties for the moment. It made Sonny's heart ache to have her staring at him with those flashing green eyes, so very like her daughter's. He avoided looking at her directly, staring instead at the floor between them.

"You're a brave little monkey." Mabh shook her head, bemused. "But not, I was led to believe, monumentally stupid. Which is why I wasn't quite sure what to make of it when we found you sleeping all alone on the edge of my lands like that."

"I wasn't sleeping—I was very unintentionally unconscious," Sonny said. "And I wasn't alone."

"Well, I suppose that lump on the back of your head is almost big enough to be called a companion, true enough."

"What happened to Fennrys, Mabh?" Sonny struggled back up to his knees.

"That lupine fellow of Gwynn's that Auberon pressed into service? I haven't the faintest idea. Nothing that *I've* done, certainly—I've never gotten close enough. Pity; he seems like my sort of creature, all brutish and bloodthirsty." She ran the tip of her tongue delicately over her teeth and shivered deliciously. "Wasn't he the one my darling Kelley had her arms all full of when I showed you the vision in the scrying pool?"

Sonny fought to remain impassive through a momentary wash of rage at her words. "He's a fellow Janus. We were hunting together, tracking the last of your Wild Hunt abominations, when you found me."

"You weren't hunting anything when I found you."

"Something hit me from behind. When I awoke, Fennrys was gone." *And there was blood on the ground. No. A lot of blood . . . Stop.* He wouldn't think of that. "Just . . . he was gone. So was my mount."

"That twitchy little kelpie?"

"Yes."

"Well, *that's* hardly surprising."

"Then everything went dark again and when I awoke— *again*—I was here." Sonny no longer cared if he seemed properly respectful. "I hate to sound suspicious, lady, but—well, I'm suspicious."

"Sweet creature." The queen laughed—a throaty, disturbing sound. "Maybe your Janus playfellow simply tired of your utterly humorless posturing. Maybe he took your horsie and wandered off in search of a bit of fun."

Or maybe he was dead.

Damn it, Sonny thought. He never should have let Fenn take off like that. Sonny briefly imagined Kelley's reaction when she found out the Janus had been killed. And that *he* had let it happen. . . .

"Speaking of fun," Mabh was saying, "let's continue along with *my* little game. I will ask you again—and, this time, you *will* answer—where is my daughter?"

193

"Why do you think I even know the answer to that question?"

Mabh raised her bejeweled fist high, the glow of her magick sparkling in the rings on her fingers.

Sonny's head fell forward, more out of weariness than surrender. He was getting tired of the taste of his own blood in his mouth. "I know she went back. That is all."

"Back where? From where? Speak sense." The queen rose and began pacing once more in agitation.

"She was here, Mabh. In the Faerie realm." Sonny blinked up at her, genuinely surprised. "Didn't you know?"

"I . . . no." Mabh frowned. "I did not know."

She *should* have known, Sonny thought. If *he'd* still been able to sense Kelley's signature, firecracker-fuse presence in his mind the second she'd come through the rift, then surely her own mother would have been able to sense that her daughter was in the Faerie realms.

"The charm she wears," he said cautiously.

"The one the Goodfellow used to hide her in the mortal world? What about it?"

"That must be it." Sonny thought back on what he'd been told by Kelley. "The leprechaun—the one Puck originally stole it from—tracked Kelley down in Central Park and cast a binding spell on the charm. To keep her from using her Faerie gifts. Probably until he could reclaim his property."

He told the Autumn Queen in a few words what he knew of Kelley's recent encounters in the park, watching with growing alarm as the blood drained from Mabh's face.

"That, then, is why my Cailleach can no longer sense her presence in the human world," the queen murmured. "And why I couldn't sense her here." She turned and peered sharply at Sonny through narrowed eyes. "So tell me this. How could *you*?"

"I don't know what you mean, lady."

Mabh laughed harshly. "Just because the Fair Folk themselves cannot lie, little Janus, does not mean we cannot tell when others do. You knew she was here."

"I knew because she came through a rift and almost landed on top of me."

"But you have a connection with her still. A bond."

I do, Sonny thought. He wondered whether Kelley still wanted that. The memory of the harsh words that had passed between them in his cottage lashed at him.

"You can *sense* her, changeling," Mabh said with growing frustration at his obvious distraction.

Sonny hesitated for a moment more and then nodded. "Aye. I can. But only when we're in the same realm and only when she is close."

"In spite of the charm?" Mabh knelt before him, scrutinizing him closely. "Even with the binding curse laid upon it?"

"Even then. She . . . sparkles. In my mind."

From the corner of his eye, Sonny could see Mabh's expression soften as she watched him. He schooled his features immediately, wondering what she had seen in his face.

"How extraordinary," she murmured. "And could you find her now? If you were in the world of men?"

"I am not."

She glared flatly at him.

"I don't know. Possibly."

For the first time, Sonny met the Queen's gaze directly.

A very strange thing happened then. Mabh looked at him—really *looked* at him—for an uncomfortably long moment. As their gazes met and locked, Mabh's eyes went wide, her hand flew to her open mouth, and she gasped as though she'd been struck across the face.

Wrenching her gaze from his, the Autumn Queen rose to her feet with a swiftness that made her dark robes swirl and blur around her like smoke. Backing away, she turned and—almost stumbling in her haste—fled to the far side of her gloomy stone hall.

"Lady?" Sonny asked, rocking himself to his feet and standing, his hands still bound firmly behind his back. "Are you all right?"

He didn't know why he should be concerned. He also didn't know why Mabh should react to him in such a way.

"Leave me." Mabh did not turn to him. She flicked her wrist, and Sonny's bonds crackled faintly with energy and vanished. He rubbed the blood back into his fingertips and took a step toward the queen. Even from that distance, he could see she was quivering with some unnamed emotion.

"Mabh—"

"Leave me!" Her voice howled through the stone hall like a gale, making Sonny wince and clutch at his head.

LEAVE ME LEAVE ME LEAVE LEAVE LEAVE . . . A maelstrom of the queen's magicks, unleashed by the fury of that cry, pummeled at Sonny, almost driving back him down to his knees. When the furious tempest abated, as swiftly as it had risen, Sonny staggered back a pace in the sudden quietude.

Mabh still stood, leaning heavily upon her rough-hewn granite throne.

And a quiet voice broke the deathly silence: "Am I interrupting something?"

Bob the boucca had materialized out of the tense air between Sonny and the Queen of Autumn—an incongruous, shimmering-green presence. Over near the grim gray throne, Mabh composed herself, her back to Sonny and this new intruder. When she turned to face them, she was cold beauty—still, contained, radiating power.

"Yes," she said. "You *are* interrupting something. So you had best have an excellent reason for the intrusion."

The boucca swept low, intoning with courtly solemnity,

"Auberon, Lord of Winter, King of the Unseelie Court of Faerie, sends his greetings to Mabh, Queen of—"

"Oh, great goddess!" she huffed. "Get on with it. What does he want?"

Bob straightened up slowly. "Help, lady."

Sonny half expected Mabh to laugh until the tears rolled down her cheeks. And, indeed, a flash of perverse merriment flashed in her eyes at Bob's words. But it was brief and in its wake flowed a calculated concern.

"From me," Mabh said, a statement rather than a question.

Bob nodded.

"Why does he need help?"

"Perhaps it is best that you ask him."

"And I shall just ride through the gates of the Winter Palace and do this?"

"I am to take you to him. Safe passage, lady. A truce."

"All right then," Mabh purred dangerously as she stalked forward. "Why does he need *my* help?"

Bob held his ground as Mabh walked right up to within an inch or two of where he stood. "For some reason—and forgive me for saying so, but I think you will recognize the truth of this—for reasons the rest of us can't quite figure out, Auberon . . . well, he *trusts* you, lady."

Mabh laughed gently. "Perhaps that's why he's king."

"Let us hope for a good while longer."

Sonny took a step toward them. "What's happened? Is Auberon—"

"Worse off than he was. Much worse." The boucca turned back to Mabh. "Lady, if you will? Haste, in this instance, would not be unseemly."

"Annis."

"Mabh."

The two Fae nodded coldly to each other. Then Black Annis stepped aside, and Mabh swept past into the chamber and across the long floor to the bed where Auberon lay. Sonny and Bob followed at a respectful distance.

Auberon was definitely worse off than the last time Sonny had seen him. The king's normal wintry pallor was gone. He looked flushed, the skin around his charcoal eyes almost purple, as if bruised from within. Sonny could see the veins in his neck pulsing.

As they approached the bed, Auberon's eyes flicked back and forth between Mabh and Sonny—coming to rest, finally, on the queen's face. A moment passed between the two monarchs that, upon reflection, Sonny could only characterize as awkward, but then Mabh waved it away.

"Do you know I found your little Janus Guard facedown on my lands?" she said. "You needn't thank me for returning him unscathed."

"That was kind of you."

"Wasn't it?" she said brightly.

"My thanks, lady. His loss would be a hardship indeed." Auberon pressed a linen handkerchief to his lips.

Sonny thought guiltily about Fennrys and the hardship of *his* loss. He wondered whether anyone would care that the other Janus was gone. *Anyone other than Kelley . . .*

Auberon fell into a rasping fit of coughing that, when it subsided, left him weak, lying limp upon the pillows like something washed ashore after a heavy sea storm. Mabh gathered her traveling cloak up and perched on the edge of the bed, reaching forward to lay her long white hands on either side of Auberon's face.

"Fool," she said, a hint of something that could almost be called tenderness in her voice. "You should have sent for me sooner."

Auberon's eyes remained closed, and his voice was a ghost shadow of his usual rich tones. "I sent for *her*," he replied. "She would not come."

"And you cannot possibly blame her for that."

"No."

"Her reaction is hardly surprising—she's your daughter, after all. And the apple—"

"Does not fall far from the tree. Yes . . . I believe I told her that very thing myself once." Auberon almost smiled at the memory. "She rather strenuously disagreed."

"The girl is stubborn unto absurdity."

200

"And in no way comes by that through *your* blood," Auberon muttered sarcastically as Mabh moved her hands gently, fingertips dancing lightly across the landscape of his ravaged features.

"Certainly not. Hush now." Mabh closed her eyes, and her face became very still as she moved her hands down his neck and across the king's broad chest. Time seemed to pass slowly. Then, suddenly, the queen hissed in pain and withdrew her hands, her movements quick and sharp. She stood and, bending low, bestowed a light kiss upon the Faerie king's fevered brow. "Rest you now. We'll be back soon."

She beckoned Sonny and the others out of the room in her wake.

"What is it that ails him, then?" Annis asked, her white eyes fixed upon Mabh as she poured a tall goblet of wine for the Queen from a table by her stool.

"Darkness," Mabh said, gulping at the wine. "Pure as any I've ever felt." She stared into the depth of the goblet as if seeking the answer to a question. "And *light*," she murmured in a wondering voice.

Annis and Sonny exchanged a confused glance. Bob didn't take his eyes off the queen. Mabh ran a dainty finger around the edge of her crimson mouth and shook her head.

"I have formidable knowledge of blood magick, I think we all agree. And this *is* a kind of blood magick. But it is far beyond even my ken. Something eats away deep at the core

201

of him—brightness and shadows all twisted together—and it is as though he is being attacked from the *inside* out. I know of no spells or charms that can do such a thing. It makes no sense—such a thing is impossible."

"Impossible?" Sonny asked.

The queen laughed briefly and without mirth. "Well, discounting the likelihood that Auberon has cursed *himself* . . . then yes. Impossible."

XVII

Rehearsal that evening was *not* going well.

It was the last rehearsal before Quentin flew to England for his "dear old Mumsy's" birthday, giving the cast a break for a week, and Kelley had really wanted to get some good substantive work done before he left. She also wanted to take her mind off the events of the past few days. Sadly, it seemed that such a thing was not to be.

"Although I joy in thee,
I have no joy of this contract tonight.
It is too rash, too unadvised, too sudden,

Too like the lightning, which doth cease to be
Ere one can say 'it lightens.' Swe—"

"*Yes!* That's *exactly* the way I want you to say that line," Quentin interrupted Kelley from the darkened house. "*If* we were doing this play as a cautionary exercise on how NOT to deliver your lines!"

Kelley sighed. "Don't mince words, chief. Go ahead. Say what's really on your mind."

"It's not what's on *my* mind, Miss Winslow, but what's on *yours*. Or, rather, what your *mind* is most definitely NOT on—and that would be *this* rehearsal and *those* words. When Juliet describes lightning"—Quentin waved his hands in the air like a Muppet—"I want to feel as if she's *actually*, at least *once* in her life, seen a *storm*. And when she says the word *joy*, I'd *like* to believe that she's capable of *experiencing* that emotion."

"Ouch," said Alec Oakland. "That's a little harsh, Q, don't you think?"

Kelley shook her head at her Romeo. "No. He's right."

"Of course I am." Quentin glared at Alec. "Even *you* were good by comparison. *Woe* betide the unfortunate director."

"I'm sorry, Quentin," Kelley said apologetically. "I'm feeling a little off my game. Maybe we should just jump to where I stab myself and call it a day?"

"Don't tempt me." Quentin spun sharply and hallooed up to the stage manager in the tech booth. "Mindi! Check the newspaper. Weather forecast."

There was a far-off rustling of pages.

Mindi's voice drifted down: "Thundershowers through the evening and into the night."

"Miss Winslow," Quentin turned on his heel, "*you* are dismissed."

". . . You're kidding."

"Your acting assignment for the evening is this: Go play in the rain. Jump over puddles. Experience the *lightning*. Experience *joy*. Just do us all a favor and *don't* stand under any tall trees. I don't have an understudy for *this* show."

She still hadn't replaced the umbrella that she was sure Bob had stolen from her during the last show. There was an ominous rumble from the skies outside, muted, but Kelley could hear it echoing down through the old converted church's bell tower. *Damned Storm Hags better not have anything to do with this. . . .*

"Kelley?" Jack knocked on her dressing room door with one knuckle and poked his head in.

"Hey, Jack—c'mon in." Kelley waved the older actor over the threshold. "Hope you weren't really looking forward to throwing me around the set tonight. I've been ordered to go play in the rain, if you can believe it."

"So I heard. Do what you gotta do, kiddo. Maybe Quentin's right—when your head's not in the game, it's hard for your heart to be."

"I really sucked out there tonight, huh?"

"No. But I would call you . . . preoccupied. Are you okay?"

"Yup. I'm good. Great." The last thing she wanted to do was talk about her present emotional state. The truth of it was that going through the romance of the balcony scene with Alec had done nothing but remind her of Sonny. All that gorgeous, poetic language and talk of "true-love's passion" and suddenly Kelley had started to feel extremely fragile. She'd had to clamp down just to keep from losing it completely. Her performance had come off as flat and unbelievable because anything else would have ended in tears. She cast about desperately for a change of subject. "Hey—are you keeping your beard like that for the part?" she asked, gesturing to the full beard that graced Jack's jawline.

"'A sable, silvered,' you mean?" he said, quoting from *Hamlet*. "Hell, yes. I'm getting too old to use Grecian Formula on my face fur. Takes too long."

"Pff." She waved away his modesty. "I think you look smashing."

"Not quite as elegant as my goateed Oberon, perhaps," Jack said and struck a subtly haughty pose.

"Best fairy king I've ever seen." Kelley smiled and spun away so that Jack couldn't see her face. She bit her lip, trying hard not to think of the real Auberon.

He's dying, Bob whispered in her mind.

He's my king. She could still see the misery in Sonny's

eyes. *What would you have me do?*

Jack put his ever-present coffee cup down on her makeup table and leaned forward. "How are you, Kelley?" he asked. "Really?"

"Oh . . . a little lonely, I suppose," she said, swallowing a watery sob and blinking back tears at the admission.

"Is this about that boy of yours?"

"Some of it. I guess. It's complicated."

"He's still not come back from . . . wherever he went?"

"Nope."

"You think he will?"

"God, Jack, I hope so. . . ." Her voice broke on the word *hope*.

"You want to talk about it?"

"Not unless I have a written promise that you won't call the guys with the butterfly nets on me." Kelley almost laughed out loud at the imagery—only because she really *did* have wings. Or, at least, she used to.

"I've heard a lot of weird stuff in my time, kid." Jack smiled gently. "Don't forget—I've been in the theater all my life."

"I know, Jack." She smiled at him. "Thanks for the offer. I just . . . my sob story wouldn't make any sense to you right now—trust me. Like I said, it's pretty complicated."

"Everything is, when you're seventeen," he said, retrieving his cup. "And I do *not* say that to be patronizing. Things just are, that's all."

"How 'bout when you're a hundred and seventeen?" Kelley murmured, not really having meant to say it out loud.

Jack just laughed. "I'll let you know when I get there."

Not if I get there first, she thought, with a pang of regret.

When she stepped out of the theater, the skies opened up.

The rain sheeted across the courtyard, blinding. Kelley put her head down and almost ran into Tyff, who was standing in the midst of the downpour, dry as a desert flower as though she held an invisible umbrella. Or perhaps the raindrops had just decided en masse that it would be to the good of all if they fell elsewhere.

Clinging to the tips of Tyff's fingers was a sticky note from the bright pink pad she kept by the phone in their apartment. It said "Meet Maddox tonight" and gave an address for an apartment on Central Park West.

"I was going to leave you the message at home." She shrugged. "But then it occurred to me that I kind of have the hots for this Maddox guy. And so I thought I'd go with."

"Uh . . . okay." Kelley took the note, watching as the ink blurred and ran in the pelting rain. "Did Madd say what he wanted?" she asked, mystified.

"He really didn't." Tyff looked at Kelley. "Are you ever going to buy an umbrella?"

Maddox opened the door to the darkened Central Park West penthouse and stepped aside for her to enter. Kelley struggled to keep it together as she stepped over the threshold. She knew instantly that this wasn't Madd's place. It was Sonny's. This was Sonny's home in the mortal realm—she could *feel* it. The very air in the room seemed to whisper to her of his presence there. She could feel him. Smell him. She swallowed to ease the ache in her throat as she imagined him walking through the wide French doors, out onto the terrace with its spectacular view of the city.

"Dark in here," Maddox said, switching on a soft glow of hidden overhead lights. "Sorry."

"Don't be," Tyff said, sweeping into the apartment after Kelley, just before Maddox closed the door. "I like the dark. It's more romantic."

"Oh." The Janus stepped back, surprised and a little puzzled to see Tyff there. "Hello, lady. When I gave you the message, I wasn't really expecting you to come along with Kelley."

"I had to give her the note in person—she seems to have misplaced all other means of communication." Tyff waved one hand airily. "I didn't mind. I wasn't busy tonight. You know—for a change. And it's Tyff. Or Tyffanwy. No one calls me lady who isn't Fae or a thrall. And you, handsome, unless I miss my guess, are neither of those things."

"Knock it off, Tyff," Kelley snapped, uneasy. "You know perfectly well he's a Janus."

"Gods," Tyff rolled her luminous eyes and took off her jacket. "She's a little touchy these days," she said to Maddox in a mock whisper.

Kelley ignored the goad. If Tyff wanted to impress Madd with her scintillating wit, she was going to have to do it all on her own. Kelley was in no mood to play straight man.

"Uh . . . yeah." Maddox closed the front door and moved to sit on the arm of the leather couch in the middle of the large living room. He looked tired. Edgy. His open, handsome face was creased in a frown. "Kelley's not the only one," he said, pushing back strands of sandy-colored hair from out of his eyes.

"What's going on, Madd?" Kelley asked. "What's wrong?"

"I'm seriously thinking of going ASAP, Kelley."

Kelley blinked. "I'm pretty sure you're not."

"A-S-A-P," Maddox assured her.

In spite of the seriousness of the conversation, Kelley had to suppress a smile. Changelings, she'd discovered, tended to achieve widely varying degrees of success when it came to getting a handle on modern slang. A few of them had only recently discovered the word *groovy*.

"If you mean *AWOL,* Maddox," she amended, "and I *think* you do, then my response to you would also come in the form of an acronym."

Maddox raised a questioning eyebrow.

"WTF?" She watched as he worked that one through and then glared at her in mild disapproval. "Sorry. Sorry . . . but what, exactly, are you talking about?"

"I'm talking about the way things have been going with the

Guard." His expression grew troubled again. "Aaneel's getting really hard-arsed about the Lost Fae. I mean—brutal."

Kelley looked over at Tyff, who'd lost her playful smile and whose eyes flashed dangerously as Maddox spoke.

"Look—I'm all for keeping things in check. And there's some among the Fair Folk—present company excluded and pardon my saying so, but— there's some Lost Fae that aren't exactly harmless. To the general mortal populace, you know?" The Janus twisted his fingers together as he spoke, cracking his knuckles. "Now, I don't have a problem dealing with that type, if you take my meaning. But I'm certainly not about to go *looking* for some stray wood nymph to chop into kindling for no good reason."

"Well, that's a great comfort," Tyff said coldly.

"We've always left the Lost Ones alone, so long as they behaved themselves. But Aaneel and Godwyn and maybe even some of the others—Ghost, probably, but he's kind of a freak anyway—suddenly they've decided to take the fight to them. I don't like it."

"Do your feelings have anything to do with Chloe?" Kelley asked quietly. "Maddox? Is that what this is all about?"

He frowned deeply. "I'm afraid for her," he said. His eyes drifted toward the closed bedroom door, and in the silence that stretched out, Kelley heard a whisper of song.

She jumped to her feet. "You brought her *here*?"

"It was the only place I could think of to keep her safe,"

Maddox protested. "It's protected by better wards than I've got set up at my place, and Sonny wouldn't mind."

"Sonny wouldn't *mind*?" Kelley glared. "Are you so sure about that, Maddox?"

"She saved your life once, you know," Maddox said softly, reading her expression. "And Mabh and Auberon both made her suffer. Dearly."

Chloe was curled up on a corner of the big bed, knees drawn up almost to her chin. *Sonny's bed,* Kelley thought with sullen jealousy. When she herself had never even set foot in that room before now. She shook her head. *Don't be ridiculous. It's not like she's here with Sonny.*

Tyff was staring at her, she knew. Kelley tried to let go of the sudden reactionary tension that thrust her shoulders up around her ears. A shaft of light, the orange glow from the city outside the window, shone through the gap in the curtains onto Chloe's face.

"Chloe? I've brought someone to see you." Maddox turned to Kelley and murmured, "She's been singing that song from the play you were in—that and another one I don't know—but those are the only things she sings now. Over and over. I don't know why, but I thought . . . maybe it would help her to see you. I didn't know what else to do." He shrugged helplessly.

Kelley couldn't imagine how her being there could possibly

help. She could barely even stand to look at the Siren.

But then, when she did look—really *looked* at her—she saw that the Faerie girl was pale and thin, almost birdlike in the way she moved. She seemed terribly fragile. And—from the way he looked at her—Kelley knew that Maddox loved her. She wondered briefly if Tyff had noticed, but the Summer Fae's gaze was fastened sympathetically on the Siren.

On the terrible scars that, Kelley finally noticed, criss-crossed her throat like claw marks.

"As I said," Maddox murmured, following her gaze, "Mabh made her suffer."

Chloe hugged herself, swaying gently from side to side and whispering thready bits of song as they approached.

Kelley stood before her. "You saved my life," she said.

Her smile was crooked; her gaze, haunted. "For a little price."

"Why?"

"Pretty, pretty music." Chloe blinked up at her as if the answer to the question were self-evident. "Almost as pretty as *his* . . ." She sang a fragment of an old song. An old Irish lullaby. The song was filled with such sadness. Such longing.

Kelley pulled back sharply—it was a lullaby that she had heard her aunt Emma sing once or twice when she'd been a very little girl. Emma had never sung it *to* her—only at times when she thought she'd been alone. And always she'd wept.

Sonny's lullaby.

Chloe closed her eyes, her expression going slack with pleasure as she sang.

"Stop it," Kelley said. "Stop!"

But the Siren was too far gone inside the music to hear her.

"Stop your damn singing!" Kelley demanded.

"Kelley!" Maddox turned on her.

"That song is Sonny's, Maddox. She has no right to that memory!"

"I know. I know." His voice was gentle, but firm. "I was there. Just remember, Kelley—he gave away that memory for you. He did it to help *you*."

That might have been true, but he hadn't *given* it away. Chloe had stolen it. Kelley bit down on her tongue to keep from hurling a curse at the Siren for that cruelty. And that intimacy.

"Tasted like wine, he did," the Siren murmured, fingers to her lips. "So sweet, like wine and forest-green shadows . . ."

Kelley had to leave. If she didn't, she was going to do something she would regret. She wrenched herself away from Maddox and moved blindly to the door.

"Take it back," Chloe whispered.

They turned to see tears pouring down Chloe's face. "Please . . . I don't want it anymore. It hurts—it's his. Not mine. I shouldn't have it. . . ."

"What's she talking about?"

"He needs it to hide. They'll *hurt* him if they find him,"

214

Chloe's voice rasped urgently through the air.

The words froze Kelley in her tracks. "What did you say?"

"I don't want him to be hurt. I'll give it back. I promise. Please tell him. . . ."

Kelley drifted back to the bedside, confused.

"Once upon a time they killed the Old Green Man." Chloe's voice was singsong, her eyes unfocused, staring up into the darkness. "They'll do it again. They'll do it again . . ."

"What does that have to do with Sonny?" Kelley asked.

"He doesn't *know,*" the Siren whispered. Her gaze was filled with regret and more than a little madness. "Just like *you* didn't know . . ."

"This is stupid. She's crazy, that's all. I'm not going to stand here and—"

Suddenly the Siren's eyes flew wide open and she lunged, grasping the sides of Kelley's head with fingers that were ice cold. Pain, sharp and shocking, lanced through Kelley's skull, and images flooded into her brain.

Sonny lay on the sidewalk. Blood flowed from holes in his chest, pooling on the sidewalk, transforming it into green, mossy ground. Streams and rivers flowed outward from where Sonny's body lay unmoving, and saplings sprang up, reaching leafy fingers toward a sky that was somehow obscured by overhanging branches and vines. A blinding burst of green light ripped through her mind, and Kelley was thrown backward through space. She landed on top of Maddox on the floor of

215

Sonny's room, shaking convulsively.

When she could see again, she looked up to see Tyff rocking the shattered Siren in an embrace, trying to shush her keening wail.

Maddox led Kelley out into the living room and shut the door behind them.

"I guess I didn't really make her feel any better, did I?" she said, a tremor in her voice.

"I guess not."

"Sorry."

"Not your fault. I should have known, I suppose. She's pretty far gone."

"Maddox . . . do you know what she was talking about?"

"I'm not sure. What did *you* see, Kelley?" He peered at her, frowning. "When she was in your head just now?"

"I don't know. It was garbled stuff." Kelley shook her head hard to dispel the image of Sonny lying bleeding on a New York sidewalk. Sonny was fine. He wasn't even in the mortal realm. "Nonsense, really. Maybe Chloe just thinks she knows something and it's just her own broken mind playing tricks on her."

"Maybe." Maddox rubbed a weary hand over his eyes. "All I know is she knew who *you* were when none of the rest of us did. Not even you."

Kelley picked up her jacket and thrust an arm through the sleeve, moving toward the door.

"Where are you going?"

"I don't know, Maddox. I sort of need to clear my head. I think I'll go do what my director told me to."

"What's that?"

"I'm going to go play in the rain."

XVIII

"We are taking you to the mortal realm," Sonny said, in answer to Auberon's query.

"No."

"We're not asking your permission, lord. Mabh and Annis concur. Until we uncover the root of what ails you, you are not safe here. If you do not believe that, at least consider this—your condition will not remain a secret much longer if you stay within these walls."

"We all agree, lord," Bob said, reaching out a hand to help his ailing king to stand. "It's far less likely that your . . . condition will be discovered there. And just possible that you may fare better away from this place. For the time being."

"I do not like the idea of hiding."

"Fair enough." Mabh glared flatly at him. "How do you feel about the idea of *surviving*?"

The king returned her stare and, relenting, struggled to sit up higher in the bed.

"I thought as much." The Autumn Queen gave Auberon a thin smile. "You're lucky, my dear, that I hold the safety and balance of the Faerie realm in such high regard that I don't treat *you* with the same courtesy that you have ever shown me. Otherwise I might just let you perish and pick up the pieces of your kingdom once you fall." Her eyes glittered with mockery even as she fetched a heavy robe from the end of the bed and tenderly wrapped it around the ailing king's shoulders.

As long as he lived, Sonny thought, he would never understand the mercurial Faerie mind. It was as though Faerie could love and hate all in the same breath and not think it the least bit strange.

"You." Mabh gestured curtly without looking at Sonny. "Help him."

"Where in the mortal realm are we taking him?" Sonny asked, as he and the boucca each got a shoulder under one of Auberon's arms and helped the king to stand.

"The only place I can think of to keep him safe," Bob said.

The palace chamber shimmered, wavering like a mirage all around them, as Mabh opened an elegant rift that drifted down to encompass the little band of travelers.

"No one will know we're there."

Darkness gave way to dim light—and silence to the sound of a thermos cup full of dark roast Colombian coffee splashing onto the floor.

"Oh. Hello, Jack," said Bob. "Damn."

"I was under the impression that there were no rehearsals scheduled for this week." Bob chatted amicably as he and Sonny took Gentleman Jack by the shoulders and steered him into the wings, perching the stunned actor on the high stool at the stage manager's station. "What on earth are you doing on your own here in the dark?"

"I was working my monologues . . ." Jack murmured. "I like the quiet. . . ."

"Now, Jack," Bob admonished gently. "You know how Quentin feels about rehearsing without his magnificent guidance. And how've you been, by the way? You're looking well. I like the beard."

"Uh . . ." Jack was a little speechless.

Bob snapped his fingers in front of Jack's eyes, trying to get his attention. "Jack? Over here, Jack."

"Who *are* those people?"

"You sure you want the answer to that question?" Bob asked. "It might be better if you just left it alone, you know."

"You . . . you all just appeared out of the air. Right out of *thin air*."

"Yes."

"How?"

"Are you *sure* you want to know?" the boucca asked again, sternly.

"And you're Kelley's young man, aren't you?" Jack turned to Sonny.

"Yes, sir." Sonny nodded.

"And that woman . . ." Jack's voice was thick with wonder. "I've never seen anyone so beautiful."

"Gods, don't let *her* hear you say that." Bob glanced back to where Mabh was settling Auberon on the center riser in the middle of the stage. "Her ego doesn't need the stroking. And if she takes a fancy to you, then you are in perishing trouble. Unless you have a fondness for drafty stone fortresses and boggy terrain."

"What in hell are you talking about?" Jack blinked up at the creature he'd once known only as a fellow actor in a play. His dazed expression sharpening finally, Jack visibly attempted to get a hold of himself. "What's going on here?"

"Are you *sure*—"

"Tell me, Bob!"

The boucca winced at the sound of his name.

"I want to know what's really happening!"

Bob and Sonny exchanged a laden glance, and Sonny threw his hands in the air. If it had been up to him, he would have tried to construct some sort of plausible tale to tell the man. What on earth that could possibly be, he had no idea. But the old actor had asked the boucca. He'd called Bob by name and he'd insisted on knowing the truth. Under those circumstances, Bob was bound to *tell* him the truth—and so he did.

Sonny knew that Bob was tempering his words with a very subtle, noninvasive form of magick—almost like a mild tranquilizer—so that the truth of what he was saying would be slightly more palatable to the human mind. It probably also meant that the boucca meant to alter Jack's memories at a later date.

All in all, Jack handled it pretty well.

Meaning he didn't go instantly mad or fall into a faint.

Bob, in his fashion, was impressed. "I've seen it happen," he murmured to Sonny. "The swooning and the crazy—even with that little bit of help. Mortals aren't anywhere near as mentally hardy as they'd like to believe. Sometimes you lay a big sack of truth across their shoulders, and the weight of it breaks them straight in two."

Jack heard the last part and raised a slow, sardonic eyebrow. "It's a hard thing to deny what I saw with my own two eyes, Bob," he said, standing.

The boucca twitched violently. "Please, Jack. I'd appreciate it if you just called me Puck."

"You're kidding." *That* bit of information did seem to shake the actor's composure. He sat back down on the stool.

"I'm really not," Bob said. "And I'd consider it a personal favor."

Jack took a deep breath. "All right. Well, let me tell you

then, er, Puck . . . I've spent a lifetime making observations. Honing my powers of perception so that I could bring some realism to my roles on the stage. I *know* what I saw. Only a fool would deny it."

Sonny looked at the old actor with respect. "I think I know why Kelley holds you in such high regard."

"She almost told me, you know. But she said I wouldn't believe her if she told me what was going on in her life. I should have known she wasn't exaggerating." Jack's gaze drifted back over to Auberon and Mabh. "So . . . *those* are . . . her folks?"

"Yes."

"I wish I'd known about the fur cloak when I was playing Oberon. I would have asked wardrobe to come up with something. . . ." Jack's voice drifted away as the significance of his newfound knowledge hammered home. He was silent for a long moment. Then he shook himself a little. "Poor man. He doesn't look like someone who's used to being sickly."

"That he is not."

Jack stood. He tugged his shirt straight and smoothed a hand over the hair at the sides of his head. Then he walked over to the table that held an assortment of props that would be used in *Romeo and Juliet* and reached for the coffee thermos he'd left sitting there. He plucked up an ornate glass goblet and filled it half full with steaming brew.

Sonny watched as the actor crossed the stage to where Auberon sat and, bowing elegantly from the waist, said, "Your Majesty. Welcome to the Avalon Grande. I thought you might like something warm to drink."

Auberon pulled himself up and, with gracious solemnity, took the offered goblet. "I thank you, mortal man. What is your name?"

"My name is Jack Savage, sir. Around here they call me Gentleman Jack."

The shadow of a smile lifted the corner of the king's mouth and he nodded. Then he took a sip of the coffee and his eyes widened in surprise. "Extraordinary," he murmured. "I sometimes forget how extraordinary mortals can be."

"I think it might be best if you left this place, sir," Sonny said quietly to the older actor once they had helped move the ailing Winter King into the actors' lounge backstage—the so-called greenroom.

"You're entitled to think whatever you like—what's your name, young man?"

"Sonny. Sonny Flannery."

"Well, Sonny Flannery, you're entitled to think whatever you like." Jack smiled. "And I appreciate the concern. I really do. But I'm not going anywhere."

Sonny sighed. He'd had a feeling that Gentleman Jack would say something like that. Crossing his arms over his chest, he silently appraised the other man. "Can you fight, Jack?"

"I used to box, some. When I was younger." Jack gave him a skeptical look.

"How about weapons?"

At that, Jack straightened up and said with a degree of pride, "Hell, I'm a certified actor combatant! I've been doing the fight choreography for this company for fifteen years."

Sonny grinned. "That's good."

"Well, now—hold on a second." Jack faltered a little, upon rapid reflection. "I might know which end of a sword is which, but there's a mighty big difference between swinging one in a choreographed stage sequence where you're trying *not* to kill your opponent, and an honest-to-god fight where you *are*."

Sonny slapped the older man on the shoulder. "If it comes to that, I'll take what I can get."

"You think there's trouble brewing?"

"I do. Mabh brought us here to be safe. But if there's even a chance that Auberon's affliction is not a natural one—if someone is willing to go so far as to poison the King of the Unseelie—then I say that, in all likelihood, there is no safe place. Not in either world. I just want to be prepared. And, if you stay here—a course of action I don't particularly recommend—then I want you to be prepared, too."

"You talk like a regular army field commander, young man. What, exactly, is it you do for a living?"

The question gave Sonny pause. He thought about Kelley and how she had called him ruthless during their argument. Because of what he "did for a living."

He turned away from Jack, so that he would not have to see the old actor's reaction as he said, "I kill Faerie."

XIX

When Kelley finally got home, there was another bright pink sticky note waiting for her on her bedroom door, scrawled in a flourishy manner with the words:

Don't bother with any of your sleeping nonsense tonight.
Come to the River. Help is waiting. . . .
T.

"Help?" Kelley muttered, staring at the note and rubbing at her eyes, which felt gritty from exhaustion.

Tyff must have gotten home before her and gone back out again.

The River was, at that moment, the last place she wanted to go. After leaving Sonny's penthouse, Kelley had spent the next few hours wandering the streets of New York. "Playing in the rain."

She'd walked for what seemed like miles, traveling south all the way past Grand Central Terminal. When she got to Park Avenue, Kelley paused and stood for a long time, looking down through the curtaining rain toward its intersection with East Fortieth Street. The streetscape seemed . . . *wrong* to her somehow. As if the office towers didn't belong there.

She peered intently through the downpour, and it was a bit like looking through a Faerie glamour. She could almost see the ghosts of the buildings that had gone before: the brick and brownstone structures, so much more elegant than the steel and glass monoliths that had sprung up in their places. For some reason, looking down that street filled Kelley with sadness.

Eventually she'd turned north again and walked toward home, letting the rain wash over her. So many thoughts and questions tumbled about in her head like puzzle pieces in a box shaken by a child who just wanted to hear them rattle.

Finally, standing on the sidewalk outside of her apartment building, Kelley had spotted one of her mother's Cailleach hovering, cloaked in a dark smudge of cloud drifting far below the rest of the stormy ceiling. It seemed as if the Storm Hag was waiting there for her to appear. Loath as she was to interact with her mother's minions, Kelley conceded to herself that they might be able to answer some of her questions. It was worth a try.

She shouted at the sky, attempting to catch the creature's attention. Waved her arms and jumped up and down. Threw rocks.

Nothing.

When a cop half a block down the street turned in her direction, Kelley gave up and ducked inside her building before she got arrested. *He* might have seen her leaping around like a lunatic, but it was quite apparent that to the Fae she was invisible. Whatever the leprechaun had done to her, whatever curse he'd cast on her charm, it had rendered her utterly nonexistent to her own kind. Even the random sparks of Faerie energy that used to escape from under the talisman's cloak were contained, it seemed. Kelley was as good as human.

In the mood she was in, Kelley seriously considered blowing off the pink-sticky-note imperative. The River was too full of flashing lights and loud sounds and people. She wasn't sure she could handle crowds just then. The encounter with Chloe weighed on her mind, as did the now-unavoidable recognition of her utterly mortal state. For someone who had once vigorously protested against her Faerie heritage, suddenly the thought of living out her days as Girl Average didn't appeal to her quite so much anymore.

She looked at the sticky note.

Help is waiting. . . .

Kelley sighed. All right. She might as well go. Maybe in the intervening hours Tyff had found some of the answers Kelley needed. She doubted it, but she was starting to realize that she was willing to give almost anything a try.

Titania wrapped Kelley in a warm embrace the moment she arrived at the River, and bestowed a kiss on her cheek. Kelley was somewhat astonished at the way Titania managed to do those kinds of things and not make the recipient of the affectionate gestures feel awkward or clumsy.

The night's festivities were in full swing, and the place was packed to capacity. Wending her way through the fashionably dressed crowd of Fae and humans, the queen drew Kelley along one of the moodily lit halls and out into the flower-filled courtyard terrace that was the centerpiece of the River. The terrace was located at the heart of the structure and was open to the sky except for the shade canopy of a cultivated vine trellis. On the surrounding walls, ivy grew thick and high-climbing, reaching almost to the very top floors of the boutique hotel, as if it would swallow the building whole.

"I have wished for this day, Kelley," Titania said, linking her arm in Kelley's. "Ever since word reached me that Auberon had brought a daughter home to his house, I have wanted to meet you. I wept on the day that you were stolen."

"Oh . . ." Kelley didn't quite know what to say.

"You think that I would have been angry." Titania interpreted her silence.

"I guess. I mean you guys were sort of a couple at the time, weren't you?"

Titania laughed. "Were, and then weren't, and then were again. We are much like the changing seasons, we Fair Folk. I may have had my differences with Auberon, but I have never not loved him, my dear." She handed Kelley a fluted glass from a silver tray on a stand. "I so look forward to getting to know his daughter and his heir."

The silvery liquid in the glass was full of brilliant bubbles, sparkling like diamond dust. Kelley took it, although she wasn't about to actually drink any of the stuff. Notwithstanding the fact that she wasn't of legal drinking age, she was also—after her encounter with Gwynn ap Nudd's Faerie hospitality—wary of offered food or drink.

"My lady-in-waiting speaks very highly of you," the queen said, as she picked up her own glass and drew Kelley toward a raised platform topped with a cushioned couch made of some exotic, carved wood.

"That's really kind of you to say." Kelley wondered exactly what kind of equivocal language Tyff had couched her "praise" in. As close as they had become, Kelley was still aware that she frequently tried her Faerie roomie's patience. "Uh . . . where *is* Tyff, do you know? I'm supposed to meet her here."

The Summer Queen glanced around as if expecting that Tyff should already be in attendance. "I sent for her, and I *did* see her arrive earlier," she said with only a faint hint of annoyance. "Ah, well. She should be along presently, I should imagine. Won't you sit with me while we wait?" Titania sank down gracefully and patted the cushions next to her. "I understand that you had a rather nasty run-in in the park the other night. A potent Fae with a grudge?"

"Oh. Yeah." Kelley's fingers automatically went to the clover charm at her throat as she sat hesitantly on the edge of the couch.

"Tyffanwy told me all about it. A binding curse—you poor thing. You must feel like a dragonfly trapped in a jar!"

More like a butterfly that's had its wings ripped off, Kelley thought.

Titania shook her head sorrowfully. "You have my sympathies, of course. And, if I may be so bold as to offer, my help if you want it. I know it is old magick—powerful magick—that binds you, but perhaps I could be of some use."

This must be what Tyff meant by her note, Kelley thought excitedly. Maybe the queen could remove the spell that held the charm fast about her throat. Give her back her wings . . .

"My own abilities are . . . not inconsequential. If you'd like, I could attempt to remove the binding curse myself," Titania said in her musical voice. "If I succeed, you'd be free to use your magicks again."

Kelley remembered what Tyff had told her about Faerie magick. She recalled with perfect clarity the sensation of that sugar-sweet venom sting of her own Faerie magick, once more coursing through her veins.

231

"Or not," Titania said, noting the frown on Kelley's face, "as you see fit. But it would be your decision, not a consequence of another's whims. What say you?"

I say "what's the catch?" Kelley thought, and was immediately ashamed of herself. But, like the wine, the very idea of Faerie-based random acts of kindness set off all kinds of warning bells for Kelley. Of course, Titania wasn't Mabh. She had been nothing but sweet and gracious, and Tyff had never had anything but glowing praise for the Summer Queen. Kelley trusted Tyff.

Where *was* Tyff, anyway?

"What say you, Princess?" Titania asked again, smiling at her.

In truth, Kelley was starting to get a little desperate. She kept thinking of the last time she had seen Sonny—beset with the horde of trolls thundering over the cliff. Fennrys had said that Sonny could take care of himself, and of course Kelley had a great degree of firsthand knowledge that such was the case. She remembered the first time she had seen him in a fight, the night he had saved her life from the Black Shuck. She shouldn't be so worried. But all she wanted was to find him again and put things right. And *that* wasn't going to happen anytime soon unless she could find a way to get herself back to the Otherworld. It was pretty obvious that Aaneel and the Janus weren't going to be any help to her. Maybe she should listen to Titania. Trust her. Let her help.

All those thoughts tumbled through Kelley's mind in the space of time it took for her to say, "That's very generous. Why would you want to help me, lady, if you don't mind my asking?"

"Because I have always believed in freedom for the Fair Folk to do as they please. That would include *you,* my dear." Titania laid a gentle arm across Kelley's shoulders, enveloping her in the sweet, subtle perfume of a forest meadow in sunshine.

Kelley felt her doubts melting. "I . . . all right."

"My lovely young actress!" The Faerie queen smiled. "Do you know, I have always wondered how *I* would fare onstage," she said, switching topics with a mercurial swiftness. Her golden eyes sparkled with merriment, and she stood, gathering her filmy robes about her.

A shaft of moonlight pierced the leafy canopy high overhead, illuminating Titania as if she stood in a spotlight.

"Out of this wood do not desire to go!" Titania's voice sang out. "Thou shalt remain here, whether thou wilt or no."

The patrons of the River fell instantly quiet. The music drifted to silence and all the partygoers stood mesmerized.

Kelley swallowed an uncomfortable feeling in her throat as she realized that the Shakespearean lines the queen had chosen to recite came from the single page sent by Sonny as a pledge to return to her. The one on her bedside table.

Coincidence? Kelley wondered silently.

Sonny had once told her that he didn't believe in such a thing.

"I am a spirit of no common rate," the queen continued, her tones soaring across the courtyard, where mortal and Fae alike had turned to watch the impromptu performance. Her gaze caught and held Kelley like the dragonfly in a jar she'd compared her to earlier. "The summer still doth tend upon my state; and I do love thee: therefore, go with me." Titania gestured with a commanding wave of her hand to the lovely waitresses who stood grouped together with their trays.

They were all Fae, Kelley noticed. The gauzy black silk of their matching tunics fluttered about their bronzed limbs.

"I'll give thee fairies to attend on thee, and they shall fetch thee jewels from the deep." The Summer Queen laughed and the Summer Girls giggled back. "And sing while thou on pressed flowers dost sleep."

The queen turned back to her, and Kelley shuddered involuntarily as Titania's eyes fastened on the charm around Kelley's throat and she said, in a voice that suddenly thrummed with unimaginable power, "And I will purge thy mortal grossness so . . . that thou shalt like an airy spirit go!" The queen's hands danced through the air, and Kelley felt the green-amber pendant grow blazing hot for an instant.

Try it now, my dear, Titania's voice whispered in her mind. Her golden eyes seemed to Kelley as if they filled the room with a wash of light. *Loose the chain. . . .*

Moving as if in a dream, Kelley slid her hands up under her hair, around to the back of her neck. Her fingertips fumbled with the clasp and a shiver of panic—irrational, unreasoning, but overpowering—rolled over her. It stopped her from undoing the catch.

Even though she knew, in that moment, that she could.

Slowly she withdrew her hands, and the chain settled coolly around her neck, the clover charm nestling back into the hollow at the base of her throat. Silently she shook her head.

Titania frowned—a brief thundercloud shadow crossing her lovely face—then whirled away from Kelley.

"Peaseblossom! Cobweb! Moth! and Mustardseed!" she cried, summoning her attendants with what Kelley knew was the very last line on that particular page of script.

"A round of drinks for everyone on the house, girls!" Titania said, smiling brightly as she dropped out of the role of grand actress and back into the part of the gracious hostess.

The Faerie girls rushed forward with trays filled with champagne flutes, and the patrons of the River applauded madly, although whether for the performance or the free drinks, Kelley wasn't sure. Titania turned back around, her questioning gaze fastened on the green-amber pendant.

"No luck," Kelley said, her voice a dry rasp.

"Are you sure?" The queen's eyes searched Kelley's face. "The clasp remains bound?"

Kelley drew upon every last ounce of her theatrical skills and lied through her teeth with apologetic conviction. "Locked up tight," she said, and gave the chain a sharp tug. Not *too* sharp. "I guess I'll just have to find some other way, your highness. Thanks for trying."

"Of course, my dear girl," Titania murmured, confusion and something else that Kelley could not quite identify swimming in her gaze. But only for an instant. "A pity. Now you will have to excuse me. I must see to my other guests, but it would please me greatly if you would stay and enjoy the festivities. At least until Tyffanwy reappears. She would be most upset to have missed you."

"Sure." Kelley nodded, forcing a smile onto her own lips. Titania's "request" hadn't sounded as though it came with the option of a refusal. She wondered if she was slipping into some kind of pathological paranoia. It was not in Kelley's nature to be suspicious, but she couldn't bring herself to trust Titania. Not yet. She needed time to think. She needed more information. She needed her roommate's sage, sarcastic advice.

Where are you, Tyff?

"Thanks again," Kelley said.

The queen inclined her head graciously and, after a last lingering glance at Kelley, turned and was soon swallowed up by a crowd of fawning admirers—mortal and Faerie alike. Kelley seriously contemplated making a break for it, but she could feel eyes on her as she moved about the lushly landscaped terrace. Whenever she turned around, she could not see who it was that watched.

Kelley tried not to look like she was pacing impatiently— which she was—until a familiar figure suddenly caught her eye. It was the enormous guy who manned the front desk. Kelley concentrated, looked right at him, and saw through the clumsy glamour—something Tyff had taught her how to do, even when wearing her charm—one of the few bits of Fae knowledge she *had* been willing to impart. As plain as day, Kelley saw the hulking shape of the ogre beneath the glamour. An ogre, Tyff had mentioned, who owed her a favor.

Maybe, Kelley thought, she could call in that favor by proxy. At the very least, maybe Mr. Ogre had seen Tyff earlier and knew where she was. It was worth a shot.

The ogre, Harvicc, led the way.

They found Tyff on another of the hotel's several private terraces. This one was on the thirteenth floor, and Tyff was there just where Harvicc said he'd left her. She was curled up in a gently swaying hammock, tucked in among garden furniture, and surrounded by potted fig trees and planters. She looked sound asleep, except for the fact that her head lolled senselessly on her neck when Kelley shook her. There was a deep, ugly bruise on the side of the Faerie's exquisite face.

"Did you do that?" Kelley asked, horrified.

Harvicc nodded miserably.

"Why?"

"Miss Tyff asked me to." The way the enormous creature mumbled around her name, it sounded almost as though he were calling her Mischief. If Kelley understood correctly—she had actually *requested* this smack-down. Maybe it was some kind of arcane Fae dating ritual, Kelley mused, although she doubted it. Why would Tyff have left her the note to come meet her, and then fling herself into unconsciousness?

"When, exactly, did you—er—knock her out, Harvicc?" she asked.

"Um . . . um . . ." The ogre twiddled his meaty fingers together. Despite his muscled bulk and fearsome appearance, he looked very much like a little boy called before the principal. "Soon after she 'rived . . . coupler hourzes ago."

"I still don't understand why, though."

"She told me she had a secret she wanted to keep and that closed eyeses was the only way to do such." Harvicc shrugged. "So she asked me to hardly hit her."

Kelley caught the gist of what he was saying; she'd told him to hit her hard. What secret? And again, why would Tyff leave a note for Kelley to come and meet her, and then demand that the ogre forcibly indispose her? It didn't make sense—any of it.

Unless, of course, the note hadn't been written by Tyff.

Kelley had never really paid much attention to her roommate's handwriting, but now that she thought back on it—and on the note that Tyff had presented her with in the rain earlier that afternoon when they'd gone to see Maddox and Chloe—she didn't think the two scripts really matched.

Scripts . . .

The note had been left on the door to her bedroom. Where her script page lay. And the note, Kelley remembered suddenly, had been signed only "T."

Tyffanwy. Or . . . Titania?

Kelley went suddenly cold, head to toe.

"Harvicc." She put a tentative hand on the ogre's arm. "Harv, do you think you could help me? You know—like you helped Tyff?"

The ogre nodded vigorously—and, in a fit of misguided helpfulness, immediately curled his hand into a monstrous, chubby fist and swung for Kelley's head.

"No!" She yelped and ducked under the thundering punch. "That wasn't quite what I meant!"

"Urm . . . sorry."

"No. It's okay." Kelley straightened up cautiously. "What I meant was—do you think you can get Tyff and me out of here without anybody finding out?"

The service elevator went all the way to the sub-basement, bypassing the main floor, where Titania held court. According to the ogre—who held Tyff as if she weighed about the same as a bag of kittens and filled every available square inch of the tiny elevator cab not occupied by Kelley—there was an old catacomb that ran from the service level to a private under-ground parking garage.

The cavernous space of the garage was dimly lit with over-head fluorescent lights that flickered and gave a greenish cast to the scattered pools of oil and water. The dankness and stench—motor oil and rotting vegetation—were almost over-powering. Kelley put her sleeve over her face and followed hard on Harvicc's surprisingly swift heels as he trotted among the hulking concrete pillars, head down and shoulders hunched so he wouldn't scrape the low ceiling. The garage was virtually empty except for one corner near the exit ramp, where a row of stalls was filled, one after the other, with an astonishing collection of vintage and collector's edition automobiles. *Cars* was too crass a word for these machines, Kelley thought. Some were shrouded in protective tarps, but a good number of them were uncovered and stood gleaming in the intermittent light as though they'd just that second been polished. Kelley's untutored eye could identify the make of the hunter-green Jaguar convertible, and the silvery-mauve Bentley, but most of the others looked either too old or too exotic for her to be able to recognize. They seemed parked according to vintage. Near the far end of the collection was a wine-red number that looked like it wasn't much younger than a Model T! On the other side of that, Kelley noticed a canvas-covered shape that stood much higher than the rest of the vehicles.

Harvicc was urging her to hurry with anxious, grunting little noises, but Kelley slowed to a stop. There was something familiar about that shape.

She walked toward it. The garage was silent except for the dripping of water and a scurrying sound that was probably a rat. Kelley reached out and grabbed the canvas drop cloth with a trembling hand. She threw it back, revealing the spoked wheels and shiny black footboards of a horse-drawn carriage.

"We Fair Folk," said a voice in the darkness, "we've always

liked to travel in style."

Kelley went numb as a shadowed figure, wiping his hands on a polishing cloth, came out from the behind the carriage. The silver buckles on his high black boots jingled with every step he took.

"Nasty greenie!" Harvicc rumbled from somewhere over Kelley's shoulder.

She glanced back to see that the ogre had unceremoniously dumped Tyff into the open backseat of the Jag convertible and was thundering toward the leprechaun like a charging bull elephant. The ground beneath Kelley's feet shook, and she saw a look of apprehension on the leprechaun's sharp face.

The tattooed Faerie recovered his composure in a flash, cracking his knuckles and opening his arms wide at the ogre's approach.

Kelley reached up under her hair to undo the clasp of her necklace. But then she faltered—she wasn't so sure she should let Hooligan-boy know that his binding curse was broken; and she *really* wasn't sure that she could do anything remotely useful with her power that wouldn't bring the structure crumbling down on top of them.

In her brief second of indecision, Harvicc swept past her, a hurricane with fists. "Run!" he roared over his shoulder at Kelley.

Kelley hesitated a moment longer. She couldn't abandon Tyff like that.

"GO!" the ogre bellowed. "I will protect!"

She turned and beat feet up the ramp as fast as she could.

Kelley hailed a taxi by way of almost getting run over by it. The startled driver's brakes were still screeching as she threw herself into the cab's backseat and slammed the door shut, giving the cabbie breathless instructions on where to take her. Kelley kept her head down and the doors locked. She didn't look out the window at the faces of the passersby when the cab stopped at traffic lights. And she began to breathe easier only when they turned down a familiar, tree-lined street at the edge of Hell's Kitchen.

She didn't know where else to go. She didn't want to go back to the apartment she shared with Tyff. If Titania had been in her room, then Kelley knew she wasn't safe there. Even if Titania herself meant no harm—something which seemed less likely with the reappearance of the leprechaun so close to the River—Kelley didn't trust a place where the Fae knew where to find her.

She couldn't go to Sonny's place. Not with Chloe still there.

She didn't trust the Janus Guard anymore—not beyond Maddox, anyway—so the park was out.

That left the Avalon Grande. It was, in her mind, the only safe place she knew.

And, thanks to the scheduling conflict that meant Quentin was back in England for his imperious mother's birthday, the theater was dark—there were no rehearsals scheduled for that week.

Kelley's fingers were still trembling as she dug around in

her shoulder bag for the key to the stage door. Inside, the familiar, slightly musty smell of the backstage hallway filled her with a sense of relief as she shut the door and threw the deadbolt lock. She was safe here. This theater felt more like home to Kelley than any place ever had.

With only the meager illumination cast by the ghost light—a bare sixty-watt bulb on a pole stand that was left plugged in and placed in the middle of the darkened stage—Kelley found her way up the stairs and onto her Juliet balcony. She reached up under her hair, slipped the catch of her necklace, and let the charm fall away from her throat. After all that time when she was unable to remove the charm, it felt to Kelley as though she stood utterly naked in the middle of the stage.

It was awesome.

She leaped up lightly to perch on the balustrade and then stepped into space.

Soft purple light flooded the darkness and Kelley spiraled up into the fly tower. She felt whole. Free. Faerie. She had her wings back. And now there was only one thing she needed in all the worlds: all she had to do was find Sonny. She concentrated, thought of forming a rift to the Otherworld in her mind, and lifted her hands in front of her. The darkened air crackled and sparked.

And a voice from far below her said, "Kelley?"

Startled, Kelley lost her focus.

Her wings sputtered, faded. She plummeted toward the stage . . .

And he caught her in his arms.

"Sonny?" She looked up into his face, certain she *must* be dreaming.

"Firecracker," he whispered, his silver-gray eyes sparkling.

His voice in the dimness was music. His arms around her were the feeling of coming home as he tightened his embrace. And his kiss . . .

His kiss was joy.

XX

"Are you rehearsing without me?" Sonny said finally, once Kelley had been forced to either come up for air or pass out (and Sonny was gratified to see that it seemed like a really tough decision). "Do I need to steal another script away from you?"

Kelley just grinned up at him as she fastened the charm once more around her neck.

Sonny ran his fingertips over Kelley's cheek and through her hair. She was so beautiful to him, and when he had seen her hovering in the air, surrounded by the darklight glow of her wings, he had felt his heart swell in his chest. Now she was in his arms and she was somehow *his*. Sonny marveled at that fact—even wondered for a moment whether he was actually deluding himself. He hugged her tightly, and the way she melted into his embrace almost made his knees weak.

"Bob told me there's kissing in this play." He frowned fiercely down at her. "I don't know how I feel about that."

Kelley's mouth curled in a slow smile. "I know how I feel about this. . . ."

She reached up and brought Sonny's face down to hers again. This time, it didn't seem as though she really cared whether she ever took time out to breathe again. Neither did Sonny. Hours could have passed and it still wouldn't have been enough time to spend locked in that embrace.

It was particularly galling that Bob's polite cough interrupted Sonny's bliss mere moments later. Startled, Kelley glanced over her shoulder.

"Hello, Princess. Fancy meeting you here."

"Bob! What—what are you doing back?" Kelley stammered, a warm blush staining her cheeks as she composed herself. She looked back and forth between Sonny and the ancient Fae. "Both of you, I mean?"

Sonny reached down and tucked a lock of Kelley's fiery hair behind one ear. He was going to have to tell her that they weren't the only ones in the theater. That not only had one of her fellow actors recently had the horizons of his world view *impossibly* expanded—but that her parents were sitting in the theater greenroom, sipping coffee.

"It's funny." Bob stepped in before Sonny had to say anything. "I was going to ask you the same thing. Apparently a 'dark' theater just doesn't mean the same thing as it used to."

Kelley stiffened, as if suddenly remembering something, and glanced reflexively over her shoulder in the direction of the stage door. "Right! I almost forgot. . . ." she glanced back at Sonny again. "Our buddy with the bad-ass boots has reappeared."

Bob gaped at her.

"But it's okay," she assured him. "I ditched him in a garage in midtown and hopped a cab. He didn't follow me. The way that cabbie drove, I'd be surprised if anyone c—"

The thunderous pounding on the stage door instantly belied Kelley's unfinished assertion. Bob cursed in a language so old, even Sonny didn't know it. Kelley nearly jumped out of her skin at the sound, and her sudden grip on Sonny's bicep was punishing. He gently pried her fingers loose and put his arm around her.

"What do we do?" he asked the boucca, pleased that his voice remained steady. Ever since the fight back in the cottage, Sonny had known that he would have to face the leprechaun again—or his brother—and he had *not* been looking forward to it.

Without bothering to answer, Bob turned on his heel and headed briskly in the direction of the back hallway.

"Bob!" Kelley called. "Stop!"

The boucca halted awkwardly, one foot frozen in midair.

"Oh, look!" he exclaimed, obviously struggling to move forward. "Can we just—for the sake of my sanity—please refer to me as Puck for the next little while, in order to avoid me unintentionally doing things—things I'll probably regret."

"Sorry—Puck—I forgot," Kelley apologized. "Carry on."

Bob's foot jerked forward and he regained control of himself. "Yes, well. It'll also decrease the unfortunate likelihood of our mortal enemies getting hold of my real name and using me against you. Which, depending on the circumstances, I might or might *not* regret!"

"*Mortal* enemies?" Kelley wondered aloud as they ran after him into the hall.

"By that, I meant 'enthusiastically pursuing our demise' mortal, not 'human' mortal," the boucca clarified in a whisper as he tiptoed to the door and made certain it was locked tight.

"I *know* that," Kelley muttered. "I was just—"

Sonny shushed her, and together they watched as Bob placed the tips of his long, knobby fingers lightly against the door.

"Oh dear." The pale greenish tinge of the boucca's skin went even paler and greener. He looked suddenly queasy— as if he was about to be sick. "It's our bully boyo, all right. How marvelously, unintentionally unkind of you to lead him straight to me." He jerked his hand away just in time before the door shuddered again under the hammer-blows of furious fists. It made for a terrible racket, but the old, solid oak door didn't budge. Bob backed toward Sonny and Kelley, murmuring, "This place doesn't have any secret entrances or open windows that I never discovered in my tenure here, does it?"

Kelley shook her head.

"Well then. Perhaps we've got a brief respite."

"Can't he just bust a window to get in?" Kelley asked.

"He could. But entering a building—especially one that used to be consecrated as a place of worship—means that he would leave almost all of his power outside."

Kelley glanced at Sonny, confused.

"Certain Faerie have certain rules about stuff like that," he explained.

"You mean—like vampires needing to be invited in over thresholds?" she asked.

"Vampires. Pff." Bob rolled his eyes. "What a lot of nonsense!"

He turned and they followed as the boucca ran in the direction of the greenroom.

They had settled the king on an ancient overstuffed couch in the greenroom, where they hoped he would be more comfortable. And, indeed, Auberon's raspy breathing had eased somewhat. He still looked like hell, though, Sonny thought. Jack was sitting in a threadbare easy chair, conversing with the Faerie monarch in low, mellow tones as if he were simply discussing a scene with another actor.

At Sonny's side, Kelley went stiff at the sight of her father.

"What's *he* doing here?" she demanded.

"I'm sorry to have had to intrude upon your life once more, my daughter," Auberon murmured. "As it was, I was in no condition to protest when Mabh brought us here to this place."

"Mabh's here, *too*?" Kelley turned an incredulous gaze on Sonny.

Auberon sat quietly on the couch, with neither the strength nor the desire to defend himself. Jack stayed quiet, too. Obviously, as much affection as he had for Kelley, this was not ground that he would tread upon lightly.

Kelley seemed to suddenly notice the actor. "Hi, Jack," she said, very quietly.

"Kiddo," he said, a worried frown creasing his brow.

"I thought I told you that you wouldn't believe any of this stuff."

"I probably wouldn't have." He shrugged. "But then I saw some things that altered my perspective."

"Yeah . . ." Kelley uttered a strangled little laugh. "They'll do that."

Like rumbles of distant thunder, the sounds of fists hammering—now at the front doors of the theater—shattered the awkward silence. All eyes turned toward Bob.

"We're safe for the moment," the boucca said, looking far too worried himself to offer the others much comfort.

"What's out there?" Jack asked.

"Don't ask," Kelley said.

"A leprechaun," Sonny answered.

"Leprechaun?" Jack almost laughed. No doubt the very word conjured up a little cartoon fellow in a green hat and short pants in the actor's mind. "You're joking. He's joking, right?"

"He's really not." Kelley sighed and blew the hair out of her eyes.

"I wish!" Bob agreed fervently. "It's too damned bad we don't have any drink stronger than coffee in this place. A single glass of liquid cheer would keep that rotten sod out indefinitely."

"What?" Kelley asked. "Why?"

The boucca was almost pacing with anxiety, his hands wringing over and over each other in a tumbling blur. "It was a curse laid on the Wee Green Men by their old dad, way back in the mists of time, when he caught them polishing off a cask of his finest whiskey. As a result, leprechauns are prevented from entering any house where a drink had been poured until every last drop is drunk."

"Why didn't you say so?" Jack said.

"Beg pardon?" Bob froze in mid-fidget.

"Sometimes it takes a little bit more than just plain coffee to get me through one of the Mighty Q's rehearsals, you know," the old actor said, fishing around in an inner pocket of his jacket. He produced a narrow silver flask and, pulling a glass tumbler down off the greenroom shelf, poured a generous measure. "It's eighteen-year-old whiskey."

Bob's eyes went saucer wide.

"Irish whiskey."

The boucca's jaw dropped. Auberon smiled.

"Does that make it better or worse?" Jack asked.

"It makes it *perfect*!" Bob cackled gleefully and smacked Jack heartily on the back. "Irish—*ha!* He wouldn't dare tempt that fate now. You old devil, Jack! I hereby dub thee an honorary boucca for this wondrously arse-saving bit of sorcery."

Jack placed the glass down on the table, and they all shuddered as they heard a pained, keening howl coming from outside. There was a rumble of thunder and then silence.

"So that'll keep him out?"

"Until the last drop evaporates. Unless he's got unleprechaunish friends, we're safe as houses. All we've got to do is wait until the little green fink gets bored and toddles off."

"That's great," Kelley said, her gaze on the Faerie king who had closed his eyes, his fine-boned hands hanging limply. "I . . ." The words caught in her throat. "I have to . . ." She turned brusquely on her heel. Brushing past Sonny, she fled down the hall toward the stage, one hand swiping at her eyes.

Sonny watched her go. He stayed standing in the doorway, unable to make himself follow. He could only listen to Kelley's retreating footsteps. He felt like a leaf floating on the surface of a river, caught between two opposing currents that would not let it drift one way or the other. Beneath the collar of his shirt, his neck felt bare and raw with cold where his missing Janus medallion used to rest. He hadn't even been able to bring himself to tell the king that he had lost it.

Auberon lifted his head and looked at the young changeling he'd raised from babyhood in his icy halls in the Otherworld. "Go to her," the king said quietly. "When all is said and done, my young Janus, you owe her far more loyalty than you do me. That's probably something she should know."

XXI

Kelley threaded her way through the rows of empty seats in the auditorium and climbed the polished wooden stairs to the Avalon Grande's balcony, still furnished with the original pews from when the place had been a church. She leaned on the balcony rail, resting her chin on her arms, and looked down, contemplating the place where Romeo and Juliet met and fell in love and tumbled headlong toward their tragic ends—victims of familial strife and ancient rivalries. Kelley tried not to draw parallels between her life and the play. There had been too many of those the *last* time.

In the gloom of the darkened stage, the support timbers of

the half-built set thrust up from behind leaning canvas flats like the remains of an ancient petrified forest. Of course, once finished and under lights, it would be beautiful. A fairy-tale town from long ago where love that was to die for could flourish. And did . . .

An illusion, she thought. *It's a lie.*

Fair Verona was nothing but a flimsy charade made of plywood and plaster, painted to look like marble and brick. The "fountain" in the town square was a lovely piece of artifice, giving the impression of water with clever light and sound effects. It was all trickery and guile. Just like Faerie.

"Kelley?"

Sonny's voice was like a finger down her spine. She shivered.

"You probably shouldn't be up here on your own. Not under the circumstances."

A safety lecture was the last thing she needed to hear.

"Kelley . . . I love you."

That was the first thing.

Sonny held her close in the darkness, silent and warm, neither of them needing any words. But then, after a long time, Sonny did speak. His voice was quiet, thoughtful. Curled into the hollow of his embrace, Kelley listened as Sonny told her stories of growing up in the Otherworld. Little vignettes—like campfire tales—glimpses of his life. He told her nothing strange or sad, and he didn't mention her father or her mother.

Instead he talked of learning to ride. Of playing at the Faerie game of hurling, chasing after a silver ball with wide-bladed oaken staves over an emerald-green field. She could hear the smile in his voice as he told her how the Fair Folk had learned very early on that the fierce little changeling boy with the silver-gray eyes was not to be coddled or pitched easy catches. Sonny told her stories of the tricks that some of the lesser fae—the fir darrig and the piskies—would try to play on him, and how he almost always managed to turn the trick around on its player.

"It does sound like a pretty wonderful place to grow up," Kelley said.

"It was. Before I knew what wonderful really was." Sonny tilted Kelley's head up until she was looking into his eyes. Something flashed deep within those silvery depths, something elusive, but she couldn't quite capture it. Then it didn't matter, because he kissed her and she closed her eyes and heard him say, "I don't care what Auberon says. I don't care what he needs, and I don't care that there are still Wild Hunt on the loose. Someone else can do the job. I'm not going back to the Otherworld. Ever. Not unless you go with me. I'm never leaving you again, Kelley. I promise. And anyone who thinks otherwise had better be prepared for a world of hurt."

Wrapped in each other's arms, Sonny and Kelley had finally given in to the overwhelming exhaustion that had been building for days. When Kelley awoke, Sonny was gone—his suede riding coat was draped over her. Lying curled up on the wooden pew, she thought she could still feel the tingle of his kiss dancing on the curve of her cheek.

She knew he hadn't gone far. He'd promised not to leave her. Besides, she knew he was worried about the leprechaun lying in wait outside. She suspected that Sonny had gone back down to the greenroom to consult with the others about what would happen next.

With Auberon so obviously out of commission, they might be in trouble. She didn't want to dwell on that—on how terrible he had looked—and anyway, Kelley thought, assuming her mother hadn't already fled back to the Other-world, surely the power of *her* shadowy throne would prove more than enough to deal with one miserable freaking leprechaun.

The backstage halls were ominously quiet and dark when she went downstairs, Sonny's coat draped over her shoulders like a cloak. Kelley saw a light bleeding out through the gap in the half-open door of one of the dressing rooms. It was flickering and vaguely purple, and she knew that it must be her mother. Drawing herself up straight, she walked forward with a purposeful step and put a hand on the door. She was going to have to face her mother eventually. *Might as well get this over with . . .*

Kelley was about to call her mother's name, but she realized that the queen was talking to someone. Not exactly prone to eavesdropping, Kelley nevertheless stayed silent and still. Peering through the gap, she saw her mother standing in front of one of the many makeup mirrors in the room, using the glass like it was some kind of mystical teleconference screen. The very reason Kelley had switched dressing rooms with Alec. She frowned and moved closer, listening. Mabh sounded upset.

Kelley held her breath. She recognized the other voice—the deep rumbling tones of Herne the Hunter, Mabh's lover of centuries past and the former leader of the Wild Hunt. Kelley had met him six months before, the night Sonny had taken her to the Tavern.

"*No* one was to know," Herne was saying. "Ever. It was the only way to keep him safe."

"Of *course*," Mabh agreed derisively. "Just so long as no one ever got close enough to look him in the eye!"

"His true nature was veiled when he was infant," Herne said sharply. "Even from himself. We cast a powerful charm over his mind—disguised as the memory of a lullaby, something he would always remember. . . ."

"Which also would have worked nicely"—the Autumn Queen's sarcasm was expansive—"*if* the boy had been smart enough not to let a Siren go digging around in his skull, eating that memory like a candied fig. Without it now, he's an open book for any of the Fae who care to read deeply enough. Which I did. I wish I hadn't."

Kelley felt the pit of her stomach drop.

Sonny . . . she's talking about Sonny.

258

"What a dangerous game you decided to play, Herne. You men. You all think you're so damnably clever, don't you?"

"You can't possibly imagine that I could have foreseen such an extraordinary chain of events, Mabh," Herne said angrily.

"Oh, Herne!" Mabh mocked him with her bitter laughter. "You of *all* people should know what twisted paths the Fates delight in making us walk." Mabh sighed heavily, and Kelley saw her sink into the chair in front of the makeup counter, her dark robes pooling on the floor around her like an oil slick. There was a long pause, and then her voice was softer as she said, "He is a handsome lad, I'll give him that."

Kelley pushed the door open just enough to see Herne's image in the mirror dip his head in a slight bow. "And she is a beautiful lass," he said, a small, sad smile on his sculpted, regal face.

"Yes. She is," the Autumn Queen said proudly. "It seems we breed lovely offspring, you and I."

"True, lady." Herne chuckled wanly. "Just not together."

"No."

"A son of mine and a daughter of yours. You are right about the Fates. Is that not their laughter I hear echoing down the wind?"

"It's certainly worth a giggle or two on their part." Mabh's own mouth twitched mirthlessly. She turned away from the mirror for a moment, as if contemplating the pattern of water stains on the peeling wallpaper. "Does *she* know what he is?

What he's capable of?" Mabh asked finally. "His mother, I mean."

An expression of old, deep pain crossed Herne's face. "When I was with her, Emmaline knew me only as a man. Just an outcast wild man living in the forest. When Sonny was born, I knew that there was something very special about him. I turned to the one person who had the power to protect him. I begged the Winter King to take my son and keep him safe."

"Auberon?" Mabh sputtered in disbelief. "You actually *trust* him?"

"Aye, lady. I do," Herne said. "And besides which—he also had a child whom *he* wished to keep safe."

"From whom?" Mabh demanded. "Not me, surely! I would never harm my own child. Great goddess, I should never have agreed to let Auberon take my daughter to the Unseelie Court in the first place."

"I do not know what Auberon's fears for the girl were, Mabh," Herne said impatiently, "only that he had them. For this reason it seemed an arrangement that was almost fated. We . . . made an agreement."

Mabh shook her head, her expression one of shocked disbelief. "So it was all a *ruse*? The theft of the boy to begin with, his poor mother driven to steal my daughter as her only means of recourse . . . like pawns on a chessboard. And *you* helped Auberon and that miserable boucca set the whole thing up!"

"Puck is blameless. Auberon simply knew his nature and

used it to best advantage. The boucca doesn't even know Sonny's true identity. No one does, yet. Except for you, Auberon, and me. It is dangerous knowledge."

"I'd say that's an accurate assessment," Mabh scoffed. "You of all people should know just how dangerous. That boy has the potential to become a grave threat—especially to anyone close to him. And yet you did not think to warn Kelley away when he brought her to your Tavern for safekeeping on the Nine Night."

"Perhaps I've grown too soft with my gathering age."

"*That* is a perilous indulgence, my love."

"He is my son."

"True. He is all that you are." Mabh's voice dropped to a harsh whisper. "All that I *made* you."

Herne went white, although with anger or fear, Kelley wasn't quite sure at first. "Do you mean to tell me, lady, that on top of everything else, he is full of *your* magicks? That not only does his blood run with the power of the Greenman, but he also carries the taint of the Wild Hunt's curse? Have you *seen* this?"

"I have."

The Greenman. Kelley felt a knot of apprehension tighten her stomach. She remembered Bob's words about the ancient nature god's power and its potential for devastating misuse. Rather like her mother's fearsome gift. *If Sonny carries both within him . . .* She held her breath and listened.

"I feared this." Herne's hand went to a small, stag-head-shaped scar at the base of his throat. He turned a fearsome glare on the Autumn Queen. "It was an ill thing you did once upon a time."

"Oh, don't lecture me, my love." Mabh spat the words back at the image in the mirror, acid on her tongue. "You were happy enough to reap the fruits of my fascination with you. Until you tired of me and my wonders, that is."

"I do not say I have no fault in this."

"Quite." Mabh's eyes sparkled fiercely. "You might also have considered the consequences of another dalliance *after* me. That is—if you were so concerned about passing on the taint of my 'gifts.'"

"I did *not* dally with you, Mabh!" Herne strained forward, and it looked to Kelley as though he would come charging through the mirror in a shower of glass. His eyes locked with the Autumn Queen's, and his face twisted with anguish. "I adored you!"

The Faerie queen fell silent as Herne gazed at her. After a long moment, she shook her head sadly and said, "You fear those that would find the boy and use his power for ill? I fear the boy himself."

Herne stared at Mabh, waiting for her to continue.

"He loves her, Herne."

"And she loves him. I know."

"I don't think you do." Mabh's voice cast a chilling pall over the tiny room. "He loves Kelley in the way that *I* once loved *you*. I saw that in him, too."

In the mirror Kelley saw Herne's face drain of all color and vitality. He looked utterly devastated.

"When I looked in his eyes," Mabh whispered, "I saw *that*."

Kelley ducked into the next dressing room as her mother turned away from the mirror, every line of her body tense with emotion.

Kelley listened as she heard Mabh's footsteps retreating down the hall. When the sound died away, Kelley burst into the other room and ran to the mirror. "Herne!" she shouted.

The mirror was empty. Only Kelley's reflection shone back at her. She hammered a fist on the glass—not *quite* hard enough to break it—and called the Hunter's name. When he didn't appear, she sank down into the chair that her mother had so recently vacated.

"You *lied* to him," she murmured to the empty room. Sadness and worry—and bitter disappointment—warred for domination over her emotions.

"I never lied to Sonny," a voice said softly.

Kelley jerked her head around and gazed into the mirror—into the eyes of Herne the Hunter. "You never told him he was *your son*," she said. "Not ever having told him that particular truth is the functional equivalent, don't you think? I thought you were better than that, Herne."

"I did it to protect him."

"I don't believe you."

"Then allow me to tell you a little story."

Kelley crossed her arms over her chest and waited.

"A very long time ago, in the days after the Wild Hunt was chained and I myself had been thrown down from the sky, retreating into the wilderness where I could lose myself, I was befriended by a god. The Greenman had been the first of Faerie to ever cross over into the world of men. He created the Four Gates of Faerie. I suppose he just felt sorry for me in the beginning, but over time we became close companions—brothers, almost. When the decision was made to move the Samhain Gate to this place, to this new young city, he was the one who did it, building the Gate into the very fabric of the park. I came with him."

"What does any of this have to do with Sonny?" Kelley said impatiently.

"He took on the guise of a mortal man, calling himself Andrew Green, in order that he might work with those constructing the park itself and accomplish *his* task as they completed theirs. That left him vulnerable. After the Gate was finished, Andrew was murdered by a thrall—a changeling slave—in what was believed to be an attempt to steal his power." Herne's face twisted with old, still fresh anger. "He was shot to death with iron bullets."

The image that Chloe had shown Kelley—of Sonny lying bleeding on a sidewalk from bullet holes—suddenly swam up before her eyes. Her insides went cold.

"Only *I* was there that day, close by, and I found him before anyone else did," Herne continued. "So, instead of someone being able to siphon off his magicks as he lay dying, the Old Man bequeathed his power to me."

"You're lying," Kelley scoffed, desperately unwilling to believe Herne's story. "The Greenman isn't dead. I saw him in your tavern."

"What you saw was a simulacrum. A sliver of his essence that I planted and tended and cultivated into a semblance of my old friend. Because I missed him." A ghost of a smile lifted the corner of Herne's lips. "But that creature, while a comfort to me, is no more possessed of the majesty and the might of the original than a painting is of its subject."

"Who killed him?" Kelley's voice was a raw whisper.

"That we do not know. The thrall's mind was gone—all he could do was babble nonsense. The New York police concluded he was insane and locked him away behind iron bars where no Faerie would dare go to seek the truth."

"What happened then?"

"After Andrew bestowed his Faerie magick upon me, in the depths of my mourning, I returned to the Samhain Gate. I used it to travel home across the sea, to where the Beltane Gate still stood open in Ireland, in the heart of that same forest where I had hidden away for so long after the days of the Wild Hunt ended. That was where Emmaline Flannery found me. Where she brought me back to myself with her kindness and beauty and the love of her wild heart . . ." Herne's eyes went cloudy with memory. "When she bore me a son, I realized that I had unwittingly passed the Greenman's power to him." He shook his head sharply, as if to dispel the remembrance. "I was a fool. I feared for the boy. And for his mother. So I left her and I veiled the power inside of him, hiding it even from himself. And then I asked Auberon to . . . to steal my Emmaline's child away."

Kelley thought of Emma. Of the silent grief that she had carried for so long.

"I did not want Sonny's fate to be the same as that of my old friend. Let us hope that no one else discovers his secret."

"Chloe knows," Kelley murmured. *And Tyff.* Tyff had stayed behind after Kelley had left Sonny's apartment. What if she'd figured it out? What if *that* was the secret Harvicc had talked about—the reason Tyff had asked the ogre to knock her out at the River? So that she could keep Sonny's secret safe from the soul-searching gaze of another Faerie?

"The Siren's mind is broken." Herne frowned. "This is what I have heard. She may possess that secret, but she can't communicate it through her madness. Let us hope she stays that way."

"Wow." Kelley glared at the mirror. "That's pretty cold."

"She ravaged Sonny's mind. I should think you, of all people, would approve her fate."

"You think wrong," Kelley said sharply, knowing even as she uttered the words that they were a lie. It was getting so very easy to lie.

"We must find a way to keep my son safe from those who would seek to use his power for ill," Herne murmured, almost as if speaking to himself. "And we must keep him safe from himself. The Greenman's power is so pure. So potent. So easily corruptible."

Like my mother's, Kelley thought. And somewhere deep inside she felt that power whisper to her, twisty and tempting. She told it in no uncertain terms to shut up.

"One need only encounter the offspring of the Greenman to know just how easily that power can rot its user from the inside."

"Leprechauns," Kelley said.

"Aye. And their vile sisters, the glaistigs." Herne's lip twisted with disgust.

"Yeah. I know all about those guys. In fact, there's one outside the theater right now."

"What?" Herne eyes snapped up to her face, filled with surprise and alarm.

"A leprechaun." Kelley crossed her arms, perversely pleased that, for once, *she* knew something that someone else didn't. It was a short-lived sensation. One that evaporated in an instant, when a thunderous sound from down the hallway heralded the fact that someone had just blown the backstage loading doors clear off their moorings.

XXII

"You look like a kid in a candy store, son." Jack smiled and twirled the big brass key on the end of his finger that had opened the treasure trove known as the prop storage room.

Sonny stood blinking, an astonished grin on his face, in front of racks and racks of swords. He'd gone in search of the actor to ask whether there was anything in the theater they could use as weapons if the need arose. He hadn't expected Jack to lead him to a room full of *actual* weapons.

"May I?" he asked, pointing at the Claymore hanging on the wall.

Jack nodded and Sonny took the sword down from its hanger, hefting the four feet of blade with an ease that made Jack nod appreciatively. "I used that one in the last production of Shakespeare's 'the Scottish play' that we did. Nice balance but a little hard on the shoulders in a prolonged fight." He reached past Sonny. "I like *this* baby, personally."

He plucked a sleek cutlass from the rack of shining steel and flourished it in a blurry-fast, side-to-side swiping move that made the elegantly curved blade sing as it cut the air.

Sonny felt the grin on his face split into a full-fledged, appreciative smile. Jack was one of the good ones, he decided.

"I used this one in a touring production of *Peter Pan*. I played Captain Hook. Six months, six shows a week, I got to know her pretty well." Jack pulled a sword belt down off a wooden wall peg and strapped it to his waist, sliding the blade home into the scabbard as if he were an old pirate. Then he reached for a long metal rasp hanging on the wall, saying, "With this, and a little elbow grease, I can even give her a bit of a cutting edge."

Sonny reached into the satchel at his side. "I think you might appreciate this."

He drew forth the bundle of three stout branches and handed it to Jack, who took the curious object in both hands and raised a questioning eyebrow.

"Oak for strength, ash for suppleness." Sonny pointed. "And thorn. For sharpness." Then he took the bundle from Jack's hand and whispered to it. The air writhed and twisted, and the branches transformed into the gleaming silver blade that was as lethal as it was beautiful.

"Odds bodkins," Jack said after a long silence. "If that isn't something else."

Sonny glanced up at the high, barred window in the little room. The sky was still dark, but his Janus sensibilities told him that morning was not far off—an hour, maybe two. If their foe outside was going to try anything, it would have to be soon. Before the sun rose and the power of the leprechaun's Faerie magick faded in the light of day. He turned back and cast an eye over the abundance of broadswords.

"What are those made of?" he asked.

"Those?" Jack shook his head. "They're not combat ready, if that's what you're asking. We just use those in productions where we have to have a bunch of guys standing around in the background looking menacing. They're cheapies—just for show. The iron content in the blades is much too high to give them any strength."

"Perfect," Sonny said. Putting away his enchanted blade, he began stacking the prop swords in Jack's arms like cordwood. He grabbed the leftover ones himself and, pulling the door shut, said, "Follow me."

"Gah!" Bob grimaced and flinched away from the pair as they walked into the greenroom bearing the armloads of swords. "Get those away from here!"

"Puck, help the king up," Sonny said curtly. "We're taking

him to the balcony."

In fact Auberon didn't need the boucca's help. The Winter King managed the entire flight of stairs under his own power, stopping only briefly to lean on the banister. His eyes had regained some of their sparkle, and the angry florid tones had faded from his cheeks—his color was almost back to its normal, healthy (for him) pallor. Sonny was pleased to see it—perhaps getting him away from the Otherworld had done him some good. It also made Sonny wonder fleetingly exactly what in the Otherworld had contributed to his lord's unease. Something to think about when he had more time.

When he reached the pews in the balcony, Sonny saw that Kelley was no longer there. She must have gone down to the dressing rooms. He would go and find her after he finished his task here. "Puck, I want you to set up a veil to hide the king."

"You really do smell trouble, don't you?"

"From everything you've told me, I'd hazard a guess and say that our leprechaun friend isn't going to quit without some kind of fight. If he can't find a way into the theater himself, he'll find someone who can." Sonny laid his swords on a pew a ways away from the king and gestured for Jack to do likewise. "And it'll be soon—there isn't much time until morning. We have to be prepared. Our first priority is to keep Auberon safe and his presence a secret—that'll primarily be your job. Our second is to protect Kelley—that will be mine. I can't do the one unless you do the other. Cast a veil over the king. Cast it well. Keep them—whoever 'they' may be—from discovering that Auberon is even here. No sense in giving the Wee Green Clan more than one target, especially if they're really looking for a fight. And in the meantime, we will ring you both round with iron. That should help keep you both safe if something does manage to breach your veiling spell."

As he spoke, Sonny moved about the balcony, placing the swords on the floor under Auberon's pew in a ring, touching pommel to point. Jack saw what he was doing and helped out, handing him the blades one by one until there was a large, roughly circular, iron enclosure marked out with the Unseelie king and the boucca at the heart of it.

Bob shuddered. "This is going to give me such a rash," he said, then closed his eyes and started to weave his veil.

Auberon, who had been quiet for some time, regarded Sonny with approval and perhaps even gratitude in his expression. But then, in the moment before he vanished from sight behind Bob's veil, the Unseelie king's gaze snapped toward the stage, and he said, in a voice like the calm before the storm, "They are coming."

The loading doors exploded off their hinges.

Sonny and Jack raced down the steps toward the stage deck, running down the aisles between the audience seating, drawing weapons as they went. Pale predawn light flooded in through the wide-open doors at the very back of the stage, casting the half-built set into shadow and silhouetting several figures standing framed in the threshold against a backdrop of sullen ash-gray sky.

The leprechaun brothers leaned indolently against a cement pylon in the loading zone outside. A drunkard and a hooligan; the Wee Green Men. If only it didn't *sound* so comical when the reality was anything but. And they'd brought company. Surrounding the brothers was a pack of feral-looking girls who crouched and perched on and around the garbage containers in the alley, every one of them dressed in a flowing green gown that left little to the imagination except their legs.

Green Maidens, Sonny thought, *glaistigs*—and he knew that the long skirts served to hide legs that belonged on goats, not girls. Sonny's predecessor in the Janus Guard had lost his life to one of those things.

"What about the whiskey?" Jack said as they ran. "Won't it keep them out?"

"The Green Maidens don't drink anything but blood." Bob's disembodied voice floated after them. "The whiskey magick won't affect them."

"Wonderful," the old actor muttered, a tremor of fear in his voice. "I should've poured a Bloody Mary."

Sonny leaped up onto the apron of the stage, Jack right behind him.

The glaistig crouching in the very front had her arms raised, and Sonny noticed that she wobbled a bit as she tried to stand, as if suddenly light-headed. She had been the one, then, to call up enough raw force to blow the doors. She saw him staring and opened her lips in a grisly parody of a smile, and Sonny saw that her teeth, long and jagged, were a bilious shade of bright green. She hissed and ran her tongue over the razor-sharp points. Then she darted into the wings.

When she reappeared, it was with the tumbler full of whiskey in her hand. She took it outside the theater into the alley, where she handed it to the leprechaun brother that had attacked Sonny in his cottage. He smiled and downed the entire glass in one long swig, groaning with pleasure and wiping his mouth on his sleeve. Then he tossed aside the glass to shatter on the pavement and, together, the sons of the Greenman sauntered toward the loading doors and on into the theater.

Beside Sonny, Gentleman Jack swallowed noisily and adjusted the grip on his sword. Sonny noted with approval that the actor's stance did not waver and his feet did not shift through any kind of dance that would have marked him as a nervous amateur. That was good. Jack would have to call on all his acting skills to keep the fiends that faced them from pegging him as easy prey.

Sonny wished fervently that they had greater numbers. With Auberon safe he didn't have to worry about him. But at the same time, taking Bob out of the ranks to ensure the king's safety reduced their available fighting resources substantially.

Sonny heard Mabh's frustrated hiss and glanced to his right to see the Queen of Air and Darkness stalking out of the wings and onto the stage. Kelley followed close behind her mother—almost running into her when Mabh halted abruptly, put her hands up, and stepped back.

"I cannot fight this battle," she said.

Sonny almost did a double take. "I beg your pardon, lady, but you have to. We need you."

"I cannot." Mabh's teeth were clenched in frustration. "Vile they may be, but the glaistig are my folk. The Green Maidens belong to Autumn."

"You're lying!" Kelley exclaimed, pointing at the lead glaistig. "I saw *that* one in Gwynn's palace."

"Faerie don't lie. Jenii Greenteeth was sent as an emissary to the Court of Spring. She serves Gwynn, but she is of the Autumn Court." Mabh sneered at the goat girl, who raised a hand and waggled her long, taloned fingers in mock greeting. "I tell you I cannot raise a hand against her—or her sisters—unless they choose to fight me first! And they are not that stupid."

"What about the leprechauns, ma'am?" Jack asked, his wary eye following the movement of their adversaries as they moved languidly to close them in a circle. They weren't in any hurry, arrogant and assured of their superior numbers.

Mabh smiled suddenly, as if she'd only noticed the two brothers once Jack had pointed them out. "Oh," she said. "You're quite right, Mr. Savage. Those naughty little boys are Solitary Fae. They belong to no Court." She raised her voice so that the leprechauns couldn't help but hear her threat. "And come they within my reach, I will set them ablaze like piles of leaves raked in fall!"

The brothers looked at each other and, in the blink of an eye, vanished—running off to hide in the shadows of the wings on either side of the stage.

Sonny turned a baleful eye on the queen. "Nice. Might I counsel against broadcasting any further stratagems you might come up with? Just to avoid giving the enemy the advantage of a heads-up?"

"Sorry."

Then there was no time for talk. The Maidens, unencumbered by the threat of Mabh, sprang suddenly into action.

The glaistigs moved with whiplash speed. Everywhere Sonny looked, it seemed as though there was yet another one skittering down the stairs from the upper platforms of the set or darting out from the wings—but they moved so fast, he could hardly count their numbers. They were blurs of motion: tornadoes of pale frenzied hair, slashing talons, and the whirling green fabric of their long, tattered gowns.

Sonny's sword whirred through the air, singing like a swarm of bees as he slashed and parried, frantically defending against the attack of the green girls with their long nails and flashing hooves. To his right, Jack fought with a kind of brilliant, adrenaline-fueled desperation, fending off the vicious Fae with his sword and his voice—his sonorous, actor-trained tones rang out, shouting threats and imprecations to good effect. But the older man's shirt was becoming soaked in sweat, and Sonny knew that he wouldn't be able to keep it up for as long as they would need to. Jack would soon tire. And Sonny couldn't fend off the glaistigs alone.

The Autumn Queen seemed to be an effective deterrent against any approach from the leprechaun brothers, at least. With a thought, Mabh had transformed her gown into a shimmering suit of finely wrought chain mail. She shone with power—the very image of a battle goddess—and the gleaming nimbus of her unfurled wings cast the entire stage in lurid illumination the color of blood and violets. Her face was a mask of fearsome glee as she cast roiling columns of dark, crackling energy at any leprechaun that came within fifty feet of her.

On the other side of her terrifying mother, Kelley had torn the clover charm from her throat and cast about with her own share of power. Her face was flushed and her eyes and fingertips flashed with dark lightning. Sonny barely recognized her. When one of the glaistigs came too close, she whirled with terrifying speed and sent the creature flying thirty feet through the air with a ball of pure, raw magick.

Distracted by the sight of Kelley fighting, Sonny allowed one of the glaistigs past his guard, and the shout of pain from his throat sounded loud in his own ears as she darted in low and raked her clawlike nails across the muscle of his right thigh. Sonny stumbled and almost went down on one knee. The pain clarified things, focused him on the task. He used the momentum of his stumble and followed in the wake of the goat girl's attack. Three steps and a downward, hacking slash of his blade—the glaistig screeched terribly and collapsed. Sonny whipped his sword back up and drove the point of the blade down between the creature's shoulder blades. There was an explosion of glowing, greenish blood, and the horrible Faerie twitched and lay still.

With a triumphant snarl, Sonny yanked his sword free, but even as he turned back to the others, he knew that they were outnumbered. The glaistigs almost appeared as if they were multiplying. Like weeds in a garden—kill one, it seemed as though two sprang up in her place.

They were going to lose.

XXIII

Kelley saw Jack hiss sharply and pull a hand back from the hilt of his sword, his forearm scored and bleeding from another glaistig attack. She would have gone to him if she'd had any kind of chance. But the Maidens just kept coming, and it took every ounce of concentration she had to fend them off. Kelley was unused to drawing on so much of her power, and she could feel herself tiring. And, even though Mabh was in her element, Kelley's mother was useful against only a fraction of their assailants— she could keep the leprechauns at bay indefinitely, but the brothers seemed more than content to hang back anyway, letting the glaistigs do the dirty work. It was only a matter of time.

Nothing for it but to keep fighting, Kelley thought grimly.

Her clover charm clenched tight in one hand, Kelley called up a fistful of magick in the other and turned back to face the next attack. She almost screamed for joy as a familiar shape—all lean muscles and menace—suddenly hurtled through the open doors, howling a battle cry. The Fennrys Wolf leaped into the fray, swinging an ax with gusto and hurling curses in an ancient Viking tongue. The gleaming circle of his blade cleared both space and breathing room for the beleaguered little band as his charge briefly scattered the glaistig.

"Fenn!" Kelley shouted excitedly.

"Where the hell have you been?" Sonny called.

"Drinking tea and eating scones," Fennrys barked. "Where else d'you think?—Behind you, Irish!"

Kelley backed off a step as Sonny feinted low and spun, dispatching another of the vile things with angry efficiency. "How'd you cross over?" he shouted at Fennrys as he dodged another running attack.

"Just followed the ladies, here," Fennrys said, positioning himself beside and slightly behind Kelley so that he could help protect her back. She gave him a grateful smile over her shoulder as she whipped a ball of crackling purple sparks at the exposed flank of a glaistig. Then she parried a running strike from Jenii Greenteeth, spinning back around in time to see Sonny dispatch another of the horrific Green Maidens with deadly grace and efficiency. His silver gaze was keen, focused—almost businesslike—as he wrenched the sword from the dead Faerie's flesh. Then he flashed Kelley a fleeting smile of encouragement, and her breath caught in her throat for an instant.

He was beautiful and terrible to watch all at once, and Kelley could not look away.

Fennrys and Sonny went back to back in a defensive posture.

"There are rifts showing up everywhere in the Otherworld," Fennrys said to the other Janus over his shoulder. "And on this side, the Gate has become massively unstable—rifts all over the place."

"Back in the shadow lands," Sonny said, sword flashing, "something knocked me out as I was about to finish off that hunter Fae. When I woke up, you were gone."

"Funny—I was going to say something similar," Fennrys said. "When I woke up, you were nowhere to be seen."

"I *told* you to watch my back!"

"Quit whining. I'm here now, aren't I? When I headed toward the Winter lands, I stumbled across this pack of darlings, moving with stealth and pretty obviously evil intent." He gestured with his chin at the glaistigs. "I thought it best to follow them. They came through one of the rifts into the park—the Janus are trying to seal them up now as best they can."

"Damn!" Sonny swore. "That sounds bad."

"Yeah," Fennrys grunted, catching a glaistig a backhand blow with the flat of his ax blade. "Remember how I said 'evil really needs to step up its game'? Be careful what you wish for. Any rate, I followed *these* lovelies—saw them hook up with those leprechaun freaks, and then the whole pack headed straight here."

"You took your sweet time following them."

"Yeah, well—I didn't want to get too close and tip 'em off. Besides, midtown traffic is a bitch."

As if on cue, they heard the sound of squealing tires. The beams from car headlights swung through the alley. Kelley looked up and saw a hunter-green Jaguar convertible careen past. Next thing she knew, Tyff came stalking through the loading doors, carrying a lead pipe in one fist and trailing a hulking menace in her wake.

"I heard there's a party going on in here," the Summer Fae sang out. "I forgot snacks, but I brought my own ogre!"

With Tyff and Harvicc's arrival the fight intensified.

The Green Maidens arrowed furiously about the stage, eyes burning red and goat hooves flashing razor-sharp. Kelley saw a glaistig lash out viciously with one foot in a high kick that tore through the sleeve of Tyff's blouse as if it were tissue paper.

That enraged Tyff, who had been wreaking havoc without slinging any magick, just the lead pipe. Now, though, Tyff spun on her heel without a second thought and, with a blast of something that looked like liquid sunshine flaring from her fingertips, she immolated the unfortunate goat girl on the spot, leaving nothing but an oily-looking plume of smoke behind.

Tyff made a disgusted sound and glared at her still-glowing fingertips as if they had somehow betrayed her. When she saw Kelley staring at her, mouth open, she shook her wrist sharply, snuffing the glow like extinguishing a match.

"Nice," Fennrys grunted.

"You have *got* to teach me how to do that!" Kelley exclaimed.

"Oh no, I don't!" Tyff snapped. "I *hate* doing crap like that! Remember what I told you, Kelley. Magick is nothing but trouble. You mark my words—duck!"

She grabbed the top of Kelley's head, pushed her down, and punched another glaistig square in the face. The goat girl squealed in pain and zoomed off into the wings, clutching her shattered nose, a trail of neon-green blood spattering on the stage deck. Tyff ran after her, hollering for Harvicc to drop whatever he was pummeling and come help her.

Their departure left a gap in the defensive ring. And suddenly Hooligan-boy, the leprechaun from the park, was there to fill it. He appeared as if from out of nowhere and ran at Fennrys from behind, hitting him with such force as to send them both hurtling far downstage.

"Now, dog . . ." the leprechaun spat, a purely vicious grin splitting his features, as he pulled the black-handled dagger from his boot. He raised his fist to bring the knife stabbing down, but Kelley's wild tackle caught him before he could do so. Her shoulder caught the Faerie a glancing blow, spinning him away from Fennrys's sprawling form, and they tumbled together, end over end across the stage, grappling desperately—face-to-face. Kelley cried out in terror as Hooligan-boy raised the knife again and it arced swiftly down toward her heart. She heard Fennrys shout, saw him move—not *quite* fast enough—and felt a dull thud followed by an immediate sensation like a thousand-volt electrical shock. The world bloomed in a starburst explosion, and Kelley felt her body go rigid and then limp.

A moment of terrible stillness.

Then the leprechaun was up and running but Kelley couldn't move. His knife lay on the stage and, through a darkening haze, Kelley saw that there was blood bright on the blade.

XXIV

Out of the corner of his eye, Sonny saw the blur of motion that carried Kelley and Fennrys and the leprechaun across the stage deck. A moment more to dispatch the glaistig that leaped for him, clawing at his eyes, and he would rush to help. Then he heard the scream. Kelley's firecracker spark flared like an exploding star in his mind's eye—and then vanished.

Winked out.

Sonny saw Kelley sprawled over by the fake plywood fountain. Her bright hair curtained her face, and her outstretched limbs splayed out at odd angles, unmoving.

No . . .

Sonny saw red on the blade of the leprechaun's knife.

He saw red everywhere.

Her spark was gone from his mind.

No . . .

A fine, crimson mist swam before his eyes, and Sonny went as cold as the ice on the lakes of Auberon's kingdom. Moving slowly, as if in a dream, he bent and picked up the clover charm that lay on the stage where Kelley had dropped it. Sonny straightened and watched as Hooligan-boy slid to a halt, turning—avarice and need blooming in his expression as his eyes fastened on the green-amber pendant.

"You wanted this?" Sonny said, holding the talisman dangling by its silver chain. His voice sounded strange to his own ears. "Is *this* what you came here for?"

From somewhere outside of him—or maybe it was inside, he couldn't think properly—he felt a surging wave of rage and hideous hatred: blind, irrational, incandescent. Sonny felt his heart begin to burn with a terrible fire.

Although it was nothing that could truly be called light, a ghastly illumination spread out from where Sonny stood—a sullen, greenish glow. It rolled across the stage like a poisonous fog.

Fear in his eyes, the Faerie leaped for his bloodied knife and threw it at Sonny's head. Sonny ducked, snarling like a wild animal, and the blade buried to the hilt in one of the wooden support timbers holding up the balcony set.

The air in the theater was heavy and deathly still. The fighting had dwindled and stopped.

Without a conscious, directing impulse, Sonny stretched out his hand, fingers spread wide, and watched impassively as the raw timbers of the wood frame set began to stretch and creak, groaning like a forest under the onslaught of a windstorm. Beneath his feet the slats of the stage decking rattled loudly, bucking and heaving like heavy seas. Out in the auditorium, behind the heavy black curtains that kept the theater dark, the arched wooden window frames shuddered and screeched, bent outward, and shattered the old stained-glass images. A shower of rainbow shards rained down on the empty seats in the auditorium.

Sonny turned to the half-constructed set and raised his other hand, almost as though he were conducting an orchestra. The wooden bones of the set stretched and shivered in response. Some of the two-by-fours grew skins of bark, some bled fresh-running sap, and others—impossibly—splintered into gnarled and grasping branches that unfurled shoots. Leaves sprouted from the heart of the dead timbers, rustling like wings.

Sonny clenched one fist, and the set timber—suddenly alive and supple as the branches of willow saplings—whisked through the air, pummeling the leprechaun mercilessly. Sonny raised his fist higher, and the living wood wrapped around Hooligan-boy's limbs and spiraled up into the set rigging high above the stage, bearing the leprechaun up into darkness. He was screaming.

A flicking of Sonny's wrist batted Hooligan-boy's skinny, tattooed body back and forth between the bars of the bare metal scaffolding forming the overhead lighting grid. Every time his flesh touched the cold wrought iron, the Faerie howled. Sonny didn't stop.

Sonny thought he might have heard a bone snap. Then another. Still he didn't stop.

From the corner of his eye he could see the other leprechaun brother—the drunkard from the cottage—step from the shadows and move toward him, seemingly drawn as if by some force outside of himself. Sonny saw surprise and recognition in the Faerie's face.

"I *know* you," the Faerie said in a whispered, wondering lilt. "I know what you *are*. . . ."

Sonny couldn't have possibly cared less what he knew. He was busy. He thrust out his other hand, fingers splayed, and lengths of heavy hempen rope used to secure scenery uncoiled, whipping through the air, lashing the leprechaun high above his head to a heavy iron crossbeam. The Faerie's eyes went wide in shock and pain. His mouth opened in a silent scream as the hated metal bit into his flesh. With his mind Sonny pulled the rope viciously tight, securing him there.

Distracted, he didn't notice that the other leprechaun had darted up the set stairs to leap at him from Juliet's balcony. Sonny heard Jack shout a warning and turned in time to see the actor come between him and the attacking Fae. But Jack was no match for the leprechaun's chaotic grace and strength. His parry was clumsy with fatigue, and the leprechaun just shoved him to one side.

Jack raised his cutlass again, but Sonny, with a bare nod of his head, sent the old actor cartwheeling painfully off to one side of the stage. This was *his* fight. He would not be denied his revenge.

The leprechaun stuttered to a reeling halt as Sonny turned an unblinking eye on him.

The Faerie began to claw at his throat as if perishing from a desert thirst, and when he opened his mouth wide, a burning verdant light poured forth from between his lips. He fell to his knees.

"Sonny!" He heard Fennrys calling out his name. "No! Don't kill him—you heard what Puck said about the Green Magick—you'll destroy us all!" The Wolf ran at him.

Sonny snarled and rage flashed green and ugly in his mind. Fennrys flew a hundred feet through the theater and crashed through the control-booth window in the balcony high above.

Turning back to his interrupted task, Sonny spread his arms wide and gathered the leprechaun's wildly coruscating energy into himself. It was *his,* Sonny thought distantly.

It had always been his.

Light flared, impossibly bright, and a wave of pressure burst outward from Sonny and the gasping Fae, like an invisible explosion. Everyone in the theater turned their faces away, squeezing eyes shut against the blinding brilliance, bracing against the shock of the blast. Sonny felt the Green Magick flood his being. He knew he stood at the center of the brilliance, glowing like a fiery comet, but the sensation elicited neither fear nor wonder in him.

At last, the drunkard leprechaun pitched forward onto his face and was horribly still. All around them, the theater groaned and creaked like an ancient forest under a hurricane wind. The air was full of splinters, sharp as hornet stings. Stage lights fell crashing to the deck and electrical cords sparked and sizzled, spitting like snakes. In the corner of the stage a canvas flat, set alight by a spark, smoldered and began to smoke. Within moments, hungry-looking flames were clawing their way up the painted wall of the Capulet's villa to engulf Juliet's balcony.

Buoyed upward on the searing wind, Sonny rose into the shadowed reaches high above the stage, to where the limp and twisted body of the other leprechaun hung lashed to the lighting grid. The ropes, he noticed vaguely, had sprouted huge, misshapen flowers and hideously overgrown leaves.

Sonny opened the fingers of his hand that held Kelley's clover pendant, and with the barest hint of a thought, he sent the talisman shooting through the air toward the leprechaun. It hung in the darkness between them, burning with a ghastly, goblin-green light. The leprechaun flinched, and Sonny narrowed his gaze and nudged the charm closer.

It struck the Faerie's chest, just beneath the hollow at the base of his throat. His cries tore through the air as Sonny poured all of the terrible magick that was in his heart and mind into the clover charm and on through into the creature. The leprechaun clawed at the talisman, writhing, kicking his booted feet at nothing, high in the air over the stage.

"Sonny!" A voice, harsh and ragged, cried out to him.

Kelley?

It couldn't be Kelley. Her blood on the knife . . . her limp, unmoving form . . . her firecracker light vanished . . .

"Sonny—stop!" The sound of Kelley's voice cut through the rage that fueled whatever terrible power kept him aloft.

Distracted, Sonny turned from the broken figure of the Wee Green Man, and the terrible forest he had conjured reacted sullenly. The vines and branches writhed and whiplashed, tossing the leprechaun aside like a broken doll. The Faerie fell through the air and slammed heavily down onto the stage deck, his limbs cartwheeling loosely as he bounced into the backstage shadows.

Below Sonny, flames licked up the stage curtains, and heavy smoke filled the air. Suddenly the ashy haze began to glow with the darkling flicker of Kelley's wings as she rose up before Sonny, one hand pressed to her side. He saw a dark trickle of blood seeping between her fingers. With the other hand she reached out to him.

An illusion.

A trick. A lie. She was dead.

"Sonny, I'm *here,*" said the illusion. He felt himself falter.

The vision distracted him, only because her tears looked so real. But he'd felt her firecracker spark snuffed out. And he would make the world burn. The whole building was shuddering now and felt alive: hungry with a need to carry Sonny's vengeance out into the mortal realm. And beyond. Sonny turned away from the illusion and, with a cry of pure wrath, bid the wood of the Avalon Grande give itself to the flames.

Then something hit him like a comet from behind, and darkness descended on Sonny like a curtain falling. The world faded to black, and Sonny plummeted to the stage, knowing full well that—because Kelley was gone—this time there would be no one there to catch him as he fell.

XXV

"**D**id you have to hit him that *hard*?" Kelley turned on her mother.

"Yes." Mabh snapped. "I did." Her pale complexion was almost ashen. The glow from her wings was barely a flicker, and she wove a bit unsteadily as she stood there.

Kelley's own wings were furled behind her. Weak. She'd barely caught Sonny when he fell, and they'd both landed heavily on the ruined stage. Out of the corner of her eye, Kelley saw Tyff moving shakily toward her. Her roommate's face, too, was white, and she was covered in tiny scrapes and cuts.

Kelley looked around at the others. They all bore wounds—

and the worst of those were *not* gotten from their foes. As for those foes, all that was left of them was the splashes of neon-green blood, painting the stage in swaths of garish color. Two of the largest canvas flats were licked with flames, and smoke boiled up into the cavernous space above the stage. The two-by-fours that Sonny's power had animated lay strewn about, snapped like broken bones.

"Where are the rest of the glaistig?" Kelley looked around, folding herself protectively around Sonny's inert form.

"Gone," Tyff said, her voice hoarse. She stooped and picked something up off the shattered stage. It was Kelley's clover charm. Tyff handed it back to Kelley, shaking her head slowly as if in denial of the images lodged in her brain. "Destroyed. In that flash of light. I saw them—he . . . they're just *gone,* Kell."

Kelley clutched the charm. It was cold in her hand.

"I need a body count, Tyff," Kelley said in a low voice as Tyff came up beside her. "How many of those . . . *things* did Sonny destroy?"

Tyff snorted. "Is 'all of them' enough for you?"

"Was it? Was it actually all of them? Think, Tyff."

Tyff's brow furrowed in concentration. "Well, there were four or five of those trashy goat bimbos in my direct line of sight when our boy went all apocalypto with the light show. And they vaporized. Utterly. I'm guessing it was the same for all of them." Her expression turned serious as she said, "And I'm pretty sure you saw with your own two eyes what happened to the leprechauns."

"No one can ever know what Sonny is," Kelley said, half to herself.

"That's a little like trying to put the genie back in the bottle, isn't it?"

"Wait." Kelley was thinking furiously. "*She* can do that, can't she? Chloe? Give him back the spell-song? The one that hides his true nature?"

"Sure." Tyff coughed in the gathering smoke. "And from what I gathered, happy to do it, too. We should really be getting the hell out of here, you know?"

"What about you?" Kelley gripped her wrist.

"What about me? I'm not about to spill the beans. And neither will Harvicc. Assuming we survive this, I'll have enough time to work on a spell for both of us that will shield that information from prying minds." She huffed. "Gods, I *hate* magick! But at least it'll be less painful than a sock in the jaw. Of course, your mortal pals are another matter all together. You could put a whammy on their memories, I suppose. But that sometimes has side effects—"

"No. No whammies. Jack doesn't even know what he saw. I'm not worried about him. And I trust Fennrys."

"That's nice to know," Fennrys grunted as he heaved himself up onto the stage from the orchestra pit. He must have found his way down from the booth by the back access stairs. He was covered in a score of lacerations from flying through the control-booth window. "You ladies staying for barbecue,

295

or can we get moving?"

Behind them, Harvicc was busy heaving aside burning flats, trying to keep the conflagration at bay. But the fire's dull roar grew louder with every passing second.

Kelley turned to her mother. "Do you have enough juice left to get Auberon out of here and back to the Otherworld? To somewhere safe?"

"Safer than here, anyway." The Queen raised her hoarse voice over the crackling of the flames. Kelley could see that there were now flames racing through the rows of audience seating, feeding greedily on the old worn carpeting. "But that spell took almost everything I had. And I can tell you that a moment later it wouldn't have been enough." Mabh stared down at Sonny with something that looked like respect. Kelley refused to believe it was fear.

"I'll take care of the others," Kelley assured her.

"And I'll take care of the boucca," Mabh said in a low voice. Kelley frowned at the possible implications of her mother's words, but she didn't have the luxury of warning Bob or asking Mabh just how she would accomplish that task. Kelley could only hope that the boucca was wily enough to escape the worst of her mother's machinations. Mabh's wings fluttered, straining against the smoke-heavy air as she rose up to the balcony.

Kelley felt a horrible stab of guilt when she saw Bob heroically cast aside one of the prop swords, breaking the iron circle so that Mabh could get to them. The boucca's yowl of agony sounded over the rest of the chaos and in the moment before Mabh opened a rift, Kelley saw him clutching his hand—as if the metal had burned him. She put a hand to where her own wound throbbed painfully. The air shimmered, and Mabh raised a hand in farewell. Kelley waved her impatiently to go, trying to ignore the expression she'd seen in her mother's gaze. The very last thing Kelley needed from Mabh was sympathy.

The air in the theater was almost furnace-hot.

Outside, in the distance, Kelley thought she could hear sirens.

She tried to lift Sonny in her arms. Her knees buckled and Fennrys caught her gently.

"I'll get him," he said.

Kelley climbed to her feet and gathered what little strength she had left. Standing beside her, Kelley felt Jack take her hand in his, giving her fingers a gentle squeeze of encouragement. A rift opened directly above them, and with an effort of sheer will, Kelley drew the crackling circle of darkness down to engulf them all as they stood huddled together in the middle of what had become a raging inferno. She lifted her chin and willed her eyes to stay dry as she left behind the only real home she'd ever known. She left it to burn.

Angry red darkness faded to a butter-yellow glow. Early-morning sunshine streamed in through the French doors of Sonny's penthouse apartment. Maddox was asleep on the long leather couch, but he sprang to his feet—shocked startlingly awake by the sudden appearance of a battered company of Fair Folk and mortals appearing out of thin air in the middle of the exquisite Persian rug.

"Seven hells!" he exclaimed. "What—"

"Hullo, Maddox," Fennrys grunted, hitching his armload of unconscious Janus Guard higher. "Stop gawping and give us a hand, will you? Which way to the bedroom?"

"Wait." Kelley put up a hand. "Maddox—is *she* still in there?"

"Uh. Yes. Well—no. I mean—" He stopped and cocked his head. "I think she's taking a shower. Um. I hear water. She takes long showers. Lots of them. For hours, sometimes." He avoided looking in the direction of Tyff's sharply raised eyebrow. "I sleep out here," he murmured under his breath.

Kelley walked over and pushed open the door. The bed was neatly made, and she nodded for Fennrys to deposit his burden. He set Sonny down on top of the coverlet and went back out.

Maddox had followed in Kelley's wake, and his jaw was hanging open. "What happened? Kelley—what happened to Sonny? Kelley . . . ?" he called after her as she brushed past him, back to the living room.

In the main room, Harvicc perched delicately on a settee that sagged under his bulk. Jack hovered near the kitchen. When the actor's eyes met Kelley's, she saw that they were full of something a little like awe. That wounded her on some level.

"I'm sorry about this. About everything," she said quietly. "I think you should go home now, Jack."

She almost expected him to argue. But he didn't. He didn't say anything. Jack just nodded and went to the door, leaving without a backward glance.

Kelley realized that her fist was still knotted around the four-leaf clover, and she opened her fingers to gaze down at the amber charm, glinting green in her palm. Without a word to Maddox or the others, she went through the French doors and out onto the terrace.

Far below, Central Park looked peaceful. She was much too high up to be able to tell whether the disturbances of the night past had left any telltale signs. Even if they had, the Janus would take care of them, she supposed. Any renegade Fae that had managed to come through would be either dead or disappeared into the city; running, hiding, waiting until nightfall, when their Faerie magick grew strong.

The Janus would be tending to wounds. Sharpening weapons. Doing damage control.

Like she needed to do. Kelley fastened her charm back around her throat. A shiver ran up her spine, and she blamed the wind.

It wasn't long before Tyff came out to join her. She'd found Sonny's first-aid kit and motioned Kelley to lie on her side on the terrace chaise, lifting the hem of her shirt high enough so that she could examine her injury.

"It's not so bad. I don't even think you'll need stitches,"

Tyff said as she crouched beside the lounge and fished around in the med kit. Tyff closed the edges of the gash along her ribs with medical tape, slathering on some sort of incredibly pungent salve and bandaging the whole area with filmy sheets of something. "Real gossamer," said Tyff. "It'll help the wound heal." Apparently Sonny's kit held more than just standard-issue medical supplies. Of course.

Kelley clenched her teeth as Tyff worked. In spite of Tyff's assertions, it still felt like the entire left side of her body had been dipped in acid. And then set on fire.

"It's the iron," Tyff explained. "You've been living so long as a mortal that you've probably built up a kind of immunity to it—and I'm guessing that charm's probably protected you, too—but a blade like that? It's deadly to Fair Folk. Getting stabbed must have been a serious shock to your system."

"I'm fine," Kelley said. She would be—physically, at least. The leprechaun's knife had only caught her a glancing blow.

It had been enough.

Enough to short-circuit her own magickal energy and make Sonny think for an instant that she was dead. And that instant had been enough to turn him into . . . *that*. Kelley had thought that what her father had done to Sonny had been monstrous enough. But what *she* had turned him into had been infinitely worse. Her shoulders heaved as she swallowed against the tightness in her throat that was half sob, half sickness.

"There's some aspirin in here," Tyff said, poking through

the kit. "I'll go get you some water." She stood and went back inside.

Magick comes from what's inside you, Tyff had told her not so long ago. *Head and heart, mind and soul.* The words echoed in Kelley's head. Sonny's heart belonged to her. That made *her* the most dangerous person she knew. As dangerous as Herne had been, once upon a time. Kelley had witnessed firsthand what her mother had done in the name of love—twisted, perverse, and every kind of wrong, maybe—but it had still been love that had made her mother conjure up a darkness so profound that it had cut a swath through the mortal realm.

Sonny's love for her, on the other hand, was a wondrous thing. Perfect, beautiful, absolutely right. And yet he had burned the Avalon to the ground with it. He had hurt her friends. Tortured and tormented her enemies. When his mind had thought that she was dead, his heart had done that. Because of her.

She could never let something like that happen again.

"So, what's next, then?" Fennrys asked.

Kelley sat up hastily, tugging her shirt back down over her bandages.

The Wolf leaned against the door frame, watching her.

"What?" Kelley asked.

"For him." He pointed with his chin in the direction of the bedroom. "What happens to Sonny?"

"He goes away," Kelley said quietly. "Into hiding. No one

can ever know what he is. What he did. Not even Sonny can know."

Fennrys stared at her silently.

"Promise me, Fennrys."

"Promise you *what*, Kelley?" His eyes were wary like an animal's. "I don't even know what happened back there. What the hell kind of power was Irish slinging around?"

"The dangerous kind. And it's not going to happen again."

"I don't understand—"

"You don't *have* to, Fenn," Kelley snapped at him, her nerves frayed. Patience at an end. World collapsing in all around her. It took every ounce of control she had not to break down in tears. "I'm sorry. Just—forget all of this ever happened. *Please*."

She waited until Fennrys nodded, accepting his silence as his word.

He crossed the flagstones to sit next to her. "What are you going to do?"

"I'll make him leave. I'll tell him he has to go back to the Otherworld. For as long as it takes, until I can figure out a way to make sure he'll be safe. From himself and others." The faint hope in Kelley's voice sounded hollow even to her ears, but it was all she had. "I found my way back to him once, Fennrys. I can do it again. I just need to know he'll be all right, first."

"Exactly how are you going to make him go?" the Wolf asked quietly.

"I don't know." That was a lie. She knew. She just couldn't say the words.

The air in the bathroom was full of steam and broken singing.

Kelley pulled a bathrobe off a hook on the door and tossed it over the top of the frosted-glass shower stall. "Come out here, Chloe," she said. And then added "Please."

Once Kelley had managed to explain to Chloe what she had wanted her to do, it was easy. The Siren was almost childlike in her eagerness to help. Together they went into the bedroom, where Maddox was sitting in a chair beside the bed. He rose when they came in, standing protectively over Sonny's unconscious form.

The big Janus crossed his arms over his chest and glowered at Kelley. "Are you going to let me in on what's going on now?"

"I . . . no." She wanted to. Desperately. Maddox was Sonny's friend and hers as well. He deserved to know. "I can't tell you."

"I see. But you can tell Fennrys, is that it?"

"I didn't tell him anything. He was *there*, Madd! And now he's in danger, too."

Kelley looked at Sonny lying on the bed. His skin was marble-pale against the dark wave of his hair spread out on the pillow, and the planes of his face showed in sharp, shadowed relief. Chloe slipped silently past Kelley and then past

Maddox, sinking down to sit on the side of the bed. The Siren's damp hair curtained her face, but Kelley caught a glimpse of her eyes—huge and dark in her delicate face—and she shivered in apprehension.

Maddox looked like he was going to lose it as Chloe leaned forward over Sonny, her hands caressing the sides of his face. Kelley steeled her own resolve and pleaded silently with him. Maddox clenched his fists and held his peace. The air in the bedroom hummed with barely audible song as the Siren turned Sonny's face toward her and lowered her head to kiss him on the mouth.

Kelley blinked but she did not turn away as Sonny's limbs went suddenly rigid and he thrashed violently, kicking his booted feet and bucking wildly. But Chloe, fragile as she looked, was stronger. She dug her fingers into Sonny's shoulders, and the music filled the room until it was almost unbearable. A moment passed and then . . . silence. Chloe gasped for air and slipped from off the bed onto the floor.

Maddox helped the fragile siren to stand and led her to the door. "Come on, Chloe honey," he murmured to her gently. "Let's get you out of here. I'll take you to my place for just a little while, eh?"

The Siren stopped in front of Kelley as she passed. She looked up at her, clear eyed, and said, "He is as he was. For all the rest, I am sorry."

Kelley swallowed and nodded, not trusting herself to speak.

"I'll be back soon," Maddox said to her, his gaze flinty. "And then you and me? We're gonna have a little chat, Kelley."

Maddox had been gone for almost half an hour, and Sonny still wasn't awake.

And Fennrys was with her on the terrace again, trying to talk sense into her—or so he claimed. "He won't leave you. You know that. He killed a whole bunch of people—"

"Those weren't *people*, Fennrys!"

"—and torched half a city block because he thought you were dead. He'll *never* leave you. Not unless you leave him first."

It sounded almost as though Kelley were talking to herself as she said, "Do you have any idea what you're asking me to do?"

His voice was carefully neutral. "I'm not asking. I'm just saying."

Tyff called her from the doorway. "Um, Kell. A word?"

"Can this wait, sunshine?" Fennrys growled at her through a forced smile.

"No." Tyff glared at him. "It can't."

Kelley went over to where Tyff took her by the arm and led her back into the living room. Someone had turned on the TV; the news coverage was all about the early-morning four-alarm fire on West Fifty-second Street that had raged for hours.

"Listen—I heard what Wolf-boy just said to you," Tyff

hissed. "Don't you think that just maybe he might have an ulterior motive or two?"

"It doesn't matter. He's right," Kelley said. "It's too dangerous for Sonny to stay here. Even if we manage to keep his secret, what about the leprechaun?"

"The *dead* leprechaun."

"I saw one of them die, Tyff. I didn't see what happened, ultimately, to the other one. And neither did you. Admit it."

Tyff said angrily, "Okay—so *what*? So I didn't see a toe tag. But I'm telling you—if he wasn't dead by the time Sonny was finished playing psycho cat to his helpless rodent, then he still had a large flaming building drop on his head."

It wasn't enough. Not for Kelley to be sure.

"I appreciate what you're trying to say." Kelley heard a noise behind her. No—not a noise. She just knew. She felt the small hairs on the back of her neck rise, and she knew he was there. So. Now or never. Showtime. "But it doesn't matter anyway." She pitched her voice so that her words were clear. Unmistakable. "I've come to understand something, Tyff."

"Really? And what's that?"

"I don't love Sonny."

"*What?*" Tyff's eyes went wide. "Kelley . . . are you all right? Did you hit your head or something?"

Kelley strained to listen.

"Kelley—"

"I just want him to go," Kelley said quietly. Too quietly.

Firecracker, she heard him whisper.

She gathered her strength, looking Tyff square in the face. "I want him out of my world. Out of my life. Sonny doesn't belong in the mortal realm anymore. I do. And I don't want him here." Kelley never in her wildest dreams thought she could be that good an actress. Skills like these would have kept her in theater school for sure. Hell—she deserved an Oscar for this performance. Her fingers touched the cold stones of her necklace. *I guess it really does make you a liar,* she thought. *Way to be human, Kelley . . .*

"Kell . . ." Tyff tried again. "Sweetie—"

"That place was my home!" She pointed savagely toward the TV, where the ruins of the Avalon Grande still smoldered. "And now it's gone. The people Sonny's used to—the person, the thing he's become . . . his kind destroy everything they touch."

Kelley took a deep breath and clutched her fist so tightly around the clover charm, the silver edges bit into her flesh.

"But you love him, Kelley—"

"No, Tyff. I don't. I barely even know him. All I know is that ever since I met him, my life has been nothing but chaos." She spoke slowly, clearly, so that there could be no mistaking what she said. "I don't love Sonny Flannery. I never did. And I never will."

Faerie don't lie.

Tyff just stared at her, not knowing how to respond.

Faerie . . . don't . . . lie, Sonny, she urged silently.

She listened to her own heart breaking as she stood there.

Moments that seemed like lifetimes passed in front of her dry eyes like a gray parade while her hideous lie did its dirty, despicable work. When she heard the front door of the apartment open and then close behind her, she waited. *It's not forever, Sonny. I'll find a way to keep you safe. I'll find a way for us. I promise. . . .*

She walked away from Tyff, back out onto the terrace, where Fenn stood waiting for her to come back to finish their conversation.

She ignored him as if he were a piece of garden statuary and walked over to the railing, looking down over the park where she and Sonny had first met. She was dimly aware that Fenn left her alone after a while, although she couldn't bring herself to care. She stood there, numb. Empty. When she heard Maddox's voice calling out in the apartment, she froze.

"Has anyone seen Sonny?" he called, an edge of panic in his voice. "He's gone!"

Kelley put her head on the balustrade and wept.

Friday, April 9
Present Day

Broken, burned, and bleeding, the leprechaun lay curled up on the floor of the carriage coach. The green blood from his shaking fingertips had marred the black lacquer of the door when he had opened it to crawl inside, and puddled on the carpet beneath him. But in the dimness of the garage, no one would see.

His rasping breath echoed through the cavernous underground room but did not disguise the sound of footsteps approaching.

The carriage door opened again, and he dragged himself up to lean on the bench seat.

"Did you get it?" From the depth of a deep-hooded cloak, eyes stared out at him.

He shook his head weakly, turning away from the flare of anger in that gaze.

"No," he gasped. "But I will. And now I know—"

"Know what?"

Everything was going dark. "I know . . . where the Green . . . Magick . . ." The leprechaun slumped to the floor. His head rolled to one side, exposing his throat—and the blackened scorch mark on his skin in the shape of a four-leaf clover.

The hooded figure leaned down and traced the outline with a gloved fingertip. The underground garage grew warm with a glow like sunshine. All around the leprechaun's spilled blood began to sprout tiny shoots, unfurling tender green leaves to the light.

Soon. Soon they would have enough power.

The hooded figure stood and cast a lingering glance at the dank, crumbling concrete of the garage. Soon the island of Manhattan would be transformed from a grim, gray mortal city into the paradise that the Fair Folk deserved. And if there was no room then for the human beasts, well . . . that was all right, too.

ACKNOWLEDGMENTS

It is humbling and astonishing to me that I get to do this for the second time: thank the people without whom you wouldn't be holding this story in your hands right now—no matter how many bright ideas I might've had. Once again, I owe a ridiculous and ever-increasing debt of gratitude and affection to a lot of people. The usual prime suspects are, of course, Jessica Regel and Laura Arnold—my agent and my editor, two extraordinary women about whom I simply cannot use enough superlatives without stepping into made-up-words territory. Thank you again to Jean Naggar and the staff of JVNLA for taking excellent care of me, along with Brendan Deneen at FinePrint. Thank you to the wonderful, wondrous crew at HarperCollins: my lovely editorial director Barbara Lalicki for her continued support; Maggie Herold, my terrific production editor, for once again making me seem as if I know what I'm doing; and Sasha Illingworth, my stellar designer, for making the whole thing look even better than it did the first time around (I didn't think it was possible)! Thank you to my two Melissas, publicists extraordinaire. Thanks to editor Lynne Missen and everyone at HarperCollins Canada for making me feel like part of the family. Thank you, Adrienne and Simon, for the support and friendship. Now, as always, I send massive love and gratitude out to my family—especially my mom. You guys are the best cheering section a girl could ever ask for. And once again . . . this could not have happened without you, John, because not only are you the reason I made it past "what if?" but, with you at my side, I got to "what happens next?" which was even better.

There is one last thank-you I must add this time around, and that goes out—from the very bottom of my heart—to you, my readers, for embracing this story and coming along for the ride. I hope it's a wild one!

Darklight

A Brief Descriptive Glossary of Certain Common Faerie Terms and Species

---

Music to Light the Darkness: A *Darklight* Playlist

A Sneak Peek at *Tempestuous*

A Brief Descriptive Glossary of Certain Common Faerie Terms and Species—
Presented for Your Enlightenment and Perhaps Safekeeping by an Eminent Gentleman Possessing Knowledge, Both Arcane and Useful, Who Shall Remain Nameless

Blood Magick: Nasty stuff. The Faerie equivalent of nitroglycerin. I'm not going to explain Blood Magick to you in any great detail. Mostly because I don't want you getting any ideas. Just . . . leave it alone. Keep your blood inside your skin. That's where it generally does the most good. Now stop asking me about Blood Magick.

Boucca: *(pronunciation: bau-kah)* One of the oldest species of Fae, boucca are rare, powerful, and dangerously inscrutable. Also devilishly handsome. Sometimes known as Phooka, bwcca, or—and only if you're a very close personal friend—pooka, they are particularly susceptible to compulsion if one is in possession of their so-called true name (a secret name the boucca traditionally chooses for him- or herself).

One of the best known of the boucca fae is the Faerie who keeps company with the Winter King. He is known as Puck, also Robin Goodfellow; however, neither of these old names holds power over the boucca since becoming common knowledge (largely thought to have been as a result of Shakespeare including them in his play. The jerk . . .). This particular boucca's current secret name is *not* commonly known.

The recommended course of action upon the unlikely occurrence of actually meeting a boucca is to be extremely polite. And maybe keep a hand on your valuables.

Cailleach: *(pronunciation: kye-lee-eck)* These creatures are also known as Storm Hags. They are loyal and biddable to Queen Mabh. To everyone else, they are an unmitigated pain in the backside. Throwing rock salt at them will repel them, but it may also provoke them enough to barbecue you with a lightning bolt. They live up to their names and are the living embodiment of inclement weather.

The Hags are mostly either unpleasantly damp or full of hot air and generally to be considered nothing more than an inconvenience. They can, however, turn dangerous in the blink of an eye and unless you're Mabh herself, or something very close to that, it's best to treat them with respect, even if it is grudging.

Also, carrying an umbrella probably wouldn't hurt. That's what I would do. Never mind where I got the umbrella.

Changeling: A changeling is a human who has been taken by one of the Fair Folk to live in the Otherworld. Usually ~~stolen~~ ~~appropriated~~ ~~pilfered~~ borrowed from the mortal realm at a young age, the changeling grows up in a world of unearthly delights. It remains something of a mystery, then, as to why so many of them seem to resent this happy fortune. Mortals can be very confusing, you know.

For the record, a Faerie child who winds up in the care of a human in the mortal realm can also be referred to as a changeling. But mostly I just refer to her as "Kelley" or "Princess."

Four Courts: There are four courts of Faerie in the Otherworld, corresponding to the four seasons and the four turning points of the calendar: Samhain, Beltain, Lunasa, and Imbolc (also see Four Gates). The Four Courts were created by the Greenman (see Greenman) after a nasty bit of business that resulted in Gwynn ap Nudd (now the ruler of the Spring Court), the first king of the Faerie Realm, being thrown down by a pair of fiery young High Fae named Auberon and Titania, aided—or hampered (according to who's telling the tale)—by Mabh.

The Four Courts consist of the two major courts, Winter and Summer (also known respectively as the Unseelie and Seelie Courts), and the minor so-called Shadow Courts, Autumn and Spring, which separate the Unseelie and Seelie geographically and calendrically—thus they are also know as the Borderlands.

It is wise—generally speaking—to avoid the Borderlands, as the terrain can be as uncertain as the seasons they represent.

Of course, if you're human, it is wise—generally speaking—to avoid the Faerie Realm altogether.

Four Gates: The Four Gates correspond to the Four Courts and were created at the same time, to serve as passages into the Mortal Realm. They are movable (although not without a great deal of effort) and have been sealed shut—with the nominal exception of the unintended cracks in the Samhain Gate—by Auberon after his infant daughter was ~~stolen~~ borrowed and spirited away from Faerie. (I'm sure you've all heard that story by now. . . .)

The fact that the Gates are sealed should in no way suggest that it is a wise thing for a mortal to spend too much time in the vicinity of a Faerie Gate. Visitors to Central Park, the current location of the Samhain Gate, are advised to keep an eye out for sudden unexplained flashes of light, and if they encounter such, to run in the opposite direction.

Even the sealed Gates are not without their share of peril, as they tend to attract Faerie to them.

The current location of Lunasa is Stonehenge—and many's the story of strange happenings in and around *that* monument. (Trust me, that recent news item? Those weren't aliens.)

The Gate of Beltane used to be known as the Hanging Gardens of Babylon, and everyone knows how well that worked out (just try and find it on a map these days). Now it is hidden somewhere in Ireland. Keep in mind that tourists tend to disappear without a trace in Ireland all the time (although local authorities do try to keep these things out of the papers).

Imbolc, the Gate of the Spring Court is . . . in the north. That's all anyone really knows with any certainty. It is as mysterious as its king. It is inadvisable to go looking for the actual location of the Gate of Imbolc. Seriously. Don't get any ideas.

Glaistig: *(pronunciation: glee-stig)* The Green Maidens may sound demure and wear long skirts and smile shyly with closed lips, but don't let them fool you. The hooves they hide under those skirts are razor sharp and the teeth behind their smiles . . . are an orthodontist's fantasy playground. Except for the fact that he'd be draped over his spit sink, bleeding from a torn-out throat if he ever got close enough to suggest so much as a good flossing.

The daughters of the Greenman, and they are unfortunately rather more numerous than their brothers, are fond of lurking near pools of stagnant water, lying in wait for innocent victims. Or, as the Glaistigs like to call them, Slurpees.

Greenman: We Fair Folk are much the poorer for his loss. The best of us. The most beloved. Wise and worldly and perhaps just a touch too trusting.

Still, the sly old coot was smart enough to figure out a place to hide the Green Magick. His influence on the mortal realm can still be seen hidden away in the details of some of the older human architecture, where his leafy mug can be seen peering out of alcoves and above doorways.

Not, perhaps, as handsome as your average boucca, but a comforting presence nonetheless. If one ignores the fact that his Magick is a little like one of those leftover World War II underwater mines that cruise ships sometimes run into. It has the potential to make a great big mess if you accidentally stumble across it . . . and you probably wouldn't even know you'd found it until after the KABOOM.

Iron: Carry it. Cherish it. Man in his cleverness has found myriad uses for this most Fae-hated of substances. And the purer the metal, the more likely it is to drive off a wayward boggart attack or discourage an ogre from considering you a handy, portable snack. Sharp iron is even better. An iron blade will cut a Faerie deep and burn at the same time.

On second thought, I'm not entirely certain why I'm telling you any of this. . . .

Kelpie: They used to be such nice, harmless creatures—gentle shapechangers who spent most of their time gamboling about in the shapes of pretty ponies. That is, until Mabh decided it would somehow be a good idea to transform one of them into an impossible thing. And then press that impossible thing into the service of pure malice. I'm sure you've all heard that story, too.

Suffice it to say, since that time all kelpies everywhere carry the taint of the Roan Horse. It makes them extremely ill-tempered and prone to lurk in waterways—tempting the unwary with the prospect of a pleasant ride, only to drown them at the bottom of a lake. Or eat them. Sometimes both.

There has only been one kelpie that I am aware of since the time of the first Wild Hunt that has shown any tendency toward rehabilitation. Perhaps this marks a turning point for the species and, like the taint of evil before it, this goodness will ultimately spread throughout the entire breed.

But I'm not holding my breath. Which is what you'd have to do if a kelpie got hold of you. Not that it would do you any good.

Leprechaun: These two brothers—and, yes, there have only ever been two Wee Green Men in existence (that is why everyone thinks they're so scarce—they are!)—truly are mad, bad, and dangerous to know (to borrow a phrase). Don't get into a drinking match with either of them. Just . . . don't. That way madness lies and I am not speaking metaphorically.

I don't really feel comfortable even talking about them. I'm sure you understand. The honey incident . . . I think I feel a rash coming on. . . .

Lost Fae: Some are here by choice, some by chance, some by misadventure. But all of the Lost Fae are still, it must be said, Fae. And although they have—for the most part—learned either to adapt to human culture or to avoid it whenever possible, they are to be treated with all due respect.

That is, unless you really want to get home from the market to find that the chicken you bought for dinner is quite capable of running around without its head for extended periods of time.

Or, after accusing the lady at the Laundromat of taking all the good dryers, you find that all of your good shirts are inside out—no matter which way you turn them.

Actions such as offering the polite words "Good day to you" and placing a coin in the cup of a long-faced homeless man (even if you suspect he may be just a hard-luck mortal) can go a long way toward avoiding incurring negative Lost Fae attention.

Nyxx: Referred to in the singular as Nyxxie, these creatures are water dwellers and tend to congregate in schools like fish. Say . . . piranha. They are difficult to describe in detail. That is because they fall under a very specific category of Faerie—that being: if you're close enough to notice minute characteristics, don't bother. Because you won't live long enough to convey them to anyone.

From a distance, therefore, accounts indicate Nyxx possess wiry, scaly limbs, seaweedlike hair, large eyes, and dusky coloration. Also, an overabundance of teeth and claws.

Best to avoid water features too deep or murky to see the bottom. Perhaps you're sensing a common element here, where the less savory among the Fair Folk are concerned? I tend to steer clear of anything much beyond a rain puddle. And I still have all my toes.

Redcap: Nasty, brutish, and short (to borrow another phrase).

This diminutive species of troll is notable for the foul habit of dyeing its long pointed headgear in the blood of its victims. The less said about these rotten little fiends, the better. Other than to perhaps point out the obvious: *avoid* at all cost.

If unavoidable, hit them over their ugly little heads with heavy objects, repeatedly. And then once more just for good measure.

Siren: Beautiful voices, black hearts. Contrary to popular belief, a siren is not a mermaid—although she can probably change her shape to look like one if she's bored. They do tend to live underwater or near water, but that's really just a by-product of historically having preyed mostly on sailors.

Why sailors and not, say, cowherds? No one really knows. Perhaps all that fresh air and sea salt lent a particularly dulcet quality to the maritime ditties that originally wafted over the waves to the sirens' ears.

Whatever the case, best to avoid yachting where unexplained drownings have occurred with any frequency. Or maybe just turn your iPod up really loud to tune out their seductive call. On second thought, sirens would probably kill to get their hands on an iPod. And no, that's not a figure of speech. So just . . . stay away from the water, why don't you?

If it hasn't yet been impressed upon you, let me suggest plainly that the human race would be much safer in general if it just stopped indulging in water sports altogether.

Thrall: A human, usually overly susceptible to one or more specific temptations, and one whom the Fair Folk have taken a keen fancy to. The end result is unlikely to be a happy one. Either the thrall becomes a mindless slave, or a mind*ful* slave to a Faerie master. Neither, any thrall will tell you, is a desirable outcome. Well—the mindless thrall might not tell you that, being mindless.

Thralldom is usually accomplished by the offending Faerie

either through bargains or offers with hidden pitfalls or—more directly—through plying the mortal subject with vast quantities of Faerie wine.

Avoid the Faerie wine.

For that matter, avoid the Faerie.

Music to Light the Darkness
A *Darklight* Playlist

I usually have a playlist for whatever project I'm currently working on, and the Wondrous Strange books are no exception. I find it enormously helpful to listen to music while I'm writing. Sometimes the songs inspire me, sometimes they provide mood, sometimes they're just there to keep me company. The songs listed below are just some of the ones that kept coming up in frequent rotation during the writing of *Darklight*.

"Manhattan"—Kings of Leon, from *Only by the Night*
Also in heavy rotation during the *Wondrous Strange* days, this song gives me such a sense of the energy of the city—the restlessness and the magic.

"The Whole of the Moon"—The Waterboys, from *This Is the Sea*
The joys of discovering the magic in another person. And, hopefully, yourself.

"Dance Away"—Roxy Music, from *Manifesto*
Melancholy, a little tragic, and the only song that actually gets a cameo in the book.

"Let It Go"—Blue October, from *Foiled*
One of those lump-in-the-throat kind of songs . . . and sadly relevant for at least one character in the story. . . .

"Evidence of Autumn"—Genesis, from *Three Sides Live*
Strange, poignant, unpredictable, a little quirky around the edges . . . remind anyone of a certain Queen of Faerie? Or, maybe, her daughter?

"Crush"—Dave Matthews and Tim Reynolds, from *Live at Radio City*
A perfect song. A perfect love song.

"Sweet Incarnadine"—Jane Siberry, from *When I Was a Boy*
Chloe the Siren's voice, in all its mad beauty.

"Electrical Storm"—U2, from *The Best of 1990–2000*
Love and longing and how all that stuff can mess you up . . . especially when you're far away from the one who's loved and longed-for.

"When Ye Go Away"—The Waterboys, from *Fisherman's Blues*
One of the most beautiful songs I've ever heard and dead-on thematic for this book, in several ways.

There are others, of course. Too many to list here, but those are some of the ones that sparked my imagination. Also, the Roxy Music album *Avalon* captures, I think, a lot of the overarching feeling of the entire trilogy. Aside from the individual songs on that album being brilliant and moody and wonderful all by themselves (and so very appropriate for the Wondrous Strange world—see Track 8: "To Turn You On," Verse 2), it's one of those albums I recommend listening to front-to-back, uninterrupted. Something that, I find, rarely happens these days in the age of "shuffle play." Give it a try. Give them all a try. You might find something that inspires you. I hope so.

Cheers,
Lesley

I

The crowd of onlookers had largely dissipated once the New York City Fire Department had finally gotten the blaze under control, though the entire block remained cordoned off with yellow police tape and the gutters ran full with soot-blackened water. Fortunately the structure had been stand-alone, unlike most of the surrounding shops and apartment buildings, and so the damage had been confined to the Avalon Grande Theatre—damage being wholly inadequate to describe the devastation wrought upon the old converted church by the fire that had started there in the early hours of that morning. Just before dawn.

Just before . . . what?

Sonny Flannery stood in a shadowed doorway across the street from the ruination and struggled desperately to remember. He knew that he had been inside the Avalon in the moments before it had been consumed by fire—holed up, waiting for morning, held under siege by malevolent Fae— and he knew that there had been fighting. Vicious Green Maidens and their leprechaun brothers. Sonny and his friends had been short on odds. And then . . . something had happened. Something bad.

And for the life of him, Sonny couldn't remember what that was.

All he kept coming up with was that one minute he'd been fighting for his life. The next, he'd woken up in his apartment with a head full of cotton wool and hobnails—only to discover that the one place in all the worlds that Kelley Winslow, the girl he loved, had truly called "home" was gone. Destroyed.

Now, standing in front of the smoking remains of the Avalon Grande Theatre on Fifty-second, Sonny had the horrible gut-twisting feeling that it was entirely his fault.

One brick wall still held bits of broken, rainbow-tinted glass in its window frames, but most of the rest of the building had been reduced to rubble when the bell tower collapsed. Over near the side alley where the stage door still hung awkwardly inside its sagging frame, Sonny saw the shattered remnants of mirrors and burned and blackened costume racks. On the end of one rack, a pair of sparkly fairy wings hung from a cord, barely singed.

Sonny turned abruptly and stumbled blindly down the sidewalk—almost knocking over a middle-aged woman in overalls and half-glasses who stood staring at the wreck of the theater, tears streaming unheeded down her face.

It began to rain, a few spattering drops swiftly turning into a downpour. Head down, shoulders hunched, Sonny walked without having a destination in mind. The wind that pushed the rain against him, soaking his T-shirt and plastering it to his chest, held a biting chill. But there was also the hint— just a taste—of green, growing things, spring buds and blossoms, that reached Sonny's nostrils, and he breathed in deeply, almost gulping the air, in an attempt to steady himself. Green things . . . and smoke? No. The smoke was in his head. A memory of . . . of what? Of a fight he couldn't remember. A battle that had set Kelley's theater ablaze, apparently. That was, at least, what he had gathered from the images on the television—video footage shot earlier that morning of the Avalon Grande collapsing in on itself, disappearing in a thick column of inky smoke, gutted. Like Sonny had been in those moments after Kelley Winslow had uttered those words.

"I don't love Sonny Flannery."

Green things and smoke . . .

He looked around, the need to run, to hide, to escape almost overwhelming.